THE PORTUGAL SAPPHIRE

An Ainsley Walker Gemstone Travel Mystery

J.A. JERNAY

CHAPTER ONE

When Ainsley Walker first arrived at the warehouse for her interview, she wondered if she had the wrong address.

A corrugated aluminum door, wide enough to accommodate a semi-truck, was rolled down and clamped tightly. Through a high window, Ainsley glimpsed industrial caged lights hanging from the ceiling. There was no sign, no logo, no marking of any type. Only a street number on the curb. It matched the one she'd scrawled in her notebook the day before.

Then Ainsley paused as she caught an odd scent floating across the air. She inhaled deeply, trying to recognize it—soft and warm, vaguely woody. It was pleasant and made her think of red wine.

Next to the corrugated garage was a small black service door. That was the entrance. Clearing her throat, Ainsley strode over and rapped on it with her knuckles. She listened to the echo faded away. After a moment, Ainsley knocked again.

She heard the click-clack of heels on the floor inside.

Then the door swung open. A mild woman dressed in a black blazer and gray pencil skirt was in the frame.

Her eyes gave the visitor a friendly once-over. "Can I help you?"

"I have an appointment with Joaquim," Ainsley replied. "Is this the right place?"

The woman smiled. "You must be Ainsley Walker. I'm Fatima. Welcome."

They shook hands diplomatically. Then she led Ainsley inside. It was a small lobby with three simple chairs and a water cooler. "Joaquim isn't quite ready for you yet," she said. "Please wait here."

Fatima left the anteroom, and Ainsley quickly checked her clothing. That morning, she'd agonized over her outfit for the longest time, finally settling upon a red silken sleeveless blouse, a white bolero jacket, a new pair of jeans, and beautifully embossed boots. It gave the correct impression of style mixed with competence.

On her finger was a small sapphire ring, a long-ago deal that she'd never regretted. On her wrist was a wristwatch that her bank account had always regretted. And on her mind were many questions.

Yesterday, Ainsley had received a phone call out of the blue, the way she got most of her business. It'd been a male voice, identifying himself only as Joaquim. He'd seen her advertisement, he'd said, and was hoping that she had time the next morning to discuss an assignment. He'd had an odd accent.

Ainsley had nearly leapt to the ceiling. Yes, she had time.

After all, it'd been three months since her last case had concluded. She'd exhausted most of her savings and had fallen two months behind in her rent. Then she'd spent three hundred dollars on the ad—a chunk of change that she was beginning to think might've been better used elsewhere.

In short, she really needed this case. To prove to herself, and others, that gemstone detective work was a viable career path.

Ainsley nervously paced the lobby, then noticed the artwork hanging on the wall. It was a picture of a grove of trees in a bucolic countryside. She squinted. The trees had been heavily stripped of their bark. That was odd.

Next to it hung a sketch of an old ship. She studied it closely: an exploratory vessel with stylishly billowing sails, blue waves chopping against its curved hull. Underneath, in loopy cursive, the artist had written *Caravel, 1490*. Whoever Joaquim was, he seemed like a man with a sense of adventure.

The door opened. Ainsley turned. It was Fatima again, in her black blazer and gray pencil skirt, an unreadable expression on her face.

"We're sorry for the wait," she said.

"No problem."

"Joaquim is ready for you now. This way."

Ainsley followed her through the second door. She found herself moving through a warehouse filled with tall stacks of what seemed to be plywood wrapped in plastic.

"Try not to touch or bump anything," said Fatima. "These stacks can fall easily."

"What do you make here?"

A man in a white hardhat drove a small yellow forklift past them. He stopped the vehicle, shoved its two arms underneath a pallet, then reversed, pulling out the stack, turned, and continued rolling out of sight.

"We don't make anything," said the woman. "We import."

"Import what?"

"Cork."

Now it made sense. These were tall stacks of corkboard, which was so light it would fall over easily. This also explained the mysterious woody scent that she'd noticed even outside.

"Where do you import the cork from?" she asked.

Fatima smiled mysteriously. "You have a lot of questions, Miss Walker."

"And not a lot of answers," Ainsley replied. "I don't know anything about this assignment."

"Joaquim can be evasive."

"Is there anything important to know before I meet him?"

She shrugged. "He is the president of the company. He's young. He's successful."

"What should I say to him?"

"Well," replied the woman, looking Ainsley up and down, "you probably won't have to say much at all."

At the rear of the warehouse, Fatima knocked at a plain office door. On the wall next to the door was a picture of an extremely handsome soccer player, wearing a red national jersey, booting the ball. Zero percent body fat, one hundred percent gorgeous.

"I'm guessing this is his favorite sport," said Ainsley, nodding at the photo.

"Absolutely," Fatima answered, "but don't mention soccer unless you want to be here all day. One more question—do you speak Spanish?"

"Yes."

"Don't mention that either."

"Why?"

"Trust me." Fatima pressed her ear against the door. "Okay, he's off the phone."

She turned the doorknob and opened the door. Ainsley took a deep breath and stepped inside.

CHAPTER TWO

It was a plain room, with brown furniture, a simple sofa, and a wooden desk. On the wall was a flag with two red and green stripes, an odd spherical insignia buried in the center.

Behind the desk, typing at his laptop, was a man.

A very good-looking man.

At first glance, he seemed to be about Ainsley's age. A head of thick brown hair, defined biceps, chest stretching his collared shirt just enough. He was facing sideways and didn't acknowledge her.

"Joaquim?" she said.

"Welcome, please sit down," he said, without glancing up. Then he added: "Fatima, could you get some coffee for us?"

The assistant nodded and left the room. Ainsley lowered herself onto the visitor's chair and studied him while he worked. His brown eyes were firmly focused on his screen. His eyes were intelligent and a little mischievous.

Fatima returned, bearing two paper cups, the aroma of coffee filling the room.

"My espresso maker is broken," he said, "so I hope drip coffee is acceptable."

"It's fine," she croaked.

Joauqim's eyes flicked up. "Are you feeling okay?"

Ainsley coughed. "I had a frog in my throat."

He reached into a drawer and dumped sugar packets, creamers, and wooden stirrers onto the desk. "Please, feel free."

"Thank you," she said. She leaned forward and took a packet of sugar and poured it into her coffee and swirled it with a stirrer.

Finally he closed his laptop and sighed. "I'm sorry for the condition of my office, but I don't spend a lot of time here. Usually I'm either on the floor, or out travelling."

She strained her ears, listening to his accent. There was a slight hint of something, but she couldn't place it.

"Me too," said Ainsley. "It's one of the job requirements of a gemstone detective."

"Is confidentiality another?" he asked.

She nodded. "Absolutely."

"That's good," he said, "because my family is in a very sensitive situation."

"I'm listening."

"Can you tell what kind of accent I have?" A small smirk appeared on his lips as his fingers ripped open a sugar packet. His eyes stayed fixed on Ainsley as he took her stirrer and used it.

"Kind of."

"I'll give you three guesses."

Joaquim didn't seem to be in any rush to get to the assignment. And, in fact, Ainsley had been trying to place his accent, but it'd been difficult. He sounded vaguely Slavic.

She sipped her coffee. "You are ... Russian."

He shook his head. "No."

"Polish?"

"Sorry."

"Latvian? Lithuanian? Estonian?"

"You're up to five now."

"Then just tell me."

His brown eyes met her own for the first time. "I'm from Portugal."

"Of course," she replied. "I should've guessed."

That was a lie. Ainsley never would've guessed that. What little she knew about the Portuguese accent came from Brazil, but Portugal was an ocean away and centuries removed from its former colony.

"The truth," he explained, "is that I was raised mostly here in the States, but my family is Portuguese, and I spent every summer over there. Now I go almost every month for business." He paused. "Do you know anything about Portugal?"

Ainsley mentally scraped her brain, seeking something, anything, to show some expertise. She remembered that it had been the home of some of the famous *conquistadores* during the age of exploration, but that had been five hundred years ago. Since then, nothing. The western piece of the Iberian peninsula seemed to have floated off into obscurity.

"I'm drawing a blank," she admitted.

She braced for the worst, but to her surprise, Joaquim smiled. "Good. It's better that way."

"It is?"

"We need a complete outsider. You don't speak Portuguese?"

"No, but—" said Ainsley, then stopped herself.

"But what?"

"Nothing."

"Let me guess. You were going to say that you speak Spanish."

"Maybe."

He softened. "It's okay. Most Americans seem to know a

little Spanish. Or they think they do. But my language is totally different."

Ainsley seriously doubted that, but she wasn't in any position to argue. "This sounds interesting. I'd love to hear about the job."

"Of course." He swallowed his coffee and stood up. "Please follow me. I want to show you something, and we can talk on the way."

CHAPTER THREE

As she trailed Joaquim into the warehouse, Ainsley became aware of the little physical changes that occurred in her behavior near an attractive man. Her heels seemed to click more insistently on the floor. Her hips swung a little more widely. Her tongue moistened her lips without her permission.

Joaquim moved swiftly through the stacked pallets of wood. "Fatima described our business to you?"

"You import cork."

He nodded. "It's *cortiça* in my language. Those panels over there"—he pointed to the left—"are flooring. We're shipping them out to San Francisco tomorrow for a large installation. This product is Portugal's biggest international commodity."

"I had no idea," said Ainsley.

"Most people don't. Cork accounted for almost seventy percent of total exports last year. And it's very environmentally responsible too. It grows quickly, is durable, and degrades beautifully." He grinned. "That's the end of my sales speech."

She thought about this. She owned a pair of cork wedges

that had been degrading beautifully in her closet for a few years now. She should've worn them more often, but they were just too summery—and Ainsley had been in some pretty wintery moods lately.

Joaquim continued: "My sister Rita runs the Portuguese side of the business. She has the relationships with all the growers in the Alentejo. But cork can only be stripped once every seven years. It's the law. I pay her what I can, but it's just a part-time job for her, depending on the season."

"Okay," said Ainsley.

"So, to pay the bills, she is also the manager of a villa. It's a historic property owned by a wealthy family, the Souzas. The patriarch is a man named Fernando Souza."

Ainsley nodded. The words *villa* and *historic property* had set her imagination afire.

"In this villa," he continued, "is a chapel. And in this chapel is a valuable mural. It's made of *azulejos*."

Ainsley scrunched up her forehead. "What are those?"

They had arrived at the back wall of the warehouse. It was dark here. Then Joaquim flicked a switch, and a row of lighting exploded from a hanging track.

Ahead of her was a mural of glazed ceramic tiles. The artistry was stunning—a blue-and-white kaleidoscopic pattern that looked almost Arabic.

"These," said Joaquim, "are azulejos. What do you think?"

Ainsley was astonished. "They're beautiful. You should import them."

He shook his head. "No, they stay in Portugal. I only brought these here to impress clients."

She nodded. "So tell me about your sister's problem."

Joaquim drew a deep breath. "The mural at the villa has one very special azulejo. It has a sapphire."

Ainsley tilted her head quizzically. "A sapphire—in the tile?"

A faraway look appeared in his eyes. "It was baked two hundred years ago, according to a very old tradition. In fact, this azulejo is even somewhat famous, mostly because it's always been privately owned, and nobody has been allowed to see it."

"So your sister has somehow lost this tile?"

Joaquim ran a frustrated hand through his hair. "It wasn't lost, Ainsley—the azulejo was stolen."

"And you don't know who did it."

He shook his head sadly. "That is what we will investigate."

Something about that sentence pricked up the hairs at the back of Ainsley's neck. "Joaquim," she said, "did you just say we?"

An inscrutable look came into his eyes. "Yes."

"Why?"

"Because we will be travelling together."

"Who?"

"You and I."

He said it as if it were the most natural thing in the world. Ainsley felt her throat go dry. "Wh...what?"

"The plan is simple. As soon as I finish with this San Francisco client, we will go to Portugal together."

She stepped backwards. "That's very presumptuous, Joaquim."

"Is it?"

"I only work alone."

He crooked his head. "So you have some ... reservations about me?"

"No, I said that I work alone."

He shook his head. "Without any Portuguese, you won't get anywhere."

She felt herself grow cooler, more insolent. "And since you mentioned it, yes, I do have a few reservations about you."

Now Joaquim was staring at her full on, a smirk curling up the corner of his lip. "Such as?"

Ainsley stammered. She didn't know how to tactfully bring up the next subject. "What are you really looking for, Joaquim?"

He smiled. "You think I am a seducer."

"I didn't say that—"

"You know, I do need someone to make me a sandwich."

"Funny."

Suddenly he grew impatient. "What do you think I'm looking for? I want the sapphire azulejo."

"That's all?"

"That's all. My business depends on it. If I wanted to seduce you, I wouldn't go through all this trouble. There are easier ways to do that."

Ainsley had to admit he was right, but she also resented his assumption that she could be easily seduced.

"How many other girls have you asked to go on this trip?" she asked.

He challenged her with his eyes. "Forty-seven."

"You're a real comedian."

"Someone has to be. The cork doesn't tell any jokes."

"Just so we're clear," she said, "you're not my type."

"Yes," he replied, "and just so it's clear, you're not my type either. See, we have that much in common." He held up his palms in a gesture of honesty. "This is professional. I promise."

"All right," said Ainsley.

"Now you have to promise me something," he said.

"Okay."

"The most important thing is that this theft must be kept a secret. If Fernando Souza, the owner of the villa, finds out that it has been stolen, my sister will be fired." Antonio swept his arm around the warehouse. "And that will affect my business."

Ainsley nodded. "Understood."

His eyes looked deeply into her own. Ainsley felt herself falling into their brown depths. It didn't help that, in her heels, she and Joaquim were the same height.

Finally she blinked, breaking the spell. "I have another question."

"Go ahead."

"Why don't you hire someone in Portugal?"

He shook a finger in the air. "There are too many tongues, too much gossip. Word will get around. We are much safer with an outside investigator who can pretend to be a tourist." He paused. "Someone like you."

Those were solid reasons. Ainsley felt a storm of excitement gathering in the center of her body. This was exactly the type of work she was meant for. There was almost no reason why she shouldn't get this job. All that was left was to negotiate price.

Joaquim seemed to read her mind. "Now, you probably want to discuss payment."

"Yes."

"It's all covered here." He handed Ainsley a yellow envelope. "Your contract. After you read it, you can tell me if you want to continue."

Ainsley accepted the envelope. She was so surprised at his abruptness that she didn't know quite what to say.

"Call me when you decide," he said, "but, please, do it quickly."

Joaquim offered his hand. She tentatively shook it. He held the grip a fraction of a second longer than necessary. Then he glanced behind her. "Fatima will help you out."

Ainsley turned. The woman had been standing quietly in the shadows behind them. She wondered how much of their conversation she had heard. How much of their eye contact she had noted.

She turned back, but Joaquim had already disappeared, the echoes of his footsteps receding into the darkness. For a moment, she allowed herself to stare wistfully into the pallets of cork.

"Ready?" said Fatima.

"Yeah."

She followed Fatima back through the small lobby and out the door. A quick farewell, and then Ainsley found herself standing outside the warehouse, blinking in the morning sun.

CHAPTER FOUR

Half an hour later, encased in gridlock, Ainsley shook her head at the license plate in front of her.

5THBENZ

She hadn't misread it. That was the driver's fifth Mercedes Benz. Ainsley felt annoyed. It hadn't been enough for the driver to merely know that she'd owned four other German luxury automobiles. She needed to alert the world, to send the message down from upon high that material status was king and she, the driver, its reigning queen.

Ainsley found herself fantasizing about ramming the grill of her car into the Mercedes' trunk. It would almost be worth the higher insurance premiums.

She watched the traffic light change from red to green, then back to red again. She hadn't moved a single centimeter. From here, she could glimpse her next stop, barely two hundred meters up the road.

Her bank.

At last she squeezed through the intersection, accelerated quickly, and pulled into the parking lot.

From her purse Ainsley pulled out her debit card, which

had been decorated with a rainbow. How ironic. It should've featured dirty fingers wrapped around the steel bars of a debtor's prison. By her calculation, Ainsley only had seventy dollars left in her bank account.

She stepped out of her car, approached the ATM, slid the card inside, and punched in her digits. The screen asked if she would like to view her account balance. Ainsley pushed no. Her poverty already weighed on her days and occupied her nights.

The screen asked for the withdrawal amount. Ainsley pushed the button marked $20, the smallest amount allowed.

The machine beeped loudly. Ainsley read the screen.

Transaction cancelled.

She frowned. That was weird. She re-inserted the debit card into the slot and repeated the process.

Transaction cancelled.

Frustrated, Ainsley kicked the machine, then felt the pain shoot up her foot. She'd forgotten that she was wearing open-toed heels.

Swearing under her breath, she limped into the bank lobby with a hard knot in her stomach and murder in her eyes. There was nobody in line. Of course there wasn't. Nobody would entrust their money to an organization whose ATM spat out lies.

A bank teller leaned into the heavy Plexiglass shield and lifted his hand. "Can I help you, miss?"

She approached the counter. "I have seventy dollars in my account, but the machine won't let me access it."

"Can you enter your account number?"

Ainsley punched it into the pad. His eyes peered through his square-rimmed glasses at his screen. "It says you only have nineteen dollars and thirty-four cents."

"That's wrong."

He looked more closely. "It seems that there was a debit yesterday."

"By who?"

His finger clicked his mouse while his eyes scanned the monitor. "Goldline Fitness. Twenty-five dollars."

That was Ainsley's health club. They billed her monthly. "Then I should have forty-five dollars," she said, her voice tightening.

"Well," he said, "that caused your balance to drop below our fifty-dollar minimum. So we charged a twenty-five-dollar fee."

Ainsley was taken aback. "There's a fifty-dollar minimum?"

"Only if you're on the regular plan. It's waived if you are a part of our Preferred Platinum Checking. Are you interested in joining? There's a one-time hundred-dollar fee—"

"No, thank you."

"Maybe you should think about it. Here." He pushed a pamphlet into the scoop underneath the heavy glass.

Ainsley pushed it back. "No thanks. So you're telling me I have twenty dollars."

"Nineteen dollars and thirty-four cents."

"But I need to withdraw twenty dollars."

"Because you're under the ordinary plan, you don't have overdraft protection, so we'd charge another twenty-five-dollar fee. Can I suggest applying for Preferred Platinum—"

Ainsley cut him off with a wave of her hand. "Tell you what. Let me just withdraw ten dollars."

She was glad that nobody else was within earshot to hear this embarrassing request. The clerk squinted at his monitor, hemming and hawing as if she were asking for the moon.

"Well, that is possible," he finally replied. "However, we will close your account if your balance drops below five dollars."

"Understood." She managed a fake smile so tight that her temples ached.

"How would you like the ten dollars?"

"It doesn't matter."

The clerk opened his drawer and withdrew a crisp ten-dollar bill. He printed out a receipt and slid both towards Ainsley in the scoop. "There you are. Have a good weekend."

The clerk smiled at her. Ainsley paused, trying to gauge if there was any subtext. She decided there wasn't any.

As she left the bank and crossed the parking lot, her phone rang in her purse. She pulled it out and checked the display. It was her friend Deirdre. Ainsley blanched. Last week, she'd agreed to let Deirdre to set her up on a blind date —and it was supposed to happen tonight.

She picked up quickly. "Oh my God. I totally forgot about that date until just now."

"I knew you would," said her friend. "Good thing is that Tom's running late. He just texted my friend to tell me that he's going to be there at six-thirty."

"Where are we meeting again?"

"Scorekeepers."

Ainsley hung her head. It was the sports pub in town, packed with prematurely fat guys shouting at much fitter guys running across television screens.

"You're kidding me," she said.

"Nope. And what's wrong with Scorekeepers? It's a decent place."

"Not for romance." She sighed. "What does he do?"

"I don't know."

"But you've met him, right?"

"No. My friend in IT knows him. She says he's a good guy."

Three degrees of separation. Ainsley heard alarm bells ringing in the distance. "I don't know about this."

"Stay positive," said Deirdre. "At least you'll get a drink and an appetizer, right?"

Ainsley leaned against her car, feeling tired. "It's not like the old days."

On the other end, the shrill scream of a toddler erupted. That was Deirdre's three-year-old son.

Her friend sighed. "I know it's not, Ainsley. Now go get those free drinks for the both of us."

"All right."

They disconnected. Ainsley mulled her crisis for a moment. Then she stowed her phone in her purse and slipped back into her car, on her way home to gussy up.

CHAPTER FIVE

As the platter of red-hot chicken wings with celery sticks and white dip passed behind her, Ainsley couldn't help but feel her stomach grumble.

She'd arrived at Scorekeepers ten minutes early and taken a stool at the bar. On the wall, six flatscreens played six different football games, guaranteeing that her eyes would always be distracted. It was football season, but Ainsley couldn't stand the sport.

Behind the bar, a young man wearing a black-and-white referee's jersey and three days' scruff slid a small cocktail napkin towards Ainsley. This was the bartender's prelude to a drink. "What can I get you, ma'am?" he said.

She winced at the word. *Ma'am*. At twenty-nine, she was already getting too old for certain establishments. "I'm supposed to be meeting somebody," she said.

"What's his name?"

"Tom."

The bartender didn't react at first. Then he poured her half a glass of cheap red wine and chucked the empty bottle into a bin. "On the house. Don't tell anybody."

Ainsley smiled. Her first free drink, and it had come from the bartender—a lot like the old days. "Thank you. How did you know that I liked red wine?"

"You don't have a beer vibe."

"Not usually. But I like liquor."

"No girl should drink liquor on a first date."

"Thanks for the advice."

She pulled her white leather purse closer to her side. Her favorite, this item had been with Ainsley through ups, downs, and everything in between. Certainly it had been with her longer than any man.

She had just taken a sip of wine when she heard a nervous clearing of a throat behind her. Then a voice said, "Are you Ainsley?"

It was showtime. She tossed her hair as she swiveled on her stool. "You must be Tom," she said.

Facing her was a white man in his forties. Ainsley's eyes quickly scanned the goods. On the plus side, he looked to be above average height, and a good weight. That was getting harder to find. On the other hand, his hairline had receded further than a Russian army, and his arms were a pair of chicken wings. Across his thin torso was a faded gray polo shirt that had seen too many washings.

In short, Tom wasn't repulsive, but he wasn't a catch either.

"Nice to meet you," he said, offering his hand.

She shook it, noticing his long, soft fingers. "Likewise."

His eyes spotted her wine. "You already got a drink?"

"Oh, the bartender just wanted to be nice to me."

"But I'm on time," he said.

"Yes, and I was early."

Tom pulled out the stool next to hers. An angry mask had come over his face. He was shedding irritation like droplets of sweat. "I was going to buy you a drink," he said, "since that's what's usually expected."

"You can still do that," she said, "if you'd like."

"Okay." Tom signaled for a couple of beers. The bartender slid one towards Ainsley with a look of sympathy.

She held up the wine in one hand and the beer in the other. "Look—now you've got me in a pair of Irish handcuffs."

Tom didn't react. Maybe women weren't allowed to be funny in his family. "Are you Irish?" he asked.

"No," said Ainsley, "but it's a fun expression."

"So what are you, exactly?"

His tone was accusatory. An open-ended question tinged with bile wasn't the best way to start a date. Ainsley tried to make the best of it.

"Oh, I'm just me," she replied lightly. "The bigger question is what are you? Deirdre didn't know what you did for a living."

"I work in IT," he said.

"Doing what?"

"Smart systems management. We're using structured algorithms to run and diagnose those systems, with the ultimate goal of being able to correct issues without human intervention. We're in beta."

Ainsley stared at him blankly. He may as well have asked her to translate cuneiform etched into a stone tablet.

"Oh," she said.

As Tom continued describing his job, she noticed that his hands were compulsively straightening his napkin so that it was perpendicular with the counter.

"So how do you earn your daily bread?" he asked.

"That's a hard one," she answered. "I've done a lot of things, and right now I'm looking for something new."

A knowing look came over his face. "Deirdre mentioned something to my friend about gemstones."

She nodded. "I do find missing gemstones."

He was trying not to smile. "So people hire you to find missing jewelry?"

"Missing gemstones."

"So you travel?"

"Yep."

She smiled nicely, trying to put a point on this. But Ainsley could see from the skeptical look in his eye that he didn't like to travel. "You must really love jewelry," he said.

"I find gemstones, Tom, and they actually have many purposes." Her voice was a little tighter than she'd meant it to be.

He wouldn't let up. "But mostly they're used in jewelry, right?"

"Yes, it's one of their many uses."

He visibly bristled. It seemed that the very mention of jewelry was a sore point for him. Ainsley guessed that he'd probably been taken to the cleaners by a greedy ex-wife.

"So have you been married before?" she said.

He instantly stiffened. "What tells you that?"

"A hunch."

Tom looked straight ahead. "Yes, I was married. Now I share custody of my nine-year-old son." He sipped his beer through slitted lips. "What about you?"

Ainsley found herself starting to explain. How she referred to her ex-husband as The Legal Weasel. How she'd supported him all through his years in law school. How he'd silently retreated out of the marriage less than a year ago, disappeared from her life.

When she'd finished, Tom was staring at her, aghast. "So your husband left you, and you don't know where he is?"

"No."

"But you're a detective."

That was a good point. "I find gemstones, not people."

Tom lifted his beer to his lips and drained half the bottle in one gulp. He dropped the bottle back on the counter. "Sounds like you made out pretty good, not getting divorced. Mine almost killed me."

"We all have problems," she said.

"Some more than others."

His eyes slid around sideways and met hers. The bitterness was almost palpable. Ainsley sensed that this would be a good time for a break. She set down her wine, and her hand wound itself around the handles of her purse.

"I'm going to use the bathroom, Tom. I'll be right back."

A sneer marched onto his face. "Really."

"Yes."

"I'll hold you to that."

She ignored the jibe and moved across the bar, aware of the stares of the young guys gathered around the pool table. In the restroom, Ainsley turned on the hot water and looked at herself in the mirror.

Her arms were well-defined, her waist still narrow, her midriff flatter than it had been for a few years. But the face that looked back at her was neither young nor optimistic. The fine lines creasing the corners of her eyes angled downwards, not upwards.

Ainsley needed to stop this downward slide, in every possible way. She would begin by breaking the bad news to Tom that their date was finished. Then she would go home, draw a bath, try to figure things out.

She washed her hands thoroughly with soap. Then held them under the hand dryer until she gasped at the heat.

When she returned to the bar, the wine and the two beers were still on the countertop—but Tom's stool was empty.

Ainsley spun around. "Where did he go?"

The bartender glanced up. "That guy you were with?"

"Yeah."

"He left. He said you'd agreed to take care of the bill."

Ainsley's felt her jaw fall to her chest. Chivalry was not only dead—it had been rolled inside a carpet, duct-taped shut, and dropped off a bridge.

"I never said that," she said.

The bartender nodded, as though he'd guessed as much. "Well, don't take it personally."

Of course Ainsley was taking this personally. This was humiliating. Tom had baggage, but he'd evidently judged that she carried even more. And Ainsley wasn't sure that he was wrong, either. She felt stabs of embarrassment in her stomach. She felt the hot flush of shame on her cheeks.

"But we just met. Jesus—"

The bartender quieted her down. "Listen, he's an asshole. He argues the bill every time he comes in here."

The bartender went back to polishing a glass. Ainsley understood why he'd offered her a free glass of wine. He'd probably guessed what was coming.

"He doesn't have to punish me," she said.

"I'll talk to him next time he comes in, ma'am." Then the bartender gently slid the black case towards her. "I put you in for the happy hour price."

Her heart sank as she looked at the bad news. It was ten dollars. The two numerals caused a pain in her stomach so intense that it felt as though someone were ripping through her intestines with a chainsaw.

Groaning quietly, Ainsley reached into her purse, produced her crisp new ten-dollar bill, and pushed it across the counter.

"Here you go," she said.

The bartender took her money. "Don't worry about the tip."

Ainsley drained the rest of her wine. "I'll give you one anyways," she said. "Don't ever go on a blind date."

CHAPTER SIX

Though she heard the crack of the starting gun, Ainsley couldn't get her legs to bolt off the starting line.

It was six o'clock in the morning, and as the first fingers of pink dawn were stretching across the sky, Ainsley was crouched on the cinder track of a high school. On her feet was an old pair of yellow track cleats, leftover from her athletic days. She'd dug them out of her closet.

Standing on the grass nearby, stopwatch in hand, was David Madradis. He'd been one of the Legal Weasel's law school classmates. She knew that David felt bad for the way her former husband had treated her. Meanwhile, he'd become so busy at a prestigious law firm, measuring out his time in fractions of hours, that the only time he could meet her was at one of his early track-and-field workouts.

David sighed. "Again, Walker? You make more false starts than a government committee."

"My shoe feels weird," she complained.

He pocketed his starting gun. "I'm not wasting any more blanks on you."

"Well, you're only two steps away. Just say go."

David held up his stopwatch again. "Runner, take your mark."

Ainsley crouched down on the block, feeling the soft vulcanized rubber under her palms. This stance brought back old memories of high school, when she'd been all-state in track-and-field. But that had been well over ten years ago, a decade filled with its own share of false starts.

"Get set..."

Now Ainsley was looking down the barrel of thirty with practically nothing to show for it. She was plagued with the nagging thought that gemstone detective was going to become just the latest entry on her already too-long resume. In her mouth was the small, bitter taste of a single-digit bank account.

"... and go."

Ainsley took off. As she tried to accelerate, it felt like her legs were pipes filled with metallic sludge. She tried to ignore the convulsions in her lungs. She concentrated instead on form, reaching out with her hands and arms, grabbing the invisible handrails, just as her coach had taught her so many moons ago.

Forty-five seconds later, she rounded the final turn and saw David at the finish line, at the far end of the straightaway, stopwatch in hand. Her esophagus was a column of fire.

Deep inside, in some pocket of primal awareness, Ainsley felt an odd twinge in her left knee—

—and then it suddenly buckled.

It was a quick demolition. In the blink of an eye, she was sprawled on the track, facedown, fifteen meters from the finish line, choked sounds crawling out of her mouth.

David clicked the stopwatch, returned it to his pocket, and walked over to Ainsley. "So you've got a bum knee. It's too bad. You would've hit sixty-five seconds. That's pretty good for age thirty, Walker."

Ainsley rolled over onto her side, her hair caught in the sweat on her face. "I'm twenty-nine."

He grinned at her. "God, this must be really unpleasant for you, rolling around on the track at six in the morning, elbows and knees all scraped to hell. There must be something you want from me."

Ainsley tried to kick him, but David wisely stepped out of her path. "Be nice," she said. "I feel like I'm dying."

"We're all dying," he said, "and running the four hundred is a reminder of that."

"Shut up and help me up."

David helped Ainsley to her feet. His arm around her shoulders, she limped to the nearby bleachers, where she collapsed.

He sat down next to her and passed her the water bottle. "The four hundred is really tricky. It's not for milers, and it's not for sprinters. It's a race for people who are somewhere in between."

"So it's for misfits."

He nodded. "Basically."

That made Ainsley feel even more miserable. Not only was she a misfit, but she hadn't even finished the misfit race.

"David, you really know how to talk to a girl."

"Hey, I'm married," he said. "I only have to watch my mouth around one woman. The rest of you get the unvarnished truth."

Ainsley's breathing had finally slowed. She was even starting to feel the first glimmerings of post-workout endorphins. Now was the time.

"David," she said, "I really need your advice."

He fixed his eyes somewhere far on the horizon. "Yeah, I figured. What's the problem this time?"

"I have a new contract, but I'm not sure about it."

He produced his reading glasses from his duffle bag. "Fork

it over. I'd hate to see you sign yourself into a lifetime membership in a Third World brothel."

Ainsley handed him the envelope. She'd read the contract at least fourteen times the night before. There was one portion that was unbelievably bad. She waited for him to find it.

David scanned the document, commenting out loud. "Hmm. Okay. That's interesting. He's got good counsel."

Then he paused. Ainsley knew that he'd come to the suspicious part.

"Ainsley—"

"The payment," she said.

"It's three thousand dollars—"

"Euros."

"—whatever. But it's one hundred percent payable upon delivery of the sapphire? Is this for real?" He turned towards her. "They're not giving you anything up front?"

"Nothing."

The lawyer grimaced. "That's baloney. Contingency is not how you want to be paid. You're not a personal injury lawyer."

"I know," she replied.

"You could work for weeks and never see a single dollar."

"Euro."

"Whatever." He looked at her. "But I can tell you want to do it anyways."

Her heart leapt. David wasn't telling her not to sign the contract. Then again, he knew Ainsley better than most. It was easier to stop a freight train with a pinky finger than to stop her from pursuing a goal.

"I do."

He tore off his reading glasses. "Then you'd better negotiate for a retainer."

"I know."

Ainsley was looking at him. She was using every cell in her

body to send the message, because she sure didn't want to verbalize it.

He looked at her. "I can tell there's something else."

Ainsley broke down. "I need a loan, David. I'm broke. Really broke."

"How much?"

"Whatever you can spare."

"Tell me a dollar amount."

She shrugged. "I don't know. It would be nice to have enough for a plane ticket."

"My school debt isn't exactly paying for itself."

She swung towards him. "David, I've got less than five dollars in cash. Five dollars."

Tears began to brim at the corners of her eyes. He raised his eyebrows. "So it's that bad," he said.

"Yeah."

The lawyer ran his tongue around his teeth, studying her. "Look, no offense, but are you sure you want to stay in this business?"

"Yeah."

He looked at her skeptically. "Really?"

She knew it sounded ludicrous, but these foreign assignments had given her a taste of honest adventure in strange lands—and that taste was more addictive than any liquor, any opiate.

She grew defensive. "What's your point?"

"No one in his right mind would hire someone just to chase after a missing gemstone."

"Then I'll just keep finding people in their wrong minds," she said. "Besides, David, most of your clients probably fit that description too."

He laughed. "Good point. You should've been a lawyer, Walker."

"Never."

"I can afford to give you two thousand right now."

Ainsley felt herself light up. "Are you serious?"

"Sure. You're a decent person. No felonies. Plus I know where you live."

She slugged him in the shoulder, but her eyes were dancing. "I'll pay it back as soon as possible, I promise."

"Of course you will. It'll be automated."

Ainsley tilted her head. "What do you mean?"

"I'll set it up through a website. Monthly minimum deducted from your bank account. You won't even have to think about it."

That would be fine. She flung her arms around him. "David, you are a prince. I don't know how to thank you."

He gingerly detached himself from her, then stood up. "Tell you what. You can start paying me back by timing me."

Ainsley stood up. "You're going to run the four hundred too?"

"Hell no." He picked up his duffle bag. "I'm doing the thirty-yard dash to my car. And if I do it fast enough, I won't be late for work."

"It's been real."

"Watch your inbox," he said.

"I will."

"And bring me something back from Portugal. I need to remember what life looks like outside of a law firm."

David saluted. Ainsley watched him run across the parking lot, climb into his car, and drive off.

Then, alone on the bench, with only the contract for company, Ainsley began to mentally gird herself for battle.

CHAPTER SEVEN

Three hours later, Ainsley tossed the contract across the desk and said, "I want a retainer."

She was sitting in Joaquim's office, her hair swept into an updo. She'd wrapped her classiest skirt around her hips, strapped her best business heels on her feet, donned her most serious jewelry on her wrists. This was how you dressed for negotiation. No man could deny a competent and glamorous woman.

In his chair, Joaquim blinked twice. "Excuse me?"

"I want a retainer. Fifty percent. I won't sign this without it."

He was looking at her oddly. "A retainer?"

"Money up front. The total is fine, but I want fifty percent to start. That's fifteen hundred euros."

A look of horror spread across his face. Ainsley felt as though she had demanded he rip the head off a live kitten. "I can't do that," he said. "We're barely hanging on here—"

"In America," she replied, "investigators get retainers."

He scratched his head, scuffed his boot on the floor. "I don't know."

She reached for her purse. "If you can't make it happen, I leave."

A look of panic flashed across Joaquim's face. He pushed the air down with his palms, as if to press Ainsley back down into her seat. "No, please, let me make one phone call. Please. Wait."

"Okay," she said.

Joaquim left the office.

Alone, Ainsley uncrossed her legs, then recrossed them the other way. She began filing her nails. They were the one thing she hadn't had time or money to fix. The cuticles were ragged, the red paint chipped. Ainsley needed a world-class manicure.

If Joaquim could meet her demand, that's exactly what she would do.

Ten minutes passed. Ainsley read old text messages on her phone until she couldn't pretend to be busy any longer. Waiting this long was a sign of desperation. She couldn't afford to lose the upper hand. It was time to walk away.

Ainsley stood and brushed off her skirt, then grabbed her purse—when he returned into the office, a weak smile on his face. "I have found a solution," he said.

She stopped. "Is it fifteen hundred euros up front?"

"No."

She felt herself growing upset. Ainsley had never been comfortable with negotiation. "Maybe you didn't understand me—"

Joaquim held up a finger. "Please, you must listen. I have just spoken with my sister. We are both very interested in your services, but she cannot afford a retainer at this time."

That begged another question: If this woman couldn't afford fifteen hundred euros now, how was she going to be able to afford three thousand euros for the final payment?

"Instead," he continued, "she is proposing to pay for a hotel room in Lisbon during your investigation."

"For as long as necessary?"

He nodded. "Yes."

Ainsley ran the numbers in her head. This offer was a pittance. They sure as hell weren't going to be putting her up at the Four Seasons.

His eyes sought her own, held them imploringly. "Please, Miss Walker."

Ainsley felt the stubbornness melting and leaking out of her head. Travel, gemstones, excitement—these things were too important to her to be thrown away for something as prosaic as a little bit of upfront cash. She would regret turning this assignment down.

The truth was that Ainsley was ready to fold—and, even worse, she had known that she would.

"Fine," she said.

"Really?" replied Joaquim.

She waved a hand dismissively. "Put the hotel payment in my contract, and I'll sign it."

His eyes grew wide. "You're wonderful."

"Go on," she said, "before I change my mind."

He turned to his laptop and typed vigorously. Ainsley studied his muscled arms, his dimpled cheeks, his heavy eyebrows.

The printer hummed, and he whipped the new contract at her. "I only changed the one line," he said. "Read it over and sign it when you're ready."

Ainsley verified the change, then signed the contract and handed it back to him. "I want a copy."

"Of course," he said. "Now, there's one other thing I have to tell you."

Ainsley froze. "What?"

"I won't be going with you."

———

Her heart dropped all the way down to her heels. "What happened?"

Joaquim sighed. "This San Francisco deal isn't ready yet, and they're is asking me to personally attend to the shipment and installation. They're our biggest client. I have to stay until it's finished."

"So I am working alone."

"Yes—for now." He rubbed his eyes and sat back. "You know, I was an actor once. Only for a year. Sometimes I think I should've stayed in it. I wouldn't have to deal with clients like San Francisco."

Ainsley ignored the background. "That's nice, but there's one problem."

"You don't speak Portuguese."

"Right."

He reached into his desk and handed her a book. It was titled *Portuguese for the English Speaker*, and looked to be older than Ainsley herself. Its cover was tattered, its edges stained with coffee, its pages tearing loose. The chapter on technology probably offered translations for typewriter and phonograph.

"My personal textbook," he said. "It's a good one. But you must learn quickly. I'm going to buy your plane ticket this afternoon. You'll leave in three days."

"That fast?"

"Three days from now, I'll test you on basic Portuguese. If you can't speak decently, I'll cancel the ticket."

Ainsley gulped. "That's harsh."

"You boasted that languages were your strength, Ainsley. Prove it to me."

She pulled herself up, tried to look on the bright side of things. "I already know Spanish, so this shouldn't be too hard."

He shook his head sadly. "Once you start studying," he said, "we'll see how long you still believe that."

CHAPTER EIGHT

Three days later, as she stared into her computer screen, Ainsley had begun to understand what Joaquim meant.

Quickly realizing that the tattered book wouldn't be enough, she had used fifty dollars of her precious remaining open credit to purchase an online language program. She'd been immersed for days.

So far, the most important thing she'd learned was that Portuguese was much harder than anybody had warned her.

The problem wasn't necessarily the grammar. The basics were nearly identical to Spanish—two numbers, three persons, three aspects, two voices. It was familiar territory.

She wasn't worried about the vocabulary either. Any English noun ending in *–ty* ends in *–dade* in Portuguese. City, for instance, becomes *ciudade*. Any English word ending in *–tion* (position) ends in *–ção* (posição). And more: *–sion* becomes *–são*, *–ble* becomes *–vel*.

No, it was the pronunciation that was making her tear her hair out.

On the first morning, at her kitchen table, Ainsley had settled into a chair and opened the first lesson on her laptop.

Against a green background, a graphical hand had lifted a vocabulary card with a single word printed on it:

Lagos.

Ainsley had pronounced it the English way: *la-gos*.

Then a woman's recorded voice had announced the correct way: *la-goosh*.

Ainsley had crinkled her nose. That was weird. The letter *s* was pronounced like *sh*. She began to consciously practice the *sh*, and the more she practiced, the more she felt like a librarian shushing people.

Then the hand had lifted another vocabulary card: *comer*. That was the same as the Spanish word meaning "to eat". So Ainsley had pronounced it the same, *co-mer*, then hit the speak button.

Wrong again. The woman's voice said *coo-mer*.

Another change: the Portuguese o. Ainsley was in the Spanish habit of pronouncing that vowel short, but the Portuguese pronounced it long. *Como* was *coo-moo*.

That evening, Joaquim had sent over his assistant, Fatima, who'd brought a small box of *natas*, Portuguese custard pastries. Ainsley's stomach rumbled to life. She'd forgotten to eat all day. The mild woman had sat quietly at the kitchen table, watching Ainsley devour them. Then she'd asked simple questions about bathrooms, hotels, and directions.

While answering, Ainsley had discovered a hazard of spoken Portuguese: the shushes and oohs built up wads of frothy spit in her cheeks. If she hadn't been careful, she would've sprayed this woman with flecks of spittle, which wouldn't have helped her cause at all.

Second day: Ainsley had woken up and headed straight back to the program, plunging even further down the rabbit hole, discovering the more obscure parts of Portuguese grammar. How personal infinitives are used to prepare for future subjunctive.

All day, she'd barely eaten, and that night, Fatima had returned with more natas and more conversation. She'd asked Ainsley to study vocabulary about gemstones and artwork. The conversation had been easier.

During a break, Ainsley had learned that Fatima was planning to leave her job next month for an extended trip to Brazil. She'd reassured Ainsley that Joaquim was a good man and a good boss—she just wanted to see Brazil, in depth, before she got too old. Joaquim had been hunting for a new assistant for weeks.

So Fatima had caught the travel bug too. Ainsley knew exactly how she felt.

Now it was the third day.

Unwashed, with no makeup, Ainsley sat in her ratty purple bathrobe, holding a cup of coffee in her hands. Her stringy hair hung in wisps across her face. Puffy pouches under her eyes. She had talked at the computer screen until well past midnight, then passed out on the couch, and dreamed of nothing.

As she sipped her coffee, her phone rang. It was Joaquim.

"So," he said, "Fatima says you weren't lying about your talent for languages."

"She has a talent for bringing good pastries."

"If it's okay with you, I'll come over at seven pm for your final test."

Ainsley froze. "To my house?"

"Yes. We can have dinner together too."

She felt her heart skip a beat. "No, that's probably not a good idea."

"Why not? We're professional. Coworkers eat together."

"I'm a pain to eat with," she lied.

"Me too. I always talk with my mouth full."

"No, I have dietary restrictions."

"We can work around that."

"It's just not a good idea."

He paused. "Okay, it's up to you. The test only."

She ended the connection and looked at her phone. Joaquim would be coming over to her home. A funny feeling of anticipation buzzed in her stomach.

Her eyes glanced towards the bedroom. Then, through an act of sheer will, she pushed her eyes back towards her laptop, crowded that dangerous thought out of her mind. It couldn't be there. It just couldn't. This man was her employer.

Instead, she started to clean.

For the next three hours, Ainsley washed every dish in the house. She scrubbed the top, side and bottom. She beat her rugs with a broom on a laundry line. She vacuumed her carpet. She polished every surface in the house with either blue glass cleaner or lemon-yellow furniture spray.

She also washed her bedsheets. After all, it'd been three days since they'd seen the laundry.

At six thirty, Ainsley dressed herself in a burgundy blazer, a scoop-neck top, and her favorite pair of skinny jeans. The blazer was to look professional, the scoop-neck top to reveal her clavicles. They were elegant, well-formed, and she'd always gotten compliments on them. But she didn't dare to dip any lower. A plunging neckline was useful only if you had something to plunge towards.

She lit a candle, then quickly changed her mind and blew it out and waved the smoke away. Nothing should look planned. It all needed to seem casual, by accident.

At six forty-five, she adjusted the lighting, straightened the remote controls on her coffee table. Then, with her apartment glistening, she perched herself lightly on the edge of a kitchen chair, crossed her legs, and waited for the knock.

It didn't come.

At seven-thirty, frowning, Ainsley called Joaquim. It rang

four times and then went to voicemail. "Hey," she said, "I thought you were coming over for my final test. Call me back."

She hung up and looked at the wall. For the next two hours, she continued staring at it, willing the phone to ring. It didn't. That's when the truth dawned on her.

She'd been stood up.

Upset, Ainsley opened a bottle of cheap red wine and poured a glass and drank it quickly. It tasted horrible. She poured another. By her third glass, neither the wine nor the rejection tasted quite as bad.

And then, at ten minutes to eleven, as she drained the last of the bottle, her phone finally rang.

It was Joaquim.

"Ainsley," he said, "I am so sorry, my meeting turned into a business dinner, it went very late, I couldn't break away, this San Francisco deal is killing me—"

Rolling her eyes, Ainsley held the phone away from her ear. Joaquim was sounding exactly like a husband in trouble.

She waited until the small voice had stopped talking, then returned the phone to her ear. "That was unbelievably rude."

His voice dropped. "It was."

"Is this how you treat everyone at your company?"

"No, not at all—"

"You haven't even paid me, and you're already treating me like this?"

"Yes, I was wrong, forgive me."

She smiled. He'd made it through the wringer, and now she would be nicer. "So the flight leaves tomorrow. Will I be on it?"

"It depends on your Portuguese."

"Where should we talk?"

He paused. "Let's talk right now. On the phone."

"Okay. What should I say?"

"Tell me about yourself," he said. "Tell me what is your favorite book, what is your deepest dream, your biggest regret, who was your first lover—"

"I won't talk about that last one."

He laughed. "Okay."

Ainsley drew a deep breath and began to speak. Then she heard herself describing, in decent Portuguese, her childhood, her athletic successes, her failed marriage, her job-hopping, her stalled career as a gemstone travel detective. The words flew out of her mouth, surprising her as much as it did him.

When she'd finished, there was silence on the other end.

"Are you still there?" she said.

"Yes." His voice was a tiny croak.

"Do I pass?"

He paused. Then: "Yes, it's good enough. Congratulations."

Ainsley threw her fist into the air in a silent gesture of victory.

"Fatima will pick you up for the airport tomorrow at noon. She's putting together the informational packet that you can read on the plane. I'll call you in the morning to wish you good luck."

"I won't count on it," she said.

CHAPTER NINE

As the late-morning sunlight streamed into her bedroom, Ainsley chewed on her fingernails and stared at her open suitcase.

The item lay innocently on her bed, a beautiful purple brocade number. It looked beautiful. But the luggage wasn't really the issue.

The problem was that she couldn't decide what to put inside the luggage—and she only had fifteen minutes before Fatima picked her up.

Packing for any international trip was always difficult. It required research of all types, meteorological, architectural, cultural. So far, Ainsley had chosen a sleeveless turquoise camisole top, an asymmetrical orange zipup turtleneck sweater, a long-sleeve black t-shirt, and a pair of cream-colored jeans. Several other finalists were circled on the bedspread.

And yet somehow none of it looked right. Not for a mystery-laced journey to a European country.

Ainsley decided to turn to accessories first, then match

her clothing that way. She rummaged through her drawers, selecting necklaces, rings, earrings.

Then she picked up an item she hadn't worn in years—a fork repurposed into a bracelet. Inherited from her grandmother, the antique utensil had been bent, shaped, and polished into a beautiful piece of art nouveau jewelry. She knew immediately that it would be living on her wrist during this trip.

Then she turned to footwear.

Fatima had warned her that the streets of Lisbon were hilly and cobbled, which pretty much nixed any possibility of wearing high heels. She didn't want to bring sneakers or hiking shoes either, because those things screamed tourist. There had to be some in-between options that were both functional and stylish, and that wouldn't announce her American citizenship quite so loudly.

Ainsley headed for her shoe closet. She yanked out stacks of the familiar cardboard boxes, flinging lids left and right, hoping to stumble upon a forgotten pair that would fill this need. She regretted not cataloguing her collection with photos of their contents.

Then, in a dusty corner, she found a pair of brown leather boots. The heels were wide and chunky, and not too tall. The name was Frye, an old American brand. Ainsley hadn't worn them for a couple of years, but she remembered that they'd been comfortable.

These would do.

She glanced at her watch. Ten minutes. Her heart was racing. She needed to make some sartorial decisions, pronto.

An enormous yawn seized control of her face. She hadn't slept much that night. With the help of three cups worth of pulverized Arabica bean, she'd stayed up until nearly five am reading about Portugal.

What she learned had been fascinating.

First, she'd read about port wine. About how it'd been one of the oldest products of the region. About how the Romans had imported the vines into Portugal two thousand years ago. How the roots stretch as much as thirty meters down into the rocky soil of the Douro Valley in search of water.

Then she'd read that the English and the Portuguese had preserved the longest uninterrupted trade agreement in European history, one that stretched back to the medieval era. Early on, it'd been based on a very simple swap of Portuguese wine for English wool.

Things had heated up later, when a seventeenth-century Portuguese abbot in Lamego invented a way to better preserve wine during its sea voyage to England. He'd added neutral grape spirit to the wine during fermentation (as opposed to afterwards, which was already common), a technique that left high levels of residual sugar.

The result: a sweet, rich, full-bodied dessert wine. It was called port wine.

And the English had loved it.

Soon the land grab was on. Throughout the seventeen hundreds, the English, extra short on wine because of its endless skirmishing with France, had swarmed Portugal's Douro Valley, buying thousands of acres, clearing the land, building terraces. Using the abbot's new technique, they'd begun producing port wine in enormous quantities, and shipped the bottles back to London. These "shippers", as they were known, still constitute the biggest names in port wine today—Croft, Taylor, Fonseca, Sandeman, Churchill, Graham, Warre, Dow.

Of course, the Portuguese themselves got in on the game too, establishing modern shippers such as Ramos Pinto, Calém, Pocas, and Real Compania Velha. But the entire port wine industry, from the very start, had been the blend of the two cultures.

To preserve their sensitive product during the long sea voyage to London, these shippers had stuffed another local product into the necks of the port wine bottles.

Cork.

And thus the wine stopper was born.

Ainsley had finally shut the books at five am to catch a couple of hours of sleep before packing. She'd forgotten to set her alarm clock and woken up at eleven am. She'd given herself less than an hour to make wardrobe decisions that usually took much longer.

The sound of a honking outside jolted her back to the present. She went over to her front window and peered outside. Fatima was parked in the loading zone outside, the engine running.

Ainsley was out of time.

She ran to her suitcase, threw all of her finalists inside, tossed an extra pair of black heels, and zipped it shut. She pulled the brown boots onto her feet and selected a black-and-white houndstooth peacoat from her closet. It was wintertime in the Mediterranean, and the coat was one of her favorites.

The car honked again.

Cursing under her breath, Ainsley quickly double checked her paperwork. Airplane confirmation number, check. Passport, check. Debit card, check. Photocopies of debit card, check. Joaquim's envelope, check. Book for airplane, check. Camera, check.

There was something she was forgetting. She knew it. But Ainsley would have to live with that.

She turned off the heat, closed the blinds, checked the sink. Then she hauled her suitcase off the bed and dragged it out into the living room.

At the front door, Ainsley paused to survey her apartment. For a moment, she felt a pang of fear. This was home. It was comfortable. It was known.

But what lay ahead offered her so much more.

CHAPTER TEN

Forty-five minutes later, as Fatima had pulled up to the departures curb, Ainsley closed her bag and looked at the driver.

"You've been wonderful," she said.

Fatima smiled warmly. "I wish you the best luck."

Ainsley took a deep breath. It was hard to leave town like this, informing nobody, saying nothing, slinking out like a thief in the night. After all, it wasn't every day that she took her first trip to Europe, let alone having no backup, barely knowing the language, and tasked with a probably impossible mission.

But she'd told nobody, except David. She'd learned that it was easier this way.

Then Fatima's phone had begun ringing. She answered in Portuguese, listening closely.

Ainsley was reaching for the door handle when Fatima, to her surprise, grabbed her arm. Her mouth silently formed the word no.

Then she ended the call. "Wait for a minute," she said.

"Why?"

A tiny smile cracked the mild woman's mouth. She glanced in the rearview mirror. "That's why."

Ainsley looked in her mirror. Behind them, a sleek, black car was tearing along the dropoff curb. It screeched to a halt just behind them.

The door opened, and Joaquim stepped out.

Ainsley felt like all the air had just been sucked out of the atmosphere. He looked good. Dressed in a trim black Italian suit, aviator sunglasses, shiny loafers, he let loose a dazzling smile that could've been the cover material for a thousand different fashion magazines. He held up an object in his hand.

"That was Joaquim who just called," said Fatima. "He said he wants to give you something before you leave."

Ainsley left out of the car and walked towards him. Her knees felt wobbly. It was hard to breathe. Until now, she'd only seen a fraction of what he was capable of. Now he'd turned on the full magnetism.

"I'm sorry for my appearance," he said, "but I have interviews all day with these San Francisco people. They are driving me crazy."

"You look fine," said Ainsley, trying not to smile.

"I wanted to apologize again for last night," he said, "and to offer a token of my remorse."

"What is it?" she said.

He handed her a black mobile phone. It wasn't a smart phone, but it did look new, and it did have a flip keyboard for texting.

"It's old," he explained, "but it's my personal phone for when I go to Portugal." Then he'd shown her how it was already enabled for Portuguese systems. She wouldn't have to bother with a SIM card or overseas billing.

"I even printed the number for you on the back."

"That is very thoughtful," she said.

Joaquim looked deep into her eyes. "I want you to come back, Ainsley."

That did it. She felt the tingling beginning to grow, first in her legs, then moving everywhere. "I will," she croaked. She caught the fresh scent of cork blended with his naturally musky masculine scent. It smelled of mystery, of travel, of a new life.

Then a misty look came into Joaquim's eyes. "Do you know about King Sebastião?"

"Who?"

"A Portuguese king who went away on a journey a long time ago. He promised his people that he would return and keep them safe."

"And?"

"He never did. He died in Africa."

"That's sad."

He nodded. "I don't want you to suffer the same fate. If you get into trouble, I promise to find you."

"Am I going to be in danger?"

"Well, that depends entirely upon you." His eyes grew mischievous. "Have a good flight. My sister will tell you everything else you need to know. She's a character."

Joaquim pulled her suitcase out of the trunk, placed it on the sidewalk, then straightened up. Then he'd squeezed her hand, for a fraction of a second longer than necessary.

"Take care, Ainsley."

"You too," she croaked.

Then Joaquim slipped into his black sedan, waved once, and drove away.

Dazed, Ainsley found herself moving inside the airport, moving through the security line, moving through customs, moving towards her departure gate. Three hours later, she dropped into her seat.

Ainsley hadn't responded when the flight attendant asked

for her choice of beverage. She'd just sat there, watching the sun drop below the horizon, hearing the other passengers snoring.

Then, three hours later, she watched the sun rise again, chewing on the complimentary breakfast croissant. Soon after that, she saw the blue corrugated sheet of saltwater appear.

Then the plane began its descent, and Lisbon came into view below her. In the yellow morning light, the sight of the reddish-orange terracotta roofs of Europe's westernmost capital took her breath away. The structures clung to the steep hills of the city, in nearly fractal patterns. These homes were real. This country was real. A thrilled panic zipped through her body.

This was Ainsley's first time to Europe.

Everybody she'd known had travelled here, on study abroad, with boyfriends, on backpacking trips, on honeymoons. But she hadn't ever taken the grand tour. She hadn't had the funds.

Now she descended here for the first time, alone, barely knowing the Portuguese language, hired for a job that might not be accomplished, by a person who might not want to pay anything. She knew this assignment was a stretch—that she was trying to thread a needle, to have it all, to both travel wildly and, just maybe, come out with some money at the other end. It was a high wire act that may or may not pay off.

But Ainsley was determined to make it a great story regardless.

The plane banked left, and suddenly she was staring straight down at gray residential blocks, parks filled with greenery, lines of antlike cars backed up in the wide boulevards. It was morning rush hour below. Ainsley felt another thrill of excitement, knowing that people so very far away nonetheless lived lives that were so very similar to her own.

Then she felt something wet clutched in her palms. She looked down. She had one cocktail napkin in each hand, balled up and soaked with perspiration. She stuffed them into the seat pocket and wiped her hands on her jeans.

As the plane's wheels finally thumped onto tarmac, the air rushed loudly over the wing flaps, and the drag caused Ainsley to pitch forward. The seatbelt bit into her midsection. That strap was literally the last restriction, the final obstacle, to the start of her gemstone adventure.

The plane slowed to a crawl, then taxied to the gate.

She was in it now. Her heart hammering against her chest, Ainsley felt the airplane jerk to a stop. They were at the gate. The pilot came on the intercom and said, "*En nome da tripulação ... bem-vindo a Portugal.*"

She unbuckled her seat belt and stood up.

On behalf of the flight crew ... welcome to Portugal.

CHAPTER ELEVEN

Anticipating the treats coming her way, Ainsley almost forgot about her greasy hair and oily face.

She had seated her dirty transatlantic self at a dainty table in the Confeitaria Nacional, a landmark on Praça da Figuiera in downtown Lisbon. The café, over a century old, was an art nouveau gem. The leaded glass windows and swooping carved lines in the brown wood were a feast for the eyes.

The nearby case of small pastries, meanwhile, was promising a feast for the mouth. Behind the glass were at least a hundred different baked sugary confections. She hadn't known the names, and they hadn't been marked either. Ainsley realized that she was engaged in an infuriating game played around the world. It was called *stump the tourist*. She'd ordered a coffee and three pastries of the café's choice and sat down to wait for them to be brought over.

The airport exit had gone smoothly. A brief wait at customs, the authoritative thunk of a stamp hitting passport, five minutes at the baggage carousel, then a taxi on the curb.

Speeding into the city, Ainsley had been surprised by how comfortable it felt. At ground level, the newer avenues near the airport were flat-out modern. Past the taxi window slid apartment towers, drug stores, cheerful dogwalkers, nervous bicyclists. Mobile phones were pressed to ears.

This didn't feel at all like the homeland of Vasco da Gama. This felt more like twenty-first-century San Francisco. Ainsley was secretly disappointed. She'd been hoping for a bit more atmosphere.

The hotel, arranged by Joaquim's family, was clean and modest, but the room hadn't been ready. The apologetic front desk clerk had offered her apologies, discounts, promises. He'd even thrust a bowl of candies towards her as a gesture of his goodwill.

Ainsley'd understood. She hadn't thought to inform the hotel of her early morning arrival. After handing her luggage in the closet, she'd given her new phone number to the clerk. He'd promised to call the moment that the room had been prepared.

Unwashed, she'd stepped out into the hustle and bustle of early morning Lisbon, the brisk blue air stinging her cheeks, the small black cars zipping by, the brown odor of carbon dioxide exhaust filling her lungs.

She'd walked down the hill to the nearest Metro stop, purchased a day pass for five euros, headed through the white-tiled underground station, down the escalators, and finally mashed herself into a crowded subway car.

While trying to avoid bumping her head on the overhead metal handles, Ainsley'd glanced at the other passengers. They looked ordinary, no different at all from any other group of Westerners—chatting, dozing, reading books, checking social media, heads nodding to invisible beats supplied by tiny white earbuds.

Ten minutes later, she'd exited at the Martim Moniz stop, emerged from the stairs into the bright yellow midmorning light. Dazed, she'd wandered down the sidewalk, through the bustling crowds, into the Praça da Figueira. Part of Lisbon's historic core, it had been the site of countless buildings, fires, rebuildings, more fires. Now it was a central plaza bordered by stores, cafes, fruit markets, and offices.

Ainsley had smiled. This was what she'd been hoping for. She'd really need a place to gather herself.

Now, at the dainty art nouveau table, Ainsley rubbed her knees in hunger. On command, the young server in nineteenth-century Portuguese costume arrived, balancing a black serving tray on her palm.

"*Bom dia*," she said. "Do you speak English?"

"Yes," said Ainsley.

The waitress nodded and set down the plate of three small pastries. "This is *bolo*, this is *bolacha*, this is *nata*."

Ainsley remembered that last one. Fatima had brought her a box of those little delights. Next, the server put down a small white porcelain coffee cup. Inside, the brown and frothy liquid told her that it'd been cut with some milk.

"And this is a *bica*," said the server. "We drink at least five every day."

Ainsley sipped the stuff. "It's strong."

"We're a nation of caffeine addicts."

Ainsley noticed that this girl's voice held only the barest trace of an accent. "Your English is excellent."

She tipped her nose ever higher. "You must be an American."

"Why?"

"The British expect that we speak their language. Only Americans are grateful when we do."

The server headed off to another table, and Ainsley was left pondering that comment. After six hundred years of constant trading, it was easy to see how the British might expect a passing acquaintance with their language.

After scarfing the pastries and gulping the bica, Ainsley

felt herself approaching a human state once again. She decided it was time to look at the materials.

Joaquim's sister, the villa manager, had asked Ainsley to call as soon as she'd arrived. Now was as good a time as any.

She powered on the phone. It worked perfectly. Ainsley didn't know why she'd expected differently. She dialed the phone number and pressed it to her ear.

"*Bom dia*," said a woman's voice.

"*Posso com falar a Rita?*" said Ainsley. The foreign phrases felt odd rolling off her tongue.

"*Quem fala?*"

"E Ainsley Walker."

There was a weird bonk. Then the woman's voice came back, this time in fluent English: "Oh, thank God you called. I dropped the phone, I was so excited. We didn't think you would actually come."

Ainsley frowned. Had Rita and Joaquim assumed that she would flake out? If so, they didn't know her. Either way, the bar had been set very low, and it would be easy to exceed expectations.

"No," she replied, "I'm here in Lisbon."

"We need to meet right away. Things are getting worse. If we don't find this sapphire, I am going to have a disaster."

Ainsley felt alarmed. Joaquim hadn't let on that things were that dire.

"I'll tell you more when you get here. Did my brother tell you where to go?"

"To Sintra."

"Do you know where that is?"

"No."

"It's outside of Lisbon. You have to go to the Rossio station and take a train. Do you know where that is?"

"Not yet."

"Bah," said Rita, "my brother is worthless. Listen, I will send my gardener to meet you. He will bring you here."

"Where should I meet him?"

"At the Praça do Rossio. The Pedro IV monument. If you can't find that, I won't hire you."

Ainsley wrote it down in a small notebook. "What's his name?"

"Lúcio."

"What does he look like?"

Rita huffed. "He's short, round, conservative. He dresses badly. Portuguese men are slow mammals. If all else fails, just look for the man with the dirty hands."

Ainsley laughed out loud. This woman sounded like a real spitfire. No wonder her brother felt comfortable leaving her in charge of the Portuguese side of their cork business.

"What about you?" said Rita. "What are you wearing?"

"Just tell him to look for the oily American girl who hasn't showered. He can follow the trail of grease."

It was time for Rita to laugh now. Ainsley felt reassured. It sounded like they might be able to get along.

"Two dirty people. Perfect. See you."

Ainsley thanked her, ended the call, stowed away the phone, and caught the server's attention. "*Outro*," she said, "*faz favor*."

"Very good," the server responded in English.

A minute later, another bica and three more pastries landed on her table. If Ainsley was going to remain a disgusting oil slick, then at least she was going to be a caffeinated, well-fed one.

CHAPTER TWELVE

At the base of the Pedro IV monument, in the Praça do Rossio, the older gentleman in the gray jacket was feeding a group of pigeons. The skin of his hands was caked brown with dirt stains.

Nearby, Ainsley sat on the edge of the base of the monument. Chin in hand, she was waiting for Lúcio to notice her. That apparently wasn't going to happen anytime soon. But she didn't want to be the first to make a move.

Twenty meters above her head, at the top of the granite column, Pedro IV himself stood majestically wrapped in his iron cape. In front of her, the plaza was a study in gorgeous tilework.

Calçadas. Pavement tiles.

They were one of the Portuguese world's signature designs, rippling waves of black-and-white tiles crossing the plaza. A similar wave pattern, equally famous, decorated the beachfront pavement in Rio de Janeiro. The geometry hurt Ainsley's eyeballs, made her feel dizzy. She looked away.

Meanwhile, the gardener had run out of bird food and

straightened up. He turned in a slow circle, hands folded on top of his belly. He was as conservative as they come, just as Rita had said.

The gardener's eyes landed on Ainsley. Smiling, she waved her fingers at him.

Lúcio didn't notice, even taking a few steps in the opposite direction. Ainsley wanted to bury her face in her arms. She couldn't have been more obvious.

Now she, the visitor, the foreigner, was going to have to introduce herself. She stood up, brushed off the seat of her pants, walked over to the confused gardener. She was a full head taller than he was.

"*Lúcio?*"

He didn't hear, so she repeated it. "*Lúcio? Do Sintra?*"

At last he turned. "*Sim?*"

"Ainsley Walker." She stuck out her hand.

"*La americana?*"

"*Eu sou.*"

The gardener's dirty hand grasped her own and slowly squeezed. On his face, an unreadable grin slowly revealed a row of tiny pebbly teeth. Maybe it was because she was somewhat attractive. Maybe it was because he'd achieved his mission. Ainsley struggled to return the smile.

In Portuguese, he said, "I am going to take you to Sintra."

"Thank you for your help," she replied.

"Sintra is not in Lisbon. It's near Lisbon. So we will take the train."

"Okay."

He repeated the information. "It's not in Lisbon. It's near Lisbon. We will take the train."

"I heard you the first time."

Lúcio fortunately missed the sarcasm. "Now I will show you the train station," he said. "It is there. That is where the train leaves from."

She followed his finger to a granite building nearby, whose entrance consisted of two impossibly ornate stone arches, like horseshoes. A granite statue of another king stood regally in the middle column, commuters flowing past his toes.

"Rossio," she said.

Lúcio didn't hear her. "That is called Rossio," he explained. "The trains leave from there. I will show you which train to take."

Suddenly Ainsley understood him. He'd been a poor listener to begin with, and working with petunias and begonias hadn't helped any. Now he had absolutely no listening skills whatsoever. Even worse, he was speaking to her the way a tour guide would a child.

"Okay," she said, "let's go to the train."

"Now we will go to the train," he repeated.

She followed Lúcio across the plaza and through the arches, the words *Estação Central* etched above her head. The gardener's pace was excruciatingly slow. Ainsley wasn't used to such strolling and cut her normal pace in half just to stay even with him.

At the ticket booth, Ainsley walked towards the teller window. "No," said Lúcio, his finger wagging in her face, "I will pay for both of us."

That could be interpreted as either sweet or chauvinistic. Ainsley guessed the latter but didn't worry too much about it. He was an old man in an old-fashioned country. Besides, according to the ticket board, the price to Sintra was only four euros.

Ainsley watched the purchase with a bemused smile. It required two minutes of conversation with the clerk, worried questions about departure times, and dirt-stained hands fumbling in a tattered brown leather wallet. Finally the tickets were slid into the tray, and the gardener turned and began a satisfied procession towards the platform. Again, Ainsley followed in silence.

The train to Sintra was already there, waiting, doors open. It was a local commuter number, small, meant for low speeds.

Inside, the car was empty, every seat was open. Ainsley seated herself next to a window, and the gardener sat himself next to her, so their shoulders were pressed together. This was natural for him, but Ainsley frowned. Her American upbringing told her that she needed personal space.

It got worse. As the doors closed, and train pulled out of the station, the gardener immediately fell asleep, his head dropping into his chest, his lower lip vibrating with each exhalation. Ainsley resigned herself to the situation and gazed out the window at the passing suburban scenery.

What was Ainsley stepping into? So far, this country felt both familiar and totally unfamiliar. No matter what, though, she was energized by travelling. The rhythms of the train, and the lack of sleep on the flight should've plunged her into sleep, but her mind was racing. There would be no sleep yet.

Fourteen stations and forty-five minutes later, the conductor's voice said, "*Sintra, próxima paragem, Sintra.*"

"Lúcio," she said.

He didn't answer. She shook him by the shoulder.

"Lúcio, we're here."

The old man's heavy eyelids jerked open. She could see him suddenly reorienting himself. Then he figured it out, and the children's tour guide returned. "This is Sintra," he said. "We will exit the train here."

Ainsley let him walk out first onto the platform, and down to the street. It was a one-lane village road, quaint, lined with gift shops and cafes. The air felt brisk and clean here. It carried the scent of pines and ocean.

A skinny middle-aged woman in a t-shirt and jeans stood before a Toyota Corolla. Black hair was piled on top of her head. She was sucking violently on a cigarette. When she saw Lúcio and Ainsley, she turned her head to the left and blew the smoke out in a long, smooth stream.

"My brother said you were attractive," she said in English. "I didn't believe him. He thinks all American women are attractive."

"If you think I'm attractive right now, then it's a pretty low bar."

"You have just defined this country. There is a low bar everywhere." She smiled. "I'm Rita."

"Ainsley."

The Portuguese woman came over and kissed her on the cheek. One skinny arm hugged Ainsley around the side, the other hand holding the cigarette far away. "I know you Americans don't like cigarettes. Nobody likes them here either. It drives me crazy."

"You can smoke," said Ainsley.

"Okay, but if you start coughing, I'll stop." She turned to Lúcio. "*Connosco?*"

The gardener shook his head no. Rita said something in rapid Portuguese, and he nodded and gestured down the street.

Ainsley watched Lúcio go down the sidewalk. "Where's he going?"

"To pick something up from the hardware store," Rita said.

"Should we wait?"

Rita laughed. "He's going to spend ten minutes at the hardware store and then four hours drinking at A Caverna with the other laborers."

"Aren't you paying him?"

"Yes," said Rita, "but I can't make these men work. I can't force their arms to dig or weed or hang drywall. They only do what they want to do. It all depends on what teams are playing in the football game this afternoon. Let's go."

That didn't happen in the States. As Ainsley slipped into Rita's car, she started to feel like she was on a real, honest-to-God adventure.

CHAPTER THIRTEEN

The Portuguese woman drove the Toyota up the short lane, around a few blind curves, and up a twisting road lined with granite statues and sweating tourists hiking uphill. Ainsley sensed that this road was leading to something spectacular.

She was right. With little warning, the road turned into an area crowded with people snapping photos. Ainsley followed their lenses. To the right side of the car was an imposing façade of a whitewashed palace, topped with red terra cotta roof through which burst a tall, cone-shaped whitewashed chimney. It was fronted by a cobblestone square.

"The Palácio Nacional," said Rita. "That's where the kings used to spend their summers. You should see the inside, if you have time."

"I'm here to work."

"Of course," she replied, "you're right. Our villa is just on the other side of town. Five more minutes."

They passed through the heart of Sintra, a blur of pastelerias, restaurants, gift shops, jewelry shops, and small museums. Then the road entered a grove of green pine trees, the shadows dappling on Ainsley's lap. She rolled down the window and inhaled deeply. The air was fragrant with pine resin and salt water.

"Sintra is the most beautiful place in the world," Rita said. "In the fifteen hundreds, the nobles built their summer homes here. In the seventeen hundreds, the tourists started to arrive. They've never stopped."

"It's magical," said Ainsley.

They swept around a curve in the road, and Rita suddenly braked. The car slowed to a stop before a tall reddish wooden gate. It was smoothly lacquered, brand-new construction, no more five years old.

Rita fumbled in her purse for a remote control. She clicked the button. The smooth gate began to slowly roll open, revealing a double-tracked gravel driveway that curved into the tall pines beyond.

"I hope you're ready for this assignment," said Rita.

"Why do you say that?"

Rita didn't answer. She took a drag off her cigarette and blew the smoke out the sliver of open window. Then she popped the clutch, put the car in gear, and pulled into the property.

The car pulled into an old forest and moved slowly down a long, dark tunnel formed by the craggy trunks of pines, the slender trunks of eucalyptus. The trees were old, mystical, living representations of the historical Portugal itself.

"The Souza family lives in Oporto," said Rita. "Their quinta is in the Douro Valley, of course, with all the other port wine producers. This is their third residence."

Ainsley thought back to her reading. "How long have they been producing port wine?"

"Almost one hundred years. They became famous for their nineteen eighty-seven vintage. It sells for over a thousand euros a bottle."

As they came around a bend, the trees fell away, and the house was suddenly displayed before them.

A small gasp issued from Ainsley's lips. For nearly two days, she'd had been trying to guess what the Souza property looked like. She'd imagined a traditional neoclassical mansion —alabaster columns, long white balustrades, old glass running in streaks down the windows. A stone cherub spitting a stream of water into a fountain.

It was nothing like that.

This was an ultramodern box. The exterior was painted a blinding white, as pure as angel's breath. Black railings clawed across the side of the house like a demon's talons. The corners were sharply perpendicular.

Ainsley stepped out of the car, gaping. "It's new," she said.

"Yes," said Rita. "They built it ten years ago but hardly ever use it."

"So it's empty."

Rita shook her head. "Not quite. The Souzas have been offering it to the public as a a vacation rental."

Ainsley was floored. "I can't imagine how much you charge for it."

"Five thousand euros a week."

"That's kind of insane."

"We haven't had too many clients." She shrugged, then took another drag on her cigarette. "Follow me, and you'll find the problem that's giving me daily migraines."

Rita guided them up the front walk. Ainsley paused at a black, shallow pond, in the center of which floated a single green lily pad. The trickling sound of water issued from somewhere nearby.

Peaceful.

Rita unlocked the front door and held it open. "Please."

Ainsley stepped into a tall atrium. The walls were painted the same angelic white, the same slashes of black railing indicating indoor balconies overhead. Further on was the living room, filled with low-slung gray sofas, porcelain white floor lamps, and reddish-brown wooden floor.

Ainsley whistled low. Rita nodded towards the patio. "The outside is even better."

She opened the sliding glass door, and Ainsley stepped onto a beautiful granite patio. A narrow outdoor lap pool, a gorgeous rectangle of electric blue, stretched alongside the home, framed by steel I-beam columns. Slingback canvas deck chairs were arranged around a modern firepit.

And then there was the view.

Ainsley found herself at the edge of a gorgeous vista—a rocky slope strewn with gray boulders, green bushes, and brown brambles. At the bottom she could see the orange roofs of a town, at the edge of which washed a jagged line of foamy surf.

Beyond the froth, all the way to the horizon, was the deep gunmetal blue of the Atlantic Ocean. The view was nearly enough to paralyze Ainsley. From this height, she could see at least fifty kilometers out, enough to notice the curvature of the planet.

Then she suddenly understood why medieval Europeans had referred to Portugal as the country at the end of the earth. The ocean must've terrified average medieval Europeans. It was still awe-inspiring to Ainsley now, in the twenty-first century, even though she had just flown across that water in a very modern way.

She turned to Rita. "I take it back. Five thousand euros a week is a steal."

Rita nodded. "Sintra down the road. The beaches of Estoril below."

"It's incredible," said Ainsley.

"You can see why there have been homes on this site for more than five hundred years."

"So where did the theft occur?"

"Over there."

The property manager pointed towards a narrow green lawn bordered by modest hedges and orange trees. At the far end, backed into a rock outcropping, sat a small white stone building, about the size of a large shed. It looked ancient.

"In there?"

"Yes," said Rita, "in the capela."

Capela was the Portuguese word for "chapel". Ainsley remembered that this was where the phrase a capella had originated, meaning voice alone, since musical instruments hadn't been allowed in Catholic churches for most of recorded history.

"Let's have a look," she said.

Rita moved down the steps, her head hung low, as if carrying a heavy burden. Ainsley followed her, the scent of moss and mushrooms hanging moist in her nostrils, the salty ocean breeze at her back, driving her across the grass and towards the mystery.

"The capela was built in the fifteen hundreds," explained Rita. "We don't know who built it. We do know that in the seventeen hundreds, it was sold to a rich trader in Oporto. He'd just returned from a decade of trading gemstones in Brazil. So, to honor the founders of Portugal, he commissioned an azulejo mural to be built inside this old chapel."

They were at the capela door, a wooden number that had been bleached by the sun. Ainsley noticed an alarm system next to the handle. Rita's fingers punched in a code on the keypad, and the small device beeped. She turned the handle and pushed the door open.

Then Rita turned to Ainsley, a weird fire in her eyes. She pulled out her phone and produced a picture. "The azulejo mural this trader commissioned was of the Knights Templar as they triumphed over the Moors. It's an important event in our history. It's the moment Portugal was born. Here, look."

Ainsley peered at the woman's phone. On the small screen, she could see a photo of the azulejo mural. She squinted, studying the image. It depicted a group of frightened Arabs, on their knees before a Christian crusader, a famous cross on his chest. His robed arm was outstretched above them, and in his hand was something glittery and beautiful. It was bright blue, and even on such a tiny screen, it was throwing the light in a hundred different directions.

"The sapphire," said Ainsley.

Rita nodded. "The trader found it in Brazil but had saved it for years. He wanted to create something beautiful. So he baked the sapphire into the azulejo."

Ainsley found herself nodding in admiration. Even on such a tiny screen, it was a gorgeous piece of art.

"Now," said Rita, "the bad news."

She moved aside, and Ainsley stepped into the chapel. The air was heavy and cool because of the thick stone walls. It would always be chilly in here, even on a hot day. Medieval builders knew how to insulate.

As her eyes adjusted to the darkness, Ainsley saw that the chapel was empty except for something on the far wall. As she crossed the floor, she saw that it was the azulejo mural.

It was stunning.

At least three meters across, it was a vivid and compelling work of art—the blues were brilliant, the finish glossy, the figures expertly drawn. She admired the frightened Moors, the proud Knight Templar, the outstretched arm—

—without a hand. Ainsley gaped.

The tile with the hand was gone. Nothing but an empty square of dried, chipped cement.

From the doorway, as if from a dream, came Rita's voice.

"Now you see my problem, Ainsley," she said.

CHAPTER FOURTEEN

Ainsley approached the azulejo mural and ran her hand over the tiles. They felt cool to the fingertips. Then she felt the missing square, the nubbly bits of dried cement, the hard outline of the edges of the other tiles.

"It was pried out," she said.

"Yes," said Rita. "But the surrounding tiles weren't damaged at all. That's not easy to do. It was very professional."

Ainsley produced her notebook and did a quick sketch. "What did the sapphire look like?"

"Emerald cut," she said. "Very large. Thirty carats."

"Do you know its estimated value?"

Rita looked exasperated. "I don't know. Nobody does."

Ainsley was no expert on Portuguese tilework, but she did know gemstones. And she guessed that a vintage eighteenth-century thirty-carat sapphire would be essentially priceless.

But the thief hadn't stolen the sapphire. The thief had taken the time and effort to dig out the entire azulejo. That meant something.

"It's worth a lot," said Ainsley, "but this thief isn't going to sell the sapphire."

"Why?"

"Because it would've been easier to just chip out the gemstone, or hack at the mural. But he removed the whole tile. Very carefully."

Rita nodded. "Agreed."

"So we can conclude that he respects art. And that he's maybe a patriot."

"True. But what does that mean? Practically speaking?"

Ainsley thought. "It means we can probably ignore jewelry stores and gemstone wholesalers. They wouldn't know what to do with a treasure like this anyways. There must've been another motive."

Rita looked glum. Ainsley scrunched up her forehead. "But who could've wanted a tile?"

"Many people," said Rita. "There is a network of tile thieves in Lisbon."

Ainsley tilted her head. "A network?"

Rita sighed. "It's a bad economy, and azulejos are beautiful artifacts. So desperate people secretly strip them from buildings at night and sell them to tourists for a few euros each."

"That's unbelievable."

"Oh, believe it," replied Rita. "In Lisbon, many azulejos within easy reach have already been stolen." She gestured around. "But here, we're far outside of Lisbon. And this is a highly protected property."

"Maybe the members of this network are getting more sophisticated," Ainsley said. "Maybe they're going outside the normal channels. Have you tried to learn about this network?"

Her eyes widening, Rita became panicked. "I don't know how to do that. I don't live in Lisbon. I don't know any criminals. And I don't have time to do anything about this—"

"Okay, Rita—"

"—not between managing these properties in Sintra and running my brother's company down in the Alentejo. I spend my life driving, Ainsley. Three, four, five times a week, back and forth, one hundred and fifty kilometers each way. I don't have any support. I'm about to go crazy!"

Fists clenched, Rita stared with sizzling anger at the mural. Then she swore in Portuguese.

Ainsley tried to exude calm. "You're going to be all right, Rita."

"And this is why you're here, Miss Walker. You have to help. If Francisco finds out, I am dead. This mural, this sapphire, is the pride of his family. They will squash me like a bug if they discover that the azulejo has been stolen."

Ainsley understood the situation better now. This woman's job as property manager was at stake. And she guessed that jobs were hard to obtain in Portugal these days. It also explained why Rita and her brother had been unwilling to pay a retainer to Ainsley. They were probably barely hanging on.

She could empathize with Rita for other reasons too. Ainsley had felt that same stress after the Legal Weasel had left her. She remembered feeling the hard, hot stone of anxiety set deep between her shoulder blades, the one that no massage could relieve. She didn't wish it upon anyone.

Ainsley cast her arm over Rita's shoulders. "Let's talk more outside."

She guided the Portuguese woman out of the chapel, back onto the narrow green lawn. The carpet of blue unrolled itself to the horizon again. It was an impossible view. If Ainsley lived here, she wouldn't get a lick of work finished.

Ainsley turned her back on the ocean, and her eyes lighted upon the security system, the one built into the wall of the chapel.

"I know this is stressful," she said, "but I'm going to have to ask you some more questions."

CHAPTER FIFTEEN

The two women returned to the patio, where they found a pair of stools at the outdoor bar near the pool. Ainsley saw that, except for the glassware, the bar's shelves were empty. She was okay with that. After her transatlantic flight, a single glass of wine would likely put her under the table.

Rita appeared to have relaxed. She was breathing more slowly. Her fists had unclenched, her shoulders slumped forward.

A short distance away, just over the edge of the retaining wall, the cliff dropped precipitously towards a slope of gray boulders and tangled green bushes.

Ainsley pulled out her steno pad. "Do you know how the thieves got past the security system? Did they destroy it? Hack away at it?"

Rita shook her head. "No, I think they used the code. Our security company would've been alerted otherwise."

"How did they get the code?"

The property manager shrugged. "Maybe they were told it. Maybe they're smart and somehow guessed it through keypad capture. I don't know."

"So who knew the code on the day of the theft?"

"Only Lúcio. And the Hampsteads."

"Who are the Hampsteads?"

"Lionel and Catherine Hampstead. They're regular guests from London. Lionel is a wealthy investment banker. They've been renting this villa every February for seven years now." Then Rita paused. "I trust them, though. They're friends with the Souzas."

Ainsley noted that in her steno pad. "So you didn't change the code after their departure?"

"No. I usually don't until the next guest arrives."

"How long is that, usually?"

"Sometimes days, sometimes weeks."

"So all the guests get full access to the chapel?"

She nodded. "It's in the rental agreement."

"What about Lúcio?"

"What about him?"

"Do you trust him?"

Rita nodded. "Lúcio doesn't know duplicity. He's simple. I am sorry to say that, because I like him, but it's the truth. He only knows trees and plants and dirt. Those things don't lie. They don't steal either."

Ainsley couldn't argue with that logic, but the gardener was still worth checking out. "Have you told anybody about the theft yet?"

"Only the police," said Rita.

"What did they say?"

"That someone named Augusto was going to call me to begin the investigation."

"Has he?"

"No. It's been a week. Very disappointing, but it's what I expected. He's even on the special task force for stolen tiles."

Ainsley was taken aback. Of all the various types of

crimes that deserve a special task force, tile theft wouldn't have made her list of top ten guesses.

"Do you have Augusto's number?"

"I have the number of the Polícia Judiciára. You can call them and try to get connected to him."

"Can I have it?"

Rita produced her phone, scrolled through the contacts list, and read off the number. Ainsley copied it down.

She eyed Rita's phone. "I'd like to talk to the Hampsteads too."

"I don't think that's a good idea," said the property manager. There was a note of pleading in her voice. "They're quite special."

Ainsley grew frustrated. Of everyone mentioned so far, she wanted to look into the Hampsteads the most urgently. But given their friendship with the Souzas, it sounded like Rita was worried that they might blow the whistle on the theft, and get her fired.

Then Ainsley heard a tiny voice speaking to her. She'd heard this voice before. It was the sound of a sneaky little plan. She was always hearing those.

"Please, Rita, give me Catherine Hampstead's number," she begged. "I have an idea. I swear I'll be discreet. Your name won't be mentioned."

Rita was looking at her skeptically, so Ainsley played her trump card. "Your brother hired me. He wants me to help you."

The property manager knuckled under. "Just don't mention the mural. Please."

"I won't," said Ainsley.

Rita pulled up the phone number and read it aloud. Ainsley quickly copied that down too. This was a good lead.

"They're in Lisbon for business right now," added Rita. "Catherine called me last week asking if the villa was available. I lied and said it was booked up. It's my only option until this problem is resolved."

Ainsley chewed on her pen. "Who do you think stole the sapphire azulejo, Rita?"

A minute crawled slowly by while the property manager reflected on the question. Finally, she said: "I don't know how they stole it, but my opinion is that it was the Framingtons."

Ainsley's ears perked up. That was a new name. "Who are the Framingtons?"

"They own a competing quinta in the Douro Valley. The Souzas and the Framingtons have disliked one another since the phylloxera outbreak of the late nineteenth century."

Ainsley listened closely. "Tell me more."

Rita sighed. "I don't know the details, but I was told that the bacteria destroyed the Framingtons' vines, bankrupting them. The Souzas took the opportunity to purchase half the Framingtons' land, then grafted American vines onto the native root stock. The vines survived and even thrived. The Framingtons have been bitter ever since."

"Okay."

"Plus, the Framingtons are English, which makes it worse. Their jealousy is always simmering just below the surface." She smiled. "Inside the port wine industry, the rivalry is a running joke."

Ainsley finished writing it all down. "Why do you think the Framingtons would have stolen the sapphire now?"

The property manager shrugged. "Who knows? I'm not in either family. Maybe spite. Maybe revenge. It doesn't really matter. In the end, they just don't like the Souzas."

This explanation smelled a little odd. This theft had been clean, precise, and very professional. It hadn't been motivated by somebody with vague dislike. Furthermore, though revenge is a dish best served cold, it's never served frozen. Almost nobody keeps a grudge for a hundred and forty years.

She closed her steno pad. "You've given me a lot of good leads, Rita."

"I hope so." The property manager's phone went off. She looked at the caller ID. "Oh no, this idiot again. I knew he would have problems." She sighed. "It looks like I'm driving back to the Alentejo this afternoon. And petrol is so expensive."

The Alentejo. The Douro Valley. Oporto. Ainsley wondered about all these places that Rita had been mentioning. But she had a more important, more pressing question, one that couldn't be ignored any longer.

She stammered, cleared her throat, unsure how to broach this topic. "Rita," she said, "we need to talk about payment."

"I know," said the woman. "My brother and I are trying to get that together. Trust me, you will be paid. But we cannot do anything right now, aside from the hotel. Please forgive us."

She looked at Ainsley with an imploring look, the same begging for debt forgiveness that people have been giving each other since the first wampum exchanged, the first coin pressed, the first paper bill printed.

"I don't usually work like this, Rita."

"Please."

Ainsley felt her icy resolve melt away. "Okay," she said.

"You are a princess," replied the property manager. "But I have to leave, and you have to begin your work. Let me drive you back to town."

CHAPTER SIXTEEN

As the odor of grilled fish from the café wafted into Ainsley's nostrils, hunger tightened its grip upon her stomach.

It'd been four hours since the small plate of pastries in Lisbon, and that had merely been a holdover. She really needed a proper meal. Her first in Portugal.

A few minutes earlier, Rita had dropped her off in the center of the village of Sintra. They'd exchanged cheek kisses across the gear shift. Ainsley'd promised to call with an update in a couple of days.

Then she'd watched Rita's car tear off down the road, towards her other job in the Alentejo, stripping cork trees or whatever she did. It was two hours away.

Ainsley knew people back home who commuted that same distance. It took years off their lives.

Now she was hiking up a cobblestone street, breathing heavily. The last of the souvenir shops and kiosks had fallen away behind her. She'd passed several tourist cafés with tempting lunch specials, but she'd been searching for a special place.

A Caverna.

Translation: The Cave.

It'd taken a few questions, a few pointed arms, and more than a few quizzical looks, but the café was finally coming into Ainsley's view. It was a ramshackle structure, the eaves crooked, a layer of blue paint reading A Caverna peeling off the gray stone. It curled into the shadows against the side of the slope like a teenager playing hooky.

This café was off the normal tourist path, but Ainsley wasn't a tourist. She had suspicions about Lúcio, and someone in this café might be able either confirm or deny them.

The sound of a roaring televised crowd greeted her ears as she stepped inside the café. She waited quietly just inside the doorway, hands folded, shoulders back. It was safe body language for a foreign woman to use when entering a bar alone, even in the middle of the day.

A Caverna lived up to its name. It was dark and damp, boasting a single fireplace crackling orange on this cool spring day. The room was packed solid with men, judging from the fifteen pairs of broad shoulders that were facing a television screen mounted on the opposite side of the room. It was playing a soccer match, small red and white figures darting across a green pitch.

She scanned the heads. None of them belonged to Lúcio. None of them was paying her any attention either, so Ainsley walked freely towards the bar. The sound of her boots on the floorboards caused a few heads to turn, a few elbows to nudge.

Behind the counter, a thirtyish man was standing over a small sink, his sleeves rolled up. He was washing a ceramic plate with a blue sponge pad. He looked a little sad.

Ainsley pulled up a seat. "Are you still serving lunch?" she said in Portuguese.

"No," he said, "we stopped ten minutes ago."

Rita had warned her that most restaurants closed their kitchens at two-thirty and stayed closed until seven. Ainsley, however, had spent thirty valuable minutes asking for directions. Now she would have to persuade him to serve her lunch.

"I'll wash that dish if you find some bread," she said.

"You don't want that job," came his reply. "Our water pressure is horrible."

"I'll wash ten more for some bacalhau."

Suddenly he switched to English. "You have funny Portuguese."

Ainsley didn't miss a beat. "I'm funny in English too. But my money is serious. And I'm hungry."

He put down the dish and disappeared through a single swinging door into the tiny back kitchen. A minute later, he emerged with a plate of crusty bread and a cup of olives.

"The appetizers," he said. "The cook said we only have enough left for one *bacalhau a bras*." He paused. "It was supposed to be my lunch."

A flood of guilt washed through Ainsley's body. She was literally taking food out of this guy's mouth. Granted, he'd allowed it.

"Is he cooking it now?"

"Yes."

"Then we'll share it."

"No. It's yours."

"No," she said, "I insist. *Partilhar?*"

He dropped his head. "Okay. We will have lunch together. And you can tell me how you found this bar. Or even why you're in this country."

He shouted something at the kitchen, then turned back to washing dishes. Ainsley swiped the crusty bread into the olive oil and gnawed on it. It took lots of chewing. Not even three pm, and the pão was already getting stale.

A couple minutes later, a whistle from the kitchen. The guy disappeared into the back. He returned carrying two dishes loaded with an unusual scrambled dish.

"I will sit next to you here," he said, rounding the bar and placing the plate under her nose. It smelled excellent. "What is your name?"

"Ainsley. And you?"

"Professor Bernardo."

"You're a professor."

"Yes, I have a doctorate in psychology. It is totally useless. As you can see, I serve beer. But the diploma helps sometimes. For example, my long study of psychological literature tells me that you would like to have a beer."

She nodded. He yanked a pair of brown bottles out from behind the bar, opened one, poured it into a glass, and slid it over to his visitor.

Meanwhile, Ainsley tentatively scooped her fork across the plate. It was basically a breakfast scramble. She lifted the food into her mouth and tasted.

"What do you think?" he said.

"It's delicious," she replied. "What is it?"

"Scrambled eggs, potatoes, black olives, and bacalhau, of course. A classic."

She commenced stuffing her face. The man tasted his own, then sipped his beer. "I think wine tastes better with this."

"A nice observation."

"I am a professor. Observations are what I do." He sighed, then glanced at the men transfixed by the soccer game behind them. "Now I am working in a bar for these sheep."

Ainsley tried to be sympathetic. "Your country is having some troubles."

"You are American?"

"Yes."

"In your country, I believe the correct term is deep shit." He swigged from his beer.

The soccer fans suddenly erupted in a long, loud *noooooooo*. Several men used their arms to throw imaginary tomatoes at the television screen.

Bernardo waited for the noise to die down. "Valencia just scored. It'll be sad here tonight." Then he reboarded his train of thought. "So are you on vacation?"

She swallowed her food and wiped her mouth. "No, I'm working."

He lifted an eyebrow. "Are you a tour guide?"

"I'm investigating a theft."

Bernardo's demeanor changed slightly. "Of what?"

"I can't say. But one of your regular clients might be involved."

He smacked his hand on the table. "Nicolau," he said. "That bastard. He steals a fork whenever he has lunch."

"It's not. This was professional."

"Who is it? Is he here?"

Ainsley glanced over at the assembled men, to see if he'd slipped in since she'd sat down. He hadn't.

"Lúcio," she whispered.

Bernardo looked confused. "The gardener? He just went home at halftime to sleep."

"What do you think? Is he trustworthy?"

He shook his head. "Lúcio isn't a professional thief. He's not even a good gardener. He killed my only tomato plant last year. But he seems trustworthy enough, yes."

"I've heard that he doesn't like to work much."

"So what? Look around." Bernardo swept a hand towards the assembled soccer fans. "I have a full café at three o'clock on a Tuesday. The match is just an excuse to avoid the work for several more hours, days, weeks."

"Sounds like the good life."

"No, it's not," he said. "See, the old people think differently than the young people. They believe that they might work, someday, if God only permitted it. But we young people are different. We think we should work, and to hell with what God wants."

Ainsley understood that. She also wondered why Bernardo was daring to talk so loudly. She figured that the older men here didn't speak English.

She mopped up the last of her bacalhau scramble. "I would love," she said, "if you could tell me everything you know about Lúcio."

"I can't."

"Why?"

"Because I don't know anything about him. He doesn't like to speak. I see him working with rose bushes on some of the old estates. That's all."

"So he's a gardener to the town."

"In Sintra," Bernardo replied, "everybody helps everybody. Everybody feeds everybody. That's why nothing ever gets done. Everybody is waiting for something to happen."

Ainsley thought about that. It was conceivable that this community could produce a person so frustrated by social inertia that he might be willing to pry a valuable tile from an azulejo mural.

Try as she might, however, she couldn't envision Lúcio being that person. She'd watched him feed birds. He'd looked happy. Then he'd fallen asleep on the train. He'd looked happy doing that too. Now he had gone home for a nap. Thieves didn't usually do those things.

And she still didn't have an inkling of a motive.

Bernardo continued: "I graduated from the University of Coimbra. I studied in England for a year. I've seen the world." He caught Ainsley's eye. "This town is different. There's no changing these people."

Which meant that the reverse was likely true: Men like Lúcio were unlikely to change anything.

Ainsley put down her utensils, wiped her mouth, and reached for her bag. "Thank you for feeding me on short notice. How much do I owe you?"

"I don't know. Half a meal?"

Ainsley fished around for her wallet. She pulled out a twenty-euro note and placed it on the table. It was too much, but he'd deserved it. "Thank you for splitting your own lunch, Bernardo. And for answering my questions."

"Come back if you want more useless knowledge about Sintra," he answered. "You haven't heard the story about how the government has promised for seventy years to fix our historic properties."

"Maybe I'll come back to listen," she said.

Stepping down from the stool, Ainsley slung her purse over her shoulder and walked out of A Caverna. Descending the steep cobblestones, she felt certain that Lúcio had nothing to do with the theft. Her female intuition told her so.

And yet there was the nagging possibility that her female intuition might, for once, be wrong.

There was only one thing for certain. Given the pathetic state of her bank account, Ainsley knew that she should start leaving smaller tips.

CHAPTER SEVENTEEN

As she peered over the security line, Ainsley could see the enormous brass armillary sphere inside the lobby of the police building.

She was standing at the public entrance to the Polícia Judiciára. It was brutal in the way of modern police structures. It'd been built during the fifty-year mid-century Salazar dictatorship.

Her purpose: to find Augusto, the head of the tile task force.

On the train back from Sintra, she'd already called the task force number. Nobody had picked up. The phone had simply rung forever. Ainsley had been warned by Rita that the police were famous for not returning phone calls, and for not doing very much at all. That's why she'd made a personal visit to this station.

Ainsley inched forward until she found herself at the front of the line. She emptied the coins and lip balm from her pockets into a small tray, put her purse on the belt for scanning, and passed through the detector.

On the other side, the black eyes of a police officer flicked at Ainsley, then flicked back to his monitor. She studied him. He was middle-aged, had a mop of brown hair. She struggled to describe him as anything other than Mediterranean.

His finger clicked on pause. Ainsley could see the image of her purse on the screen. His black eyes squinted as he analyzed its contents—her compact, lipstick, wallet, breath mints, birth control, camera, passport.

The black-eyed police officer glanced at her again. Then he smiled at her. His finger clicked a button and the belt began moving again.

Ainsley didn't know how to feel. He was either a weirdo or romantically interested in her, or both. Granted, there was sometimes a thin line between the two.

She picked up her coins and lip balm, then submitted to a mandatory wanding from a female officer, her arms held out sideways from her body. Finally Ainsley collected her purse and stepped into the lobby.

The armillary sphere was at least three meters high, its brass rings encircling the globe, representing lines of latitude and longitude. The device had been introduced centuries earlier by a Moorish man named Al-Andalus. It had since then been embraced by the Portuguese as a symbol of their naval dominance in the Age of Discovery.

Beneath the sphere stood the police desk, behind which sat a stern row of official heads. A smaller line of people had queued before the desk, waiting for help.

Ainsley joined the end of the line. She gazed around the room. On the bench lining the walls was an elderly woman dressed in black. Ainsley took that to mean that she was a widow. She sat motionless, her face as cragged as the wall of an excavation pit. It was carved with suffering and wasn't the type of face seen in the modern world. Ainsley guess that she was probably from a rural area.

The line moved forward slowly. Ainsley felt a swimming

sensation in her head. It was a dizzy spell. She leaned against a concrete column and closed her eyes. She'd felt this before, knew its name.

Jet lag.

It was impossible to fly halfway around the world, get only two hours sleep on the airplane, plunge herself into a foreign city, begin the investigation of a gemstone theft, and pretend that it was just another ordinary day at the office. She'd been swinging a metaphorical mallet at her body. Sleep was going to pounce soon, whether she gave her permission or not. A glance at her watch told her that it was only five pm.

Ten minutes later, she had reached the front of the line. Behind the counter, a bored-looking police officer lifted his pencil towards her. Ainsley approached.

"Yes," he said in Portuguese.

"I need to speak to Augusto," she replied in Portuguese.

"Last name."

"I don't know. But he's on the azulejo task force."

The officer betrayed no emotion. "I can give you his phone number."

"I already have his phone number," Ainsley answered. "I would like to speak to Augusto personally."

"I can leave a message for you," the officer said. He reached for a pad of paper. "What is the problem? A theft?"

"I would prefer to discuss it with him in person. Can I see him?"

"No, it's not customary," he said. Ainsley was surprised by his politeness. In other countries, she would've felt the rude swat of dismissal by now.

The officer wrote down a number on a piece of paper. "This is the task force telephone number. You can call him."

"I already called that number. Nobody answered. I need to speak with Augusto now."

"Please, there is no rush," he replied. "Besides, it is almost five pm. If you come back tomorrow, you may have a better chance of catching him."

The officer's face was open but impassive. Ainsley couldn't read his motivation. It felt like friendly obstruction.

"Thank you," she said. Disappointed, she turned away from the desk. On the other side of the lobby, just before the exit, she ripped up the paper and dropped the pieces into a garbage can.

Then Ainsley felt a prickling sensation on her neck. There was someone watching her.

She straightened up, glanced around the bustling floor, and found the eyes immediately. They were black, and they belonged to the security officer manning the monitor behind the conveyor belt.

To her surprise, he crooked his finger. He wasn't disguising his interest now. Ainsley felt a little worm of disgust wriggle through her belly. The man was the type who might abuse his power to land a foreign tourist, but she knew he wouldn't do so in the headquarters. Plus, Ainsley couldn't disobey a police officer. He might even help her.

She walked around the security entrance, past the wanding, and stood before him in the narrow entrance to his workspace.

He swiveled ninety degrees in his chair and faced her. "You like to destroy paper?"

"What?"

"That note was property of the polícia." He nodded to the garbage can. A thin smile cracked the edge of his mouth.

Ainsley finally understood. He was flirting with her. The context was odd—the security line of a city police headquarters—but this was flirtation. She would be wise to return it.

"I love to break the law," she replied. "It excites me."

He suddenly grew still, and Ainsley wondered if she'd overstepped her bounds. In English, he said, "You can't get anything done in this department without someone on the inside."

She switched to English too. "It's the same everywhere."

"Who are you looking for?"

"Augusto. The head of the azulejo task force."

He steepled his fingers, nodding his head. "They told you to come back tomorrow, right?"

"Yes."

He shook his head. "Augusto is never here. He is always out."

"I need to talk to him."

He suddenly snapped to attention, as though he'd made an internal decision. "I am going to assist you. What is your name?"

"Ainsley Walker."

She glanced at the security line. The conveyor belt had frozen still. Several pairs of eyes were accusing her of the stoppage.

The officer was oblivious to the backup. He'd turned to his computer screen and was typing on the keyboard. "Miss Walker, Officer Augusto Oliveira can be found attending Mass every morning at the Sé. He likes the eight o'clock mass. He sits in the back row, on the left." He looked up. "Are you going to write this down? Because I'm only going to say it once."

Ainsley scrambled for her notebook and scrawled the information.

"Now," he continued, "you probably want to know what Augusto looks like."

"I would appreciate that," she said.

"It's going to cost you a phone number." That same small smile cracked the edge of his mouth again.

"Any number?" she answered. "I can give you the number of the azulejo task force."

"No," he said, "I want your phone number. And then dinner this Friday."

He produced his own cell phone and waited for the digits. His eyes looked up at her matter-of-factly. Ainsley smirked. This man assumed the sale, but she wondered if his confidence was a byproduct of his police uniform. In street clothes, he probably wouldn't have half as much bravado.

"You win," she said. She read off her phone number to him, and he entered it into his own phone. Then she saw him hit send. A second later, her phone began to ring in her purse. It startled her.

Then the ringing stopped. He pocketed his phone. "You're honest, Ainsley," he said. "If you had lied to me, I would have arrested you for giving false information to a police officer."

Ainsley couldn't tell if he was kidding. "How fortunate," she replied. "Now where is the picture?"

"I can only keep this page on the monitor for a second," he said. "Notice I'm speaking in English too. Ready, look."

Onscreen came a headshot of a fat older man. Dark purple sacks of flesh hung from his eyes. His earlobes were fleshy nubbins. And his soul gazed sadly out from behind his eyes. He seemed deeply and profoundly sad.

"Augusto," said the police officer. Then he closed the picture.

"You have been very helpful," she said.

"And you will be helpful as well," he replied, "but in a different way. I'm Officer Silva. You must pick up when I call you."

"Of course I will," Ainsley lied.

Officer Silva's eyes fixed on hers. "Remember that I can find you."

As Ainsley left the lobby, she could feel those black eyes burning into her back of her pants. She wasn't totally opposed to the date. But she didn't want to derail herself from her goal, especially before the end of her first day.

As she hailed a taxicab and climbed inside, Ainsley consoled herself with the thought that very soon she was going to wrap herself in a very different set of arms, belonging to someone closer, more dependable.

The arms of sleep.

CHAPTER EIGHTEEN

The next morning, on the rooftop of her hotel, Ainsley sipped her cappuccino streaked with chocolate and blinked the sleep out of her eyes.

Last night, Ainsley'd fallen facefirst onto her bed, pausing long enough to kick off her shoes, and slept like the dead for eleven straight hours.

Now, from this alfresco dining area, she could look across the rooftops of Lisbon.

Stretching below her was an elongated green park, one end of which featured an enormous water fountain. Then she noticed that it was as dry as a bone. Empty. The public works had evidently shut it off.

Ainsley drained her coffee, swallowed her last pastry, and stood up to begin her first task of the day.

To find Augusto.

Having consulted the map over breakfast, she retraced her steps from the previous morning: out the hotel, down the hill, towards the subway station. It'd felt good to stretch her legs, to stride with purpose. She bought another Metro daypass for five euros, then moved through the white-tiled station and mashed herself again into another southbound subway car on the red line.

She exited at Martim Moniz again, but instead of going to the Praça da Figueira, she headed down Avenida Magdalena for six blocks, then made a quick left on Pedras Negras. A few seconds later, Ainsley found herself facing the Sé.

It was stunning.

The Sé was a church that looked more like a Romanesque fortress. Forbidding, impregnable, its stony front façade lorded over the narrow street like a stern bishop looking down on the heads of the peasants. She'd read that the church had been built on the site of a former mosque after the Reconquista, as a dare to the Moors to try to retake the city. It'd served its purpose well. The structure's only concession to lightness or beauty was a single beautiful rose window —and even that was flanked by twin crenellated stone towers.

Ainsley ignored the side tourist entrance, which led people into the cloisters for a small fee. Instead, she crossed to the main entrance and stepped into the church.

Catholics have always known the value of sensory experience in religion, and the Sé took full advantage of that. The church was nearly pitch black. The smell of incense enveloped her nostrils. Down the red-carpeted aisle stood the altar, where a priest lifted a golden chalice over his head, chanting in Portuguese, the loose white sleeves of his robe dangling.

The attendees were elderly and few. A quick head count showed less than a hundred parishioners, their gray hair thinning, their shoulders wracked with age and defeat.

Ainsley stepped lightly along the back of the church, passing the holy water, trying to keep her boots from clacking too loudly on the stone floor. She scanned the back row. It didn't take long to find him.

The pudgy face. The purple hammocks swinging below each eye. The fleshy earlobes.

Augusto Oliveira.

He was sitting alone, holding rosary beads in his hands, which were crossed on his belly. His gut was large and betrayed years of inactivity.

Ainsley casually slipped into the pew and seated herself next to him, as though it were the most natural place in the world to sit. Augusto's eyebrow lifted. He scanned his visitor up and down, then edged away slightly.

Ainsley moved closer. He edged away again.

"What do you want?" he said in Portuguese. His voice was low and deep.

"There has been an azulejo stolen," she whispered. "I'm Ainsley Walker. You need to help me find it."

Augusto smirked. "This is an inconvenient time. Leave a message for me at the police station."

"You don't return phone calls."

"That's not true."

Ainsley faced him directly. "You're going to listen to me, Officer Oliveira, whether you like it or not."

At that moment, several booming cracks sounded through the church. Ainsley was startled, until she realized that it was the other parishioners dropping their wooden kneelers.

With difficulty, Augusto bent over and lowered their pew's kneeler, then dropped himself to his knees with a grunt. Ainsley followed suit. Immediately she felt the strain in her abdomen and in the twin columns of muscle lining her spinal column. With prayer rites like this, Catholics must have the best core muscles of any religion.

"Please, Augusto," she said, "I know this is unusual."

"No it's not," he replied. "There have been at least ten thousand azulejo tiles stolen this year. What makes yours special?"

"There is a sapphire baked into it."

The police officer paused, staring at her. Ainsley heard the parishioners starting to recite the Lord's prayer in Portuguese.

Then he whispered: "The Souza azulejo has been stolen? From the Sintra estate?"

"Yes. But it's a secret. The Souzas don't even know yet. Their property manager hired me to find it."

Augusto looked pained. "I don't know what I can do."

"You have to do something. You're the head of the police task force."

The fat man shrugged. Ainsley began to understand the dynamics here. His position was a sinecure, a meaningless job given to somebody who was dead weight. He didn't look like he'd investigated anything more threatening than a slice of cake.

"Give me some time," he said. "This will require much careful thought."

An elderly usher had arrived at the edge of the pew. He gestured with one arm towards the altar.

Ainsley followed his arm. A line of parishioners were shuffling down the center aisle, hands folded, heads bowed. At the head of the line, the white-robed priest was solemnly placing communion wafers in their mouths.

Augusto planted his hands on the back of the facing pew, then hoisted himself to his feet, groaning. Ainsley stood and kicked up the kneeler.

"You can stay here," he said.

"Sorry," replied Ainsley, "but I'm not letting you out of my sight."

Shrugging, the fat man waddled down the cathedral's nave. Ainsley followed him, feeling incredibly self-conscious. They joined the rear of the communion line. Ainsley stood demurely, her hands folded, looking straight out across the heads of the people. She was nearly a full head taller than everybody here.

At the front of the line, Augusto stepped forward to the priest.

"*Corpo de Cristo*," the priest said.

"*Amém*," replied the police officer. He obediently opened his mouth and took the wafer.

Ainsley took a deep breath. She wasn't Catholic. She'd never been baptized. She was probably going to burst into flame as soon as it hit her tongue.

"Corpo de Cristo," the priest said, holding the communion wafer up. The flesh of Jesus, transubstantiated right there, for her eternal salvation.

"Sure," she blurted.

Ainsley opened her mouth. She felt the unleavened bread touch her tongue. It melted quickly in the saliva of her mouth.

She stepped to the side and started to make the sign of the cross, the way everyone else was doing, but she wasn't sure which way to go. Was it top, bottom, right, left? Or top, bottom, left, right?

Next to the priest, an assistant offered a chalice of wine. The blood of Christ. She frowned. The rim was probably lined with millions of viruses. She ignored the offer and walked to the back of the cathedral.

The back pew was empty. Ainsley spun around. Augusto was nowhere to be found.

Then she heard a quiet clunk. She whirled. The side door to the cathedral had just closed shut. The bastard had slipped away while she'd been distracted with saving her soul.

Slinging her bag across her shoulder, Ainsley ran across the cathedral floor and out the same door.

She found herself standing in a narrow cobblestone street outside the Sé, blinking in the bright sunlight. Springtime buds were sprouting on the tree branches overhead. A small car blared its horn as it zipped past her, mere inches from her feet.

Ainsley scanned the bobbing pedestrian heads until she spotted Augusto. His wide, bulky body was hurriedly waddling back towards Avenida Magdalena.

She took a deep breath and broke into a run across the cobblestones. It wasn't anything like the hundred-meter dashes that she'd performed countless times during her youthful track-and-field career. This sprint could end in a sprained ankle or wrist.

Fifteen seconds later, she arrived alongside the police officer. "I knew you were going to escape," she said.

Augusto didn't look pleased, and neither did he stop walking. "I always leave after communion. I am a very busy man."

"Where do the thieves take the azulejo tiles?"

"You will have to leave a report at the station, Senhora Ainsley."

"No," she insisted. "I need to know who buys them. I need to know where they buy them. How much they pay."

Augusto stopped in his tracks. She was afraid that she'd pushed him too far. "Do you really want to see?" he said.

"Yes."

"Meet me here tomorrow morning. I will show you."

"Seriously?"

"Yes. There is an event that will help you on your quest."

That could be a way to get rid of her. Or it could be a genuine offer. Either way, she'd harassed the man long enough.

"Thank you," she said.

"And don't be late. I only go to this event once a month."

"I won't."

Augusto held her gaze a moment longer than necessary, as though he were wary of opening up his great big honeypot of a soul. She offered her hand. He grasped it. His hand was soft and flabby.

He turned and disappeared into the sea of pedestrians.

CHAPTER NINETEEN

A half-hour later, on the bank of the Tagus River, Ainsley was looking at her phone, trying to summon the courage to make her next call.

The contacts page was open. The name Catherine Hampstead had been selected. Her finger was poised over the call button. All she had to do was press it.

Ainsley couldn't do it.

She was sitting on a concrete pylon here in the Praça do Comércio. Around her, a neoclassical arcade of staid government buildings served as a reminder that Lisbon was indeed the center of the Portuguese national government. Every so often, she had glimpsed a couple of harried-looking bureaucrats crossing the square, clutching briefcases, worry lines etched into their foreheads. Ainsley sympathized with them. She was nearly broke, yes, but these people were grappling with a level of macroeconomic debt so insidiously high that she could barely conceive of it.

Hence the word austerity. It was quite popular around here.

She glanced at the middle of the square. There, surrounded by pigeons and tourists, was a statue of the Marquês de Pombal, sitting on horseback, snakes crushed beneath its hooves. She remembered reading about him. Marquês de Pombal had, in 1756, created the Douro Wine Company to regulate the wine trade with England. The company's first decision was to delineate the Douro region as the only area in the world that could technically produce wine labeled and sold as port.

Today, this declaration still holds true. California, Argentina, Spain, and Italy all produce and sell fortified dessert wines. But none of them are allowed to label the product port wine. That's the result of a nearly three-hundred-year-old Portuguese law that continues to be internationally respected.

Ainsley turned and faced the fourth side of the square. It was wide open to the Tagus River, the brownish-blue waters glinting in the morning sunlight. A few kilometers to the west, the river took a final jog around a bend before flinging itself into the Atlantic. Ainsley felt her heart swell in her chest. She could envision the thousands of explorers who'd sailed their caravels along these very banks, five hundred years ago, on their way to Africa, to India, to China, to Brazil, to sickness, to danger and disappointment, to fame and fortune, to death.

She jerked herself back to the present. The plan that she'd been concocting was a good one, but executing it would require major fortitude, probably more than even she possessed.

Ainsley pressed connect and lifted the phone to her ear. On the other end, the phone rang and rang. It felt like an eternity.

Then, on the fourth ring, someone finally picked up.

"Hello?" a woman's voice said.

It was a plummy British accent, one that betrayed years of proper schooling, of pale blonde hair, of casual aristocracy.

"Is this Catherine Hampstead?"

"Speaking."

Ainsley took a deep breath. "Mrs. Hampstead, my name is Ainsley Walker. I'm a guest at the Souza villa right now."

"Yes," said the woman.

"The one in Sintra. You stayed there recently."

"Oh, of course we did, dear. We adore that property. My husband and I were trying to get it this week, actually."

"Quite sorry about that."

"Heavens, don't be—it's not my property. Have at it."

Ainsley breathed out and launched into the lie. "I'm calling you because Rita, the property manager, gave me your number. We think you may have left behind a piece of jewelry in the home."

There was a moment of surprise. "Is that so? I don't think I'm missing anything."

Ainsley glanced at the antique fork bracelet on her wrist. "It's a bracelet. Quite lovely too."

"What does it look like?"

Ainsley bit her lip. "It's rather hard to describe. I think it would be better if I were to bring it around to show you. Rita said you're in Lisbon right now?"

"Yes, until Sunday."

"Well, I'm in Lisbon for the day." Then she added: "Shopping, of course."

That was a wise choice. "Oh how splendid," said the Englishwoman. "The boutiques are just fabulous. Have you been to the Avenida da Libertade?"

"I'm planning to this afternoon. It's always good to save the best for last."

"Be sure to visit Gauge de Stijle. They produce the most

ethereal blend of Portuguese and Dutch elements, especially the vases."

"Thank you, I will." Ainsley went for the kill. "Catherine, would you mind if we met for a quick coffee? This way, you can see the bracelet for yourself. If you don't recognize it, we can be on our separate and merry ways."

There was a choke, then an odd silence on the other end of the phone. Ainsley had guessed that this type of spontaneity would be difficult for a wealthy Englishwoman. It was the real stumbling block in the conversation. Catherine probably required an appointment three weeks in advance just to chat with her own daughter.

"I don't know," said Ainsley.

"Rita asked for it."

"I suppose that would be all right," she answered.

"Oh good," said Ainsley. "Where should we meet?"

"There's a café on the north end of the street. Café dos Chaves."

Ainsley wrote it down. "Three o'clock pm."

"That'll be acceptable," said Catherine. "You're going to quite a lot of trouble for a stray piece of jewelry, Miss Walker."

Ainsley smiled. "I just want to see this bracelet find its proper home. Call me the Mother Teresa of wayward jewelry."

That got a brief laugh. Then Catherine Hampstead said goodbye and disconnected. Ainsley looked at her phone after the call ended.

Her ability to bullshit was even better than she'd thought.

CHAPTER TWENTY

At three o'clock pm, Catherine Hampstead entered the relaxed interior of Café do Chaves.

Ainsley set down her coffee and spotted her immediately. It didn't take a rocket scientist. Catherine Hampstead was tall, elegant, finely dressed, aged well in her fifties, and sporting a head full of fine blonde hair. She wore an expensively tailored cream pantsuit. Around her neck hung a turquoise pendant in a vintage setting so exquisite that Ainsley swore she'd once seen it mounted in an art museum.

In short, Catherine Hampstead was the picture of modern British wealth, the image of the powerful pound sterling, and Ainsley began doubting the wisdom of this plan. Trying to bait this woman with a bracelet began to feel juvenile. If this Englishwoman had a brain cell in her head, and if she had anything to do with the theft of the azulejo, she'd see right through Ainsley's little scheme in the blink of an eye.

But since Ainsley had already arranged this coffee klatch, she would see it through.

"Catherine?" she said.

The Englishwoman looked up. "Miss Walker?"

"You can call me Ainsley."

The woman's eyes roved Ainsley from crown to heel. Evidently she must've passed her test, because Catherine at last held out her hand like a present. "Charmed, Ainsley."

"Delighted," replied Ainsley, shaking it.

"You know, actually, I'm glad you called. My husband and I were hoping to get the Souza property again this month, and I wanted to meet my competition."

The wording was accusatory. It puzzled Ainsley.

"Here I am," said Ainsley, "enemy number one, pleased to make your acquaintance."

Catherine's eyes scanned Ainsley. "At least I know that you have good taste."

"Three years in art history at Oxford will do that," said Ainsley.

Catherine paused for a half a second. "Did you say Oxford?"

"Yes."

"Oxford Uni?"

She meant the university. "Of course," said Ainsley.

This was another lie, but it had the intended effect. "My husband went up to Oxford too. Which college?"

"Balliol," said Ainsley. She'd cooked up this lie earlier in the afternoon. She'd even looked up the history of Balliol College in a bookstore.

"That's quite respectable," said Catherine.

Ainsley sighed. "I somewhat regret it now. The diploma is wasted on Americans. Nobody seems to understand its prestige."

Catherine placed her purse down on the counter and visibly relaxed. "My husband read economics at Christ Church College. He's never regretted it, not for a second."

"It's quite a cross to bear."

"Absolutely. People have no idea how difficult it is at the top."

"I've already ordered a coffee. What would you like?"

That was too much, too soon. Catherine Hampstead clutched her purse and reared back like a spooked horse. "Oh, I can't, I'm heading out to meet some friends—"

"Please, Catherine," said Ainsley, "this one's on me." She motioned to the barista behind the counter. "*Uma bica, faz favor.*"

Catherine folded. She returned her purse to the counter and her shoulders slumped forward. She looked suddenly older. "Well, that's quite decent of you, Miss Ainsley, thank you. And your Portuguese sounds quite decent as well."

"No," said Ainsley, "I'm just a beginner. In fact, I'm only here for another week."

"On holiday?"

Ainsley nodded. "I'm divorced. Trying to figure out what to do with my life."

"Lucky you," said Catherine.

"I don't feel lucky." Ainsley sighed theatrically. So far, she was delivering a masterful performance, worthy of an Oscar. "Are you ready to have a look at the bracelet?"

"I'm not entirely sure that it's mine," answered the Englishwoman.

"Let's find out." Ainsley reached into her purse and produced a soft purple velvet bag.

"What a lovely sack," said Catherine. "Where did you find it?"

"This? I brought it from the States."

That was another lie. Ainsley had spent the afternoon on Avenida de Libertade, scoping the jewelry boutiques. She'd finally found a jeweler and bargained hard for just the bag, *só saco*, a phrase that the jeweler had purposefully continued to misunderstand by trying to sell her jewelry to go inside of it.

Eventually he'd grown so annoyed with the ludicrous negotiation that he'd finally handed Ainsley the sack and told her to leave.

Ainsley gently tugged the jewelry out of the bag. "And here it is."

She placed the piece on the countertop. Her own precious grandmother's bracelet, polished silver, the fork's tines reworked into a beautiful, curvy piece of art nouveau. "I found it on a side table in the foyer," said Ainsley. "It looks like someone forgot it on the way to the door."

Catherine Hampstead didn't react. She didn't touch it. But she tipped her nose up slightly; her eyes studied the piece.

"That," she announced, "is most certainly my bracelet. I can't believe that I left it at the villa."

Ainsley felt her stomach drop to her shoes. It took all of her restraint to not smack her across the face. This rich bitch was claiming a bracelet that she knew wasn't hers. Her seven-digit bank account didn't matter. She was no better than a sticky-fingered teenager in a department store.

Still Ainsley managed to keep her game face. "Oh, thank God. I just wanted it returned to its rightful owner."

"Curses on me for forgetting it," said the Englishwoman. Then she scooped the bracelet up, examined it in the light, and dropped it into her purse. "And bless you for calling me."

"Where did you get that piece?" said Ainsley.

Ainsley kept a serious look plastered on her face while the Englishwoman stuttered and groped around for a good story. "My friend Julia produced it. She's a jeweler. She said the fork was found in the rubble of a building after the blitzkrieg during the war." Catherine lowered her voice. "She said it had been found in the hand of a corpse."

Visions of blood spattered on a cream pantsuit entered Ainsley's mind. "That's quite a story," she said evenly.

"Indeed. Imagine the person, having an innocent piece of beef ... Oh my goodness, now I'm going to get emotional." She dabbed her eyes. "I can't imagine how to thank you, Ainsley."

"You can tell me more about the Souza property," said Ainsley. "I don't know much about it. I rented it on a lark, and Rita promised to explain to me, but she hasn't had time."

The Englishwoman made an ugly face. "That woman. So low-class." She sipped her bica, then dabbed her lips with a napkin. "We've been going there seven years," she replied. "It's been an absolute dream. My husband has even discussed purchasing it, but Mafalda insists that it's not for sale."

"Who's Mafalda?" asked Ainsley.

Catherine looked at her quizzically. "You don't know her? She's the lady of the estate, Mafalda Souza. She's married to Francisco Souza."

Ainsley shrugged. "I found the property through a rental agency."

"How serendipitous."

"They'd be foolish to sell," said Ainsley.

"Indubitably. I can't imagine the price they would ask. And with that gorgeous azulejo mural in the chapel..."

The Englishwoman's voice trailed off, her eyes staring at the far wall. The time seemed right to break the news.

"Did you know," said Ainsley, "that the azulejo has been stolen?"

She watched the Englishwoman's reaction closely. Catherine's eyes snapped to attention. "Stolen? How does someone steal a mural?"

Ainsley shook her head. "Not the whole mural. Only one tile. The thief chipped it out. It has some sort of gemstone baked into it."

Her face grew ashen. "Oh, my heavens. Someone has stolen that tile?"

"Apparently."

"It's a sapphire," said Catherine. "A knight is holding it in his hand." She looked suddenly ashen. "That is terrible news. It's a very historic piece of art. I admire it every day that I'm there."

"Rita won't let me into the chapel. It's closed."

"That's terrible," she said. Then added: "Lourenço is going to be upset." She sipped her bica.

"Who's that?" said Ainsley.

Her tone was either too aggressive, because Catherine waved a hand. "I really shouldn't be telling you all this."

Ainsley leaned forward. "No, please, continue—Rita tells me nothing."

The Englishwoman looked skeptically at her, then relented. "Lourenço Souza is a cousin of the Souza family. He sits in the Portuguese Parliament. He's the head of some committee. He loves that azulejo."

Ainsley felt panicked. "If it's all the same to you, Catherine, please don't tell him, or anybody else. Rita made me promise to keep it a secret. She's not even reporting it to the police yet."

"Why not?"

"I think she wants to hire someone to pursue the tile."

Catherine grimaced. "Good luck to her with that. This city is full of thieves." She paused, then said: "My lips are sealed."

"So, Miss Walker, you're here in Lisbon alone?"

"Sadly."

"I remember what that was like. My first few visits were unbearably lonely."

"That's why I've been shopping."

Catherine laughed. "Could I interest you in some tea?"

Ainsley felt the surprise ripping up and down her spine. "I'm flattered, Catherine—where do you have in mind?"

The Englishwoman's eyes took a long tour of the ceiling. This was a wrenching act of spontaneity. "I don't normally invite strangers to the Kensington Club, but your generosity has been overwhelming and I feel obliged to return the favor."

"What is the Kensington Club?"

"Oh," she said airily, "it's just a little pavilion where we British like to gather and have a drink and discuss the affairs of the day. You might even recognize a classmate or two from Balliol."

"That sounds fabulous," said Ainsley, "but I don't think I'm dressed appropriately."

A flash of jealousy flashed across the older woman's eyes as she looked Ainsley from head to toe again. "Oh, please—you look smashing. Besides, it's just a little tea on the patio."

Ainsley straightened up and acted as blasé as possible. Then she pretended to have made her decision. "Oh, why not. You're good company, and it'll be a nice break from this endless shopping."

Catherine emitted a short, sharp bark that passed for a laugh. "Shopping is tiring, isn't it?" Then she sighed. "Goodness, sometimes I wish I could just take a day off and be someone else. There's no end to this keeping up with society."

"Would you like to hail the cab while I settle the bill?"

Catherine Hampstead looked confused. "Oh no, dear—my driver is waiting."

My driver. It was clear now just how high this woman lived. She was a part of the one percent bubble.

And even though she'd just stolen a bracelet, she'd welcomed Ainsley inside.

CHAPTER TWENTY-ONE

In the backseat of the chauffeured Mercedes, Ainsley was starting to enjoy the role of the wealthy, globe-trotting sophisticate.

The character had been simple: Ainsley had presented herself as a rich woman who had rented the Souza villa at five thousand euros a week, who shopped indiscriminately on Avenida do Libertade, who was so wealthy that she returned lost jewelry as if it were borrowed lipliner, who had graduated from Oxford University.

All lies.

In real life, Ainsley was broke and living in a shitty one-bedroom apartment. She'd borrowed money to fly to Europe, to work without a retainer, to chase a stolen gemstone that may never be found. Her rent was a week overdue and no safety net was stretched below to catch her if she fell. She'd never been to Oxford University, though she had read *Brideshead Revisited* once.

No matter. Ainsley was regaling Catherine with spectacularly bullshitted stories of wild spending, of men loved and men dumped, of brushes with politicians, financiers, athletes.

At this moment, Ainsley was basically a fraud—and yet the fakery felt good. She understood why pathological liars invented wild personas and insisted on their truthfulness. It gave her a kick. But while sociopaths lied for their own gain, she had invented this persona to accomplish her task.

Catherine had begun to share her own stories. Her life was controlled by a household staff of five, packed with expensive weekends in Gstaad and the Amalfi Coast, grown children who didn't call, and a frustrating lack of control. She said that she felt like she had been trapped on a cruise ship for decades.

Ainsley barely noticed when the automobile slid to a stop, or when she stepped into a beautiful Manueline portico, or when she floated up the steps into the Kensington Club.

At the front door, a stiff man in a tuxedo stood behind a podium. He had olive skin but spoke in a perfect British accent.

"Good afternoon, Miss Hampstead," he said.

"I have a friend today, Alastair," Catherine replied. "She needs to sign in."

He turned a leather book towards Ainsley and handed her a fountain pen. "Very good, ma'am."

Ainsley smiled inside. A person has too much money when she hires someone to tell her *Very good, ma'am*.

Ainsley signed her name on the register. The pen was heavy in her hand. When she'd finished, Alastair turned it back around. "Very good. The reception is on the patio, straight through the dining room. Oh, Ms. Haverford left a message for you, Ms. Hampstead."

Alastair handed her a small piece of stationery. Ainsley smiled at the quaintness of the practice. Women were sending millions of text messages to one another on a daily basis—but these special women, in this special club, were still leaving small squares of paper with the concierge as though it were the nineteenth century.

Catherine read the note. "This is unbelievable."

"What is it?"

"Nothing." She stuffed the note into her purse and managed a smile. "Let's make an appearance, shall we?"

Ainsley followed her into the clubroom. It felt subtly British—modern chocolate brown banquettes, blue leather chairs, cream tablecloths. The tangy smell of HP sauce in the air. Behind a bar, a row of wooden handles displayed exclusively English beers.

"I should warn you about the men here," said Catherine. "They often get a bit too fond of their spirits."

"That's not a problem."

Catherine regarded Ainsley over the top of her glasses. "It very well could be. I take it you've never encountered the British on vacation."

Ainsley waved it off. "I'm sure I'll manage."

"No doubt about that," said Catherine, glancing at Ainsley's figure. "They'll be circling you like vultures."

The jealousy in Catherine's voice was almost palpable. Ainsley suddenly sensed that she wasn't the only one with an ulterior motive.

As they stepped outside, the bright light temporarily blinding her, Ainsley soon found herself on a patio paved with red bricks. It was enclosed by high strands of purple and green bougainvillea. Square and immaculate.

A large tea service had been laid out on a side buffet table —scones, pots of jam, clotted cream, fresh butter, small tea cakes. There was a large silver cistern with a tap at the bottom. That was the hot water.

"There's the foodstuffs," said Catherine, "but mostly we just socialize. Let me introduce you."

About thirty guests were milling around the patio in small

groups, holding beverages. A few looked uncomfortable. Others revealed bad dental histories in their wry smiles. All had white skin, reddened cheeks, and the same grayish-blonde hair as Catherine.

Ainsley looked at their tumblers. Most had ice cubes and lime wedges and smelled faintly of gin. Ainsley guessed that very little tea had seen the inside of a glass so far today.

A fleshy woman with small nostrils and watery blue eyes approached Catherine. They exchanged air kisses. The woman was very drunk. She was wearing a boater hat and swinging a glass of champagne around the patio like a weapon.

"My dear, I thought I was seeing a ghost," she said. "You said you wouldn't visit again till June."

"Oh, you know what they say about plans," replied Catherine.

"And who's your young friend?"

"Her name is Ainsley Walker. She's renting the Souza residence right now. And she's an Oxford girl."

The woman held out her hand. "Doris. Welcome to the Kensington."

Ainsley shook her puffy hand. It was slick with sweat. Her skin was fish-belly white and her empire waist dress wasn't quite hiding the swell beneath, the spare tire that told of a few too many desserts.

"It's a beautiful facility," said Ainsley.

The woman waved off the comment. "This shack? You should see the Factory House in Oporto."

"You've been there?" said Catherine.

"Of course," said the woman. "They ask me to a dinner at least once a season. It's been delightful meeting you, Ainsley."

Catherine took Ainsley by the arm and wheeled her away. She whispered, "An utter lie. It's impossible to get an invitation to supper at the Factory House. They don't like to admit women."

The next group was a group of three paunchy men dressed in contoured British suits. The ties were absent and their collars open. They looked pleasantly pickled.

"Who's this lassie?" said one.

"Looks like Catherine's found a new friend," said the second.

"A new bird to help pass the time in the boutiques," said the third.

"It wouldn't be to try to impress you," Catherine answered. "Say hello to Ainsley Walker."

The men's bloodshot eyes flicked towards her. Catherine put her arm around Ainsley, tossed her hair, and dipped her leg slightly—

—and that's when it dawned on Ainsley. The English-woman had invited her here to shore up her own social status. Having a relatively young, attractive girlfriend was a sign that Catherine Hampstead was not in fact over the hill, that she was still young and vital.

So they were both using one another. That was the blunt truth.

"Hello, lovely," said one.

"You look in sore need of some male company," said the second.

"And I've got the bigger company," said the third, reaching for Ainsley's waist.

Catherine steered Ainsley away. "Cretins, one and all," she whispered.

Nearby, another knot of conversation beckoned. At the edge was a short, balding man with olive skin and a bulbous nose. He was wearing a rumpled gray suit. In his hand was another gin-and-tonic. He looked a little out of place.

"Catherine," he said, turning.

"Lourenço," she replied, "how is Mafalda?"

Ainsley's ears perked up. This was the Souza cousin whom Catherine had described earlier, at the café.

"I don't know," he said, shrugging. "I've been too busy trying to convince people that cuts in social spending are in their best long-term interest."

Catherine's hand fluttered like a bird between them. "This is Lourenço Souza, member of the Portuguese Assembly. Lourenço, this is Ainsley Walker. She's staying at the villa in Sintra this month."

A childish look of wonder appeared on Lourenço's face. "You're a lucky woman. It's my favorite place on earth. How do you say it—my happy place?"

"It's astounding," said Ainsley. "How fortunate that your family owns it." She hoped that Catherine would keep her mouth tightly sealed about the theft.

"I lived there every summer when I was a child," he continued, "before Mafalda married into the family and renovated everything. It was much more historic then."

Ainsley played it casual. "Well, the capela hasn't changed."

A flame roared in his Portuguese eyes. "I love that chapel. The azulejo mural is a treasure."

"Why don't more people know about it?"

He smiled mysteriously. "We've fought hard to keep it a secret. I don't want anybody else sharing my happy place."

That was a ringing clue. Clearly he had a strong connection to the sapphire azulejo.

"I can't imagine having your job right now," said Ainsley, "with all the financial difficulties."

The politician winced. "That's why I come here. No pressure. All these English people—and none of them can vote for me."

"Lourenço is the head of an important committee in the

Assembly," said Catherine. "He proposes trade regulations —right?"

The Portuguese man nodded sadly. "It's a mess. We're trying to figure a way out of the present situation."

Ainsley knew a euphemism when she heard it, and *present situation* sounded like another way to say "flat broke".

"So how do you two know one another?" he said.

"We're old friends," said Catherine, casting an arm around her.

Ainsley shot her a dirty glance. "We don't know one another that well."

Lourenço looked back and forth between them. "You two should probably get your story straight."

"It's complicated," said Catherine, trying to save face.

He lifted an eyebrow. "Indeed. Well, it's been a pleasure. Enjoy yourself at the villa. I've got to visit the chapel again. It's been too long." He shook Ainsley's hand, then moved away.

When he was out of earshot, Catherine lifted her drink to her mouth. "I would appreciate it if you didn't openly disagree with me."

"Catherine," replied Ainsley, "just don't tell people that we're old friends. It's not true."

"I can say whatever I like," said the Englishwoman, "without any editorializing from you." She put down her drink, opened her compact, and dabbed her lips with a napkin. "You can see yourself to the door at your convenience."

"Maybe I'll stick around," said Ainsley.

"Maybe you will," said Catherine, "but it makes no difference to me."

She snapped her compact shut, stowed it in her purse, and turned her back upon Ainsley.

Nobody excludes, ostracizes, and cold-shoulders quite as

well as a wealthy Englishwoman. Twenty minutes later, Ainsley found herself exiled to a corner of a patio, unable to even make eye contact with anybody except the three lecherous men. She finally threw in the towel.

Arriving back at her hotel that evening, Ainsley was sure of two things. One, acting like a pathological liar was exhausting. Two, this mystery was going to be harder to crack than she'd expected.

CHAPTER TWENTY-TWO

At eighty-thirty the next morning, Ainsley closed her umbrella and ducked into the front door of the Sé.

She shook off the rain but couldn't shake the fuzz out of her brain. The same gloomy interior greeted her, though there were about two hundred worshippers this time. Then she spotted Augusto quickly—he was standing in the same pew.

He was a man of his word.

She remained behind a tall concrete pillar, waiting for communion to begin. She watched Augusto stand up from the kneeler and head down the aisle and receive his wafer on his tongue from the priest.

Then, when the police officer made his post-communion dash for the side exit, Ainsley was already there, waiting.

"I knew you would come back," Augusto whispered.

"Of course," she answered.

They stepped out of the cathedral into the rain. Little cars zipped by on the cobblestones, splashing dirty rainwater onto their shoes.

Ainsley popped open her umbrella. "What are you going to show me?"

"Many of the stolen azulejos are for sale," he said. "Every Tuesday and Saturday."

Ainsley counted the days on her fingers. "Today is Saturday."

He nodded.

"So where are they being sold?"

"At the Feira da Ladra. I will show you. It's not far."

Augusto turned and began walking up the cobblestones. Ainsley watched him, trying to translate those words. *Feira* meant "fair". *Ladra* meant "thief".

The fair of thieves. That sounded promising.

She hurried to catch up, her boots becoming more soaked with each step. As they moved through the neighborhood, the police officer explained the history of the feira. How it had been held twice a week for four centuries now, and possibly longer. How it'd been originally established by thieves selling stolen goods, as the name implied.

"So it's still thieves today?" Ainsley said.

"They're mostly gypsies," he said.

"Aren't gypsies thieves?"

He made a fifty-fifty motion with his hand. "It's complicated."

They were passing through the winding streets of the Alfama, the medieval district that had survived the enormous earthquake of 1755. Augusto explained that it'd survived because the buildings were high enough to avoid the tidal wave that had rolled in from the ocean, flattening two-thirds of the city.

As they walked through the narrow alleys, the storm tapered off, and the torrents of water gushing out of the gutters became a trickle. It didn't matter, though, because Ainsley quickly became lost in the maze of lamps, corners, and cobblestones. The smell of grilled fish danced between the raindrops. From the narrow second-floor balconies, water dripped from hanging laundry. Ainsley halfway expected to see a purple-robed Moor with a scimitar.

Suddenly Augusto pointed straight ahead. "There. Under the Santa Engracia Church."

Ainsley saw a white dome of a small cathedral. It looked newer than the rest of the medieval neighborhood.

"That's the feira?"

He nodded. "We can enter down here, but if we go up to the top, you can come in through the Arco do Sao Vicente. That will be the best way to enter the market."

They huffed and puffed up a steep street and soon arrived at the top of the fair. A plain arch denoted the entrance, tourists pouring beneath its arch. He stopped beneath the arch.

"There," he said.

Before them was a narrow pedestrian lane lined with vendors sitting beneath umbrellas or rain ponchos or even clear plastic sheeting. On the ground lay the goods for sale. The lane extended along a tall yellow wall, down and around the curving slope of a hill.

"No tables?" she said.

"We are not a wealthy country," said Augusto. "And many of these people are gypsies, with their own customs. But they sell azulejos. That's why I've brought you here."

"You've tried talking to them."

He shrugged. "Not directly, no."

"Why not?"

"It won't do any good. The gypsies won't say where the tiles come from."

"It's worth a try."

He shrugged. "It doesn't matter. We know they are

connected to the pickpockets through someone named O Paizão. He's the mastermind."

Ainsley wrote it down in her pad. "I will listen for that name."

"You'll never find him."

"I can try."

Augusto shook his head. "O Paizão is the center of the thievery network in Lisbon. He has his fingers in everything."

The police officer shrugged, his hands hidden deep into his pockets. He didn't look particularly agitated. Maybe he'd been exhausted by years of fruitless investigation. It would explain his listlessness.

"I'll be sure to look into it," said Ainsley.

Augusto gave a knowing smile. "I wish you luck. Also, when you come back into the Baixa, be very careful on Tram 28. We've identified about seventy pickpockets who work that line. Because of the economic troubles, their numbers are growing, and they target the tourists. They'll take anything that isn't tied down. Keep your bag closed."

"I will."

"Good. That's everything I know."

"No, it's not."

He smiled. "That's everything I will tell a stranger."

"I'm not a stranger. I told you that I'm working for the Souza family."

"Oh, I know. I called Rita yesterday to check on you. But you're still an outsider. Enjoy yourself at the feira."

"So you're going to leave."

"Of course." He gestured to the gypsy vendors. "They might recognize me. I'm an important man." The police officer pulled himself up his full height. "And besides, I'm planning an event here next week."

"What type of event?"

"There will be arrests made, in the name of the law. In

fact, I've been planning it for two years. You will not find a single azulejo for sale here after next Tuesday." The police officer rubbed his fat hands together in anticipation.

"Can I ask you more questions later? If I have them?"

Augusto lifted his hands. "I can't stop you. You know my church."

"You could switch churches," she said.

"Never."

Ainsley grinned. "Have a good day, Augusto."

"And you too."

They shook hands, and the heavy man turned and walked away, the raindrops bouncing off his broad back.

"And thank you," she shouted.

"I'm just doing my job," he replied, then disappeared down the lane.

It sounded like a humble comment. A minute later, however, Ainsley remembered that Augusto was, in fact, notorious for shirking his job, for avoiding phone calls, and that she'd had to corner him at his place of worship just to get the clue about this fair from him.

But it was a lead.

She turned and headed into the Thieves' Fair.

CHAPTER TWENTY-THREE

Ainsley plunged into the Feira da Ladra playing the tourist. Wide-eyed, innocent, exuding naïvete, she strolled along the yellow wall,. Every item a cause for exclamation.

It was all an act.

She couldn't believe the junk that these people were selling. There were plain wall clocks, old PC monitors, silverware that had crusted brown with age. There were crates of old record albums, mostly *fado*, the covers bearing pictures of sad men in black suits with acoustic guitars. There were yellowed hardcover books urging political revolution. There were racks of old clothing, gray and brown shirts and pants, plainly cut, not a sequin or a spangle to be seen. A few sellers didn't have racks and had merely flung their old castoffs across the tables. She even saw someone trying to sell a rock.

This was a flea market.

No, it aspired to become a flea market. Right now, it was just gray mass of crap.

Then, halfway down the lane, where the feira expanded into the Campo Santa Clara, she spotted the first ones.

Azulejos.

They were stacked in a clear plastic bin, which lay discreetly on the cobblestones next to an array of cracked compact discs and plastic children's toys. A small sign read €10. This bin would be easy to miss unless you were hunting for it. That was probably the point.

She looked at the vendor. He was a skinny man with a sharp nose and a pair of hawklike eyes. He wore a black shirt and a black overcoat with a black winter cap. An iridescent shell hung from a string around his neck. A cigarette burned to a nub between his rounded knuckles. His eyes were weirdly hypnotic, and he appeared to be locked in a trance.

He was a gypsy. He had to be. Ainsley hadn't ever seen anyone quite like that before.

"Good morning," Ainsley said.

The gypsy didn't respond. She crouched down and rifled through the bin. The tiles were abstract and geometric, in the typical Moorish way. Historically, Muslims had been forbidden from depicting God or even human figures and had instead perfected the art of geometric designs.

Ainsley turned them over. The back of the tiles featured chipped bits of concrete. That was the smoking gun. They'd probably been gouged out of walls.

She kept up the innocent act. "These are gorgeous. Where did you find them?"

The gypsy looked down at her, tilted his head, flapped his elbows—and then chirruped like a bird.

Ainsley groped for a reply. "Excuse me?"

In response, the gypsy chirruped again, even more loudly. He unleashed a stream of unintelligible sounds—squawks, cheeps, and even a few syllables of some bizarre language. Then he cackled wildly. His eyes were dancing wildly.

Ainsley felt her hopes sinking. Still, she decided to play along with the loon.

"Thank you, birdman," she said. "Can you tell me where the humans found these azulejos?"

The gypsy lifted his face to the dark clouds and began issuing a rhythmic guttural sound. A nearby vendor was watching him with a sly grin on his face.

Ainsley swore to herself. This man was utterly certifiable. She'd have better luck questioning a tabernacle.

She decided to try one more time. "I would love to know the history of the azulejos before I buy one. Can you tell me?"

The gypsy snapped out of his trance and giggled. "Buy one!" he said in English. "Buy one buy one buy one buy one buy one buy one! Buy one! Buy one buy one—"

He danced bizarrely, arms flung in weird angles around his head and neck. Ainsley closed her eyes. He wasn't lucid enough to answer a question, let alone conduct a transaction.

She gave up. Moving down the lane, hearing his strange squawks recede into the distance, Ainsley feigned interest in the old transistor radios, the cheap bracelets with paint flecking off.

Then she saw a second group of azulejos. They were spread out on a blanket, and this time the vendor looked considerably saner. He was wearing jeans and a red zippered red soccer warm-up jacket. He was leaning back in a chair against the yellow medieval wall, playing with his phone.

Ainsley fingered an azulejo. It was the usual kaleidoscopic pattern.

"Those are beautiful," she said in Portuguese.

"You like them?" he said in English.

She switched to English too. "I do. Where did they come from?"

"From that guy." He pointed back towards the gypsy, several tables away.

"He's insane."

The vendor chuckled. "He's very special."

"Do you know where he gets them?"

The vendor shrugged. "I don't know. He doesn't tell us. Do you want to buy one?"

Ainsley hesitated, then plunged in. "Well, I'm looking for a certain azulejo. I was wondering if you might be able to find it for me." She laid a twenty euro note on his table, but kept her fingers on it.

The vendor stowed his phone into his pocket. The sight of money had earned his attention. "What does it look like?"

"It's a hand. In the hand is a gemstone."

He looked puzzled. "A gemstone?"

"A real gemstone. It's baked into the azulejo. Have you heard about anything like that?"

The vendor seemed to grow nervous. "I don't know anything about that."

"Do you know someone who would know?" She slid the note closer to his side of the table, but still didn't take her fingers off of it.

His eyes glanced down at the money, then up at her. "Nobody here. We don't sell expensive objects like that."

It was a good point, but Ainsley was asking for inside information. So she produced a second twenty-euro note and slid it underneath the first. "That's forty euros. Just for an honest conversation."

He cleared his throat, wiped something from behind his ear. "Do you want something else here? I can sell you some nice plates, maybe?"

Ainsley sighed. He was protecting his sources, like any good distributor. She wondered how many more euros would be needed to get him to talk.

She pulled her money back, thanked him, and wandered off. Over the next half-hour, she found two other vendors selling azulejos. Neither would speak about their sources. One even turned his back upon her.

When Ainsley had reached the bottom of the feira, she looked back up the hill, at the blankets cloaking the cobble-stones of Campo Santa Clara. She'd visited every table. There'd been grand total of four vendors selling azulejos. None of them had been willing to reveal anything to her.

That was okay. Cracking into in-groups was always an uphill battle, but this fair took place twice a week, every week, all year long. She would come back on Tuesday, then the Saturday after that. She would earn the vendors' trust.

Unless there was a better way.

CHAPTER TWENTY-FOUR

O Paizão.

Leaning against the black wrought-iron railing, Ainsley tilted the tiny ceramic cup against her lips and tasted the bitter espresso before it slid down her throat. Then she stared at the notepad in her hand.

Translation: *The big daddy*.

He was the king of the azulejo thieves. She pictured him as an older man, gray streaks in his hair, a single ostentatious pinky ring, sizing up azulejos in a plush office hidden inside a dilapidated warehouse. O Paizão. Sophisticated and ruthless, yet a connoisseur. The ultimate game player.

Staring across the orange rooftops, she wondered how she could find out something about him.

Ainsley was perched at the best view in the city. She was near the feira at a lookout known as Portas do Sol. It was a half-moon of tables along a railing, with a small kiosk in the middle selling drinks and snacks. From this patio, everything on the southern half of the city was visible in a hundred-eighty-degree panorama, the gently undulating Alfama district, the warren of white medieval homes sloping down towards the slate-gray river, the 25 de Abril bridge, and the far-off Cristo-Rei statue inspired by the majestic crucifix in Rio de Janeiro.

This patio would be stunning on a sunny day. But right now, the gray clouds had dampened everything, including her spirits.

The feira had done a good job of that too. She'd gotten nowhere at the tables, not even the tiniest bit of a lead. She knew that she needed to be patient. Detectives sometimes took days, weeks, months, even years to find the cracks in a case. She wondered if she really had that kind of patience.

Ainsley finished her coffee and left the small ceramic cup on a nearby table. She was out of leads for the moment and felt a little bit of window shopping might bring something into clearer relief. Retail girls were notoriously chatty, and they were sure to speak English. Maybe one would offer a good idea about where to search.

Catherine had said that Bairro Alto, or "high neighborhood", was the most stylish place in Lisbon. She'd also said that it was the neighborhood where all the carousing starts, early in the evening, since it's easier to walk downhill as the night rolls on and the legs get wobblier.

A quick glance at her map told Ainsley that the best way to get there—on the other side of the valley of the Baixa—was to take the Tram 28. Augusto had mentioned that tram too. He'd said it was home to seventy known pickpockets.

Then she heard a tremendous rattling sound. She looked over.

Clattering loudly down the narrow tracks was a tram. The bottom half was yellow, the top half white framed windows. The trolley pole itself dragged along the live electrical wire overhead. On a simple placard above the front of the tram were the words Bairro Alto 28.

Suddenly she recognized it from her research. This was

Tram 28, the famous elétrico that crossed Lisbon dozens of times per day. It was one of the most recognizable icons of the city.

Ainsley slung her purse under her arm and walked over to the tram stop. It clanked to a halt before her and opened its doors. She stepped aboard. A driver sat squarely in the middle of the car, an enormous round steering wheel flat over his legs. He nodded at her. She swiped her Metro daypass through the meter, then stepped past him into the interior.

The tram was indeed old, its brown wooden trim nicked with decades of use. The seats were filled with tourists, mostly British and Irish, judging from the reddened cheeks and pale skin and the blue eyes that stared out at her. Cameras hung from nearly every neck. Nobody offered her a seat.

That was fine. Ainsley took a standing position in the middle of the trolley. Her hand clung to the brass pole as the tram suddenly lurched forward into the narrow streets of the medieval district, and she was thrown backwards on her feet.

Soon the yellow tram was whipping around the curves. Ainsley planted her legs wide and tensed her thigh muscles. It was like standing on a children's roller coaster, all lateral movement. Outside the window was a blur of stone walls, tiny wooden doors, bright flowers, green ivy.

A loud screeching, and Ainsley was thrown forward. Her shoulder hit the brass pole and she folded around it like an umbrella.

The tram had stopped.

The doors opened, and a small, thin man with an odd limp stepped into the tram, his condition that made walking very, very difficult. On his foot was a black shoe that was turned painfully inwards. It looked like prescription footwear, but she imagined nothing could really help that condition. He wore a simple black jacket and didn't look at anyone in the eyes.

He heaved himself past Ainsley and stopped behind her. His hand came out and gripped the brass pole just above her own. She was surprised that nobody had stood up for him. Ainsley felt her heart go out to the man. He should've been given a seat.

The tram lurched forward. Ainsley had found her sea legs this time and managed to keep her balance. The clubfooted man leaned on the pole.

She glanced at the riders' eyes. Most of the tourists were fixed on the clubfoot. There were looks of empathy, of pity, of disgust, of contempt, of all the human emotions that an extreme physical handicap can summon.

The tram was winding downhill now. Ainsley recognized the Sé on the left, and then, when the tram slammed to another grinding halt a moment later, she recognized the Praça do Comércio, the square at the heart of old Lisbon.

Several tourists rose from their seats and descended the steps of the elétrico 28; just as many more piled in. The club-footed man didn't try to take a seat. Ainsley wondered why.

Meanwhile, the sun had pierced one part of the steel-gray cloud cover. A single white ray of sunlight shone onto the flat water of the Tagus. It was a compelling photo. Ainsley reached into her purse for her camera, lifted it to her face for the photo, then replaced the camera in her pocket. The long cord with the butterfly decal at the end dangled out of her pocket, so she stuffed it back in.

The tram quickly started forward. Ainsley didn't have a hand on the brass pole and fell backwards into the clubfooted man. She quickly got her footing back.

"*Tenho muito pena*," she said.

"*Está tudo bem*," he replied.

Mortified, she kept to herself while the tram tilted uphill, winding through the streets of the Chiado, past the fancy European stores, their windows showing the latest and greatest in scarves, knits, and coats. Ainsley leaned forward, feeling the workout in her abdominal muscles.

The tram screeched to a halt again. This time, the club-footed man began hobbling towards the steps. Ainsley shook her head sadly. He was a pathetic sight. When the door opened, a gust of cold, damp air rushed into the tram. It already felt colder at this elevation. She instinctively stuck her hand into her pocket.

It was empty. Her camera was gone.

And then she remembered that she had stuffed her wallet in the same pocket, after taking out her Metro daypass. Her wallet was gone too.

With her passport in it.

Ainsley's breath caught in her throat. She twirled around, head down, searching for it. The floor was clean. There was nobody standing near her. Only one person could've taken it.

She leaped down the steps and out of the tram just before the doors closed.

CHAPTER TWENTY-FIVE

She landed on the crowded sidewalk. Unlike the feira in the Alfama, this was a modern part of the city, with glass-fronted boutiques and clean curbs. A street sign said Praça do Camões. Ainsley quickly scanned the pedestrians, the dark mops of hair, the hunched shoulders, the phones held to ears, the gray scarves.

There he was.

The clubfooted man had opened a black umbrella. She hadn't remembered him carrying one. He had crossed the street and was lurching out of the crowded plaza.

Ainsley sprinted across the lanes. A taxicab screeched to a halt. She patted the hood as she strode past. She only had eyes for the clubfooted man.

Her quarry had slipped down a side street. She slipped in behind him. It was darker, narrower, emptier than the plaza. A hazy gray light lit the street from four stories above. The irregular black cobblestones felt hard beneath her feet. This street felt suddenly older.

The clubfooted man heard her footsteps and turned

around. His eyes landed on Ainsley. His face broke into a grotesque smile—

—and then he broke into a run.

It was a long, loping stride. The fluid gait of a normal, symmetrical person.

Stunned, Ainsley stopped walking. She saw something black in the man's hand. It was his shoe.

The clubfooted man wasn't clubfooted at all. It was a disguise.

Rage descended upon Ainsley. Her whole field of vision went red. Her nostrils widened, her lips tightened. She heard David's starting gun fire in her ear.

A half second later, she was bolting, hot on his heels. Her legs flying down the alley, her cheeks puffing out like a blowfish, her arms reaching out in front of her, pulling at the invisible handrails.

Her quarry had begun sprinting too. He was fast, but Ainsley was faster, gaining on him with every step.

A few seconds later, he must've come to the same conclusion, because he suddenly dodged sideways into a doorway. His body went perpendicular in the space of a single stride. It was a feat of lateral movement.

Ainsley tried to slow down, but she still overshot the doorway and instead bashed her shoulder into the doorjamb, stopping her momentum. Breathing hard, she burst inside, stopping in the middle of the shop.

It was an odd little place. There was a narrow copper countertop that comfortably could fit three people, maybe. There were no stools. Two glass jars of a deep red liquid sat on the counter. A paunchy man stood behind them, casually drying a small shot glass with a yellow rag. It felt like a tiny, empty bar.

"Ginginha?" he said.

"What?" Ainsley replied.

"Doce o la otra?" He pointed to the two jars of liquid.

Ainsley caught a movement out of the corner of her eye. She whirled. Behind her, the clubfooted man had been hiding behind the door—and now he'd just dashed outside again.

She raced out of the shop, back into the alley. Up ahead, she saw the black heel of the clubfooted man flashing around a corner.

Ainsley summoned all her energy and sprinted full-speed to the corner, rounded it—and stopped again.

There were only two shops in this alley—a boutique and a hair salon. Past them, it stopped in a dead-end. A giant wall, at least five meters high, dared anybody to try to climb it.

He couldn't have climbed the wall. He had to be in one of the two shops.

Ainsley chose the boutique first. Inside were exactly five racks of women's clothing. She glanced at the dressing room. There were no legs showing beneath the partition. The air felt undisturbed.

A bored-looking salesgirl was leafing through a fashion magazine at the counter. She was twirling a coin between her fingers.

"Did a man enter here?" said Ainsley.

"I just started working an hour ago," came the reply.

"I mean, in the last minute."

"No."

Ainsley turned and left the boutique and crossed the street to the hair salon.

There were only three people inside the salon. A female client with pieces of aluminum foil in her hair, and a girl in stilettos standing over her holding a towel stained black. Ainsley had interrupted a coloring session.

The third person was sitting in another chair, a newspaper lifted to its face. The sleeves were all black. The pants were black. The person was skinny.

It was the clubfooted man.

"I'll be right with you," said the hairdresser.

Ainsley ignored her. "You son of a bitch," she heard herself say. She stalked across the room and snatched the newspaper out of his hands so fast that it ripped in two. "You're a thief, and may God damn you to eternal hell."

The wrinkled face of an elderly woman stared back at Ainsley. Her face was the picture of shock. Then Ainsley noticed the black habit on the ground next to the chair.

It was a nun, waiting to get her hair done.

"I am so sorry," said Ainsley, picking up the shredded pieces of the newspaper. "I thought you were somebody else."

"Who? The devil?" croaked the nun.

All three women were staring at Ainsley. She wanted to crawl down a sewer. Over their shoulders, through the glass window, Ainsley glimpsed a skinny figure in black slink out of the clothing boutique. He was climbing the five-meter wall at the dead end of the street.

"Oh hell no," Ainsley said out loud.

She dashed out of the hair salon. The thief had scaled the wall quickly. His foot was about an arm's length above her head, and his long, grabby hands were grasping for purchase on the stones of the old schist wall.

Ainsley leaped for his heel but missed. He was too high already. She found herself scrambling after him. This was unfamiliar territory. She'd always avoided those fake rock climbing walls. Now she was regretting that.

Using footholds, she successfully got about a meter off the ground, then reached her peak. Ainsley had always been afraid of heights, and the gravity, no pun intended, of the climb was too daunting.

"Give me my stuff back," she said.

No response.

"The game is over! Stop trying to escape."

He said nothing.

Furious, Ainsley began cursing at the thief instead, in English, Portuguese, Spanish, in every language she'd ever learned. She pounded her fist on the rocks. She even threw a pebble at his butt.

A giggle from below caught her attention. Ainsley looked over. The hairdresser, the client, and the nun had stepped outside the shop to watch this frozen mockery of a pursuit.

Ainsley noticed them. "He stole my money and my passport," she said.

"Where are you from?" said the client with aluminum foil in her hair.

"The U.S."

The nun muttered something. The other two laughed.

"What did she say?" said Ainsley.

"She said that you shouldn't ride tram 28. She also said she doesn't want to visit your country. You're too crazy."

Ainsley ignored the gibe. The situation felt hopeless. His long body was just a little out of reach, spread across the wall like a praying mantis. She could see the butterfly clip of her camera cord dangling out of his pocket.

"He can't come down unless you get down first," said the hairdresser. "You're in his way."

That was a good point. Ainsley gave up the chase and hopped backwards off the wall onto the cobblestones. She landed off-balance and fell on her backside. Groaning, she pulled herself to her feet and brushed off her coat.

That's when the nun stepped forward. Producing a crucifix out of her robes, she lifted it towards the thief. Her thin lips became a stern ring and from her throat issued a stern order:

"*Desce.*"

That was easy to understand: get down.

From the thief's hidden face came one muffled word: "No."

The nun frowned. Her voice grew sterner, her arm stronger, the crucifix higher. "*Em nome de Deus, dar a esta mulher louca o seu dinheiro e passaporte.*"

Translated: In the name of God, give this crazy girl her money and passport.

The thief lowered his arm slightly, revealing half his face. One skittish eye looked down upon the nun. She kept the crucifix up.

The gambit worked. Slowly, the thief climbed backwards down the wall. Then he hopped to the ground, turned to Ainsley, and bowed deeply, as though he'd just completed a performance.

"You," he said in perfect English, "are not a typical tourist."

CHAPTER TWENTY-SIX

Ainsley stepped back and got a better look at her thief. His eyes were sharp beneath his heavy brow. His left foot was in a black sock. He'd dropped the shoe somewhere during the chase. He stood completely still but those eyes had a sort of dancing madness behind them.

She knew his type. He was a shapeshifter, an actor—pliable, stretchable, amoral but not harmful. She'd known men like him over the years, and they were always compelling but untrustworthy.

"You're lucky," he said in English.

"I would love to know why you think I'm lucky," Ainsley replied.

"Because usually we work in pairs," he said, "but today my partner is out of town visiting his mother. If we had done our usual trick, you never would've caught me."

"You're not helping your case."

The smallest crack of a smile curled his lip. "You're not the police."

"I can have them here in a moment," she said.

The thief grew very calm. Reaching into his pocket, he

produced Ainsley's wallet and camera and pushed them into her hands. She looked through the wallet, taking a quick inventory. "The money is gone. I had ninety-three euros in here."

She looked up at the thief. He reached into his other pocket and produced a pile of paper and shoved that at her too. She counted it. "This is ninety euros. I had ninety-three."

He reached into his back pocket and ceremoniously dumped a single euro coin into her outstretched palm.

"That's ninety-one."

He nodded towards the clothing boutique. "I gave two euros to that girl to let me hide in the dressing room."

Over his shoulder, Ainsley saw that the girl had closed and locked the door. She was staring out from behind the register.

"I looked in the dressing room," she said.

"I was standing on the seat."

That was so she couldn't see his legs. Ainsley felt like a poor investigator.

Then she remembered the name that Augusto had mentioned. The same name that she'd repeated to herself on the overlook. Big Daddy, the mysterious head of both the pickpocket and azulejo networks.

"I want you to do something for me," she said.

"What?"

"Take me to O Paizão."

She watched his reaction carefully. A flash of surprise passed across his face.

"Who is that?" he said.

"You know who that is."

"I don't know anybody like that. Me and my brother, we are independent."

The fact that he was protesting his independence showed Ainsley that he knew damn well who O Paizão was.

Ainsley began cooking up a plan in her brain. She took

her camera and looped her hand through the long cord. "Give me your hand," she said.

"No."

"Give her your hand," said the nun. "You must pay for your sins. God demands it."

The thief dropped his head and held out his hand. Apparently the nun's command had worked.

Quick as a mongoose, Ainsley grasped his hand, looped the rest of the camera cord around their wrists, twisted it three times, and cinched it tightly. They were now bound together by camera cord. To outsiders it would look like they were a couple holding hands.

"You're going to take me to O Paizão," she said.

"No, I'm not," he said.

Ainsley was ready for that. She'd already pulled her phone from her pocket and pulled up Augusto's name on the contacts list. "See that name?" she said. "Augusto? He's with the Polícia Judiciára. He's the head of the azulejo task force. He's also very interested in the pickpocket network."

The thief blanched. He twisted his wrist around to escape, but Ainsley held fast to his hand. "Don't resist," she said. "We'll end up on the ground wrestling. Then you'll be arrested and questioned for sure. And I'll tell them everything. I'll even make up things."

The chorus of women *ooohed*. Ainsley was providing the most excitement they'd seen all day.

"Okay," he said at last, "but there is no guarantee that he will meet you."

"I don't care," said Ainsley. "Just lead the way."

CHAPTER TWENTY-SEVEN

Strolling hand-in-hand with the pickpocket down the steep staircases of the Bairro Alto, Ainsley felt that she may very well have crossed the line.

Chasing a known criminal through a foreign country was one thing. Physically tying herself with a cord to that same criminal was quite another. Her palm was growing slippery with sweat. She felt embarrassed about it, especially since his hand felt cold and defined.

"I'm surprised you haven't tried to chew through the cord," she said.

"We're in public," the pickpocket replied.

"Do you have a name?"

"I do, but if you ask, I will give you a different one."

"Then that would be pointless."

"Yes."

"Maybe I'll call you clown."

"You can call me whatever you want," he answered.

"Would you prefer idiot?"

"I have no opinion in the situation."

Ainsley knew what he was doing. Keeping his head low,

playing along nicely, which would lead to underestimation, which could lead to possible escape. She needed to keep a strong frame.

"Listen," she said, "why don't you show me how smart you are and tell me exactly where we are going."

"We're going to the Baixa. It's where O Paizão lives."

"Where is that?"

They had come to the upper deck of an outdoor elevator. A sign over the sliding wooden door read Santa Justa Elevador. An attendant stood nearby.

The pickpocket led her to the railing and pointed at the flat ground below, the bustling sector of Lisbon located on the plain between the Bairro Alto on one side and the Alfama on the other. "That's the Baixa," he said. "What kind of tourist are you?"

"I'm not a tourist," she answered.

A moment later, the elevator door opened. Ainsley approached the attendant.

"Two," she said.

"Ten euros," he said.

She turned to the pickpocket. "You can pay him. Taking this elevator was your idea."

"I don't have any money. Why do you think I'm a pickpocket?"

That made sense. Ainsley reluctantly handed the attendant a ten euro note. "I can't believe I'm doing this," she said.

As they boarded, the elevator attendant explained, in slow, deliberate English, that the Baixa was the neighborhood in the center of Lisbon. Because it was at sea level, it had been wiped out by the massive tidal wave triggered by the great earthquake of 1755. Under the Marquês de Pombal, it had been rebuilt along Enlightenment ideas of reason, logic, and perpendicularity—straight avenues, uniform building codes. In other words, much unlike the rest of older Lisbon.

Ainsley stood at the window of the old iron carriage, feeling the faded wood under her one free hand, looking out the frosted glass of the elevator as they descended.

She noticed an elderly woman next to her. She was a tourist, judging from her pale face, large buck teeth, and camera around neck, at the ready. She was smiling at Ainsley. Her eyes glanced at their tied hands.

"That's how you keep a good man," she said. "Don't let him get away."

"Too bad he isn't one."

"Oh, be nice," replied the old woman.

The door opened, and she and the pickpocket slipped outside and plunged into the commercial neighborhood of the Baixa.

As he led her into the neighborhood, Ainsley drank it all in. The Baixa was laid out in a grid, like Manhattan, and most of the buildings were five stories high. The ground floors were always commercial, floors two through four had nondescript windows, and the top floors featured a wrought-iron balcony that ringed the building.

That's when Ainsley felt the tip of something sharp dig into her ribcage.

It was the thief. His free hand was inside his coat, and he was pushing something into her side. A cold look had chilled his eyes.

"ATM," he said.

That, Ainsley thought, is a knife.

She wanted to kick herself in the head. A smart detective would've frisked him first. Now she'd tied herself to a known criminal with a knife, gone from the hunter to the hunted.

And she knew that there wasn't any way to get out of it.

"You're crazy," she said. "I'm completely broke."

He pushed harder. She felt the tip through the fabric. It was driving into her skin.

"Okay," she said.

He led her to an ATM. It was inside a glassed-in kiosk. He held the door open gallantly. She walked in, glaring at him. The thief followed and stood close alongside her, once again pressing the knife to her ribs. From the outside, they looked like a couple who couldn't bear to be apart, not even for a withdrawal.

With her free hand, Ainsley reached into her wallet and fumbled for her credit card. She slid it into the machine. The screen beeped and asked for her choice of language. She chose English.

"Take the maximum," he said. "Five hundred euros."

Her heart, already hammering, doubled its speed. That would deplete her bank account enormously.

"I don't have enough," she lied.

He pushed the knife harder. "Do it."

She punched in five hundred euros. A whirling ball on the screen indicated a transaction in progress. She felt a tear coming to her eye. How could she have been so stupid?

The screen lit up: Transaction failed.

Ainsley exhaled, smiling. Finally her poverty was paying off.

The thief crinkled his nose. "Two hundred fifty."

"It's not going to work," she said. Ainsley already knew that the amount wasn't the problem. The problem was the fact that she'd forgotten to inform her bank that she was travelling abroad. The bank's security department had blocked her transaction. For once, she gave thanks for being ill-prepared for a journey.

Still, she tried again, to satisfy the thief. Transaction failed.

"One hundred," he said.

Same result. Ainsley turned away from the screen and faced him. It felt bizarre to be holding hands with this man.

"The only broke tourist in Lisbon," he said, shaking his head at his bad luck. "Listen, give me the cash. Ninety-one euros."

"I only have eighty-one left, thanks to your dumb elevator ride. I'll split it with you if you take me to O Paizão."

"No."

"Yes."

He started to reach inside his coat for the knife. Ainsley grabbed at the coat first, feeling around the outside with her fingers. The knife was right there, long and thin and circular.

"That's not a knife," she said.

He answered quickly. "Yes, it's a knife, very dangerous—"

Quick as a snakebite, Ainsley shoved her hand inside his coat. He tried to resist, but she had already found the object in the inside pocket and removed it.

It was a blue pen.

CHAPTER TWENTY-EIGHT

"I knew it," Ainsley said, throwing the pen on the ground. "You are pathetic."

A sad look fell across the pickpocket's face. "My brother is out of town—"

"No excuses. As a criminal, you suck."

"I don't understand *suck*."

"It means you are a bad criminal."

"I'm a pickpocket. We are all bad."

"Not bad," she said, "but incompetent. *Incompetente*."

That was a guess, but it must've been dead on, because the thief looked wounded. "Please, senhora, I don't have a job. Life is very difficult here."

"Take some pride in yourself," she said. "Commit. Whatever you do, be the best. Don't let strangers stick their hands into your coat."

"But my brother is out of town—"

"Please stop talking about your brother." For a moment, Ainsley honestly considered letting this guy go.

"Listen," she said, "if you lead me to O Paizão, my offer of splitting the eighty-one euros still stands. For your trouble.

Do we have a deal?"

The thief moped. "I don't know," he said. "It's not as good as a wallet."

"No thievery necessary."

With a small nod, the pickpocket finally acquiesced. Ainsley guessed that two heists gone flat in the same day probably pushed him into that decision.

They exited the ATM enclosure and walked for three more blocks. The pickpocket halted at the corner of Correeiros and Doura. He pointed at a building. It was like the other structures in the Baixa, two and a half centuries old, in need of repair, cracked panels falling off the front. The windows on the second, third, and fourth floors were dusty and cracked. Nobody had lived there in years.

"O Paizão lives there," he said.

"That building is empty," answered Ainsley.

The thief shook his head. "The top floor."

Ainsley looked up. On the fifth floor, trailing out of a window, hung a line of fresh white laundry.

"He really lives there?"

The thief nodded.

"And you've met him?"

"Of course."

"Then lead the way."

They stepped into the small lobby. It was dark and smelled like a bucket of worms in black earth. It was also narrow enough for Ainsley to stretch out her arms and touch both walls, which were lined with rough concrete patches. She guessed that these had once boasted azulejos.

Ahead, a creaky staircase with a wooden banister beckoned. This part was barely wide enough to walk single file.

"This is where we have to break up," said Ainsley.

The thief shrugged. "My heart will never recover."

She unclasped his hand. Then Ainsley unwound the

camera cord that had bound them together for the last ten minutes. Free of her burden, Ainsley rubbed her wrist until sensation began to return. She lifted her hand to her face and smelled it. The residue of his sweaty palm was still there.

She gestured to the staircase. "Please, you first."

"You're the boss," he replied.

The pickpocket walked ahead of her and slowly began climbing the stairs. His legs were long, and he bounded up the steps two at a time, turning quickly at each landing. Ainsley hurried at double time to keep up with his ascent. She didn't want to let the thief out of her sight.

On the second floor, she passed a door with a broken window. On the third floor, she saw a small green plant thriving on the tiled floor, its roots in the cracks between the squares. This building hadn't been inhabited for years.

By the fourth floor, her thighs were hurting, her lungs gasping. She understood why, before the invention of the elevator, buildings didn't go very high. A trip to the super-market could kill an older person.

"You're almost there," said the pickpocket's voice, floating down the stairwell. "Only one more flight."

Ainsley stopped, her ears pricking up. She detected a certain note of glee in his voice. She wondered if he was plan-ning something devious, if this were an enormous improvised setup that she had, ironically, helped to set up. Maybe a gang of vicious thugs awaited her. Given Lisbon's peaceful reputa-tion, she doubted it, but stranger things had happened, and would happen.

She needed to leave, fly home, get a real job at a credit union or restaurant. Why had she thought that she could play this role? Laughing with the jetset, muckraking with the unsavory, analyzing gemstones, even acting as an amateur linguist—foreign travel required the skills of at least four different women. A pang of embarrassment knifed through her belly.

But Ainsley reached deep down, knowing that she was those four women, or at least she could be, at different times. And she wouldn't give up. She couldn't live with herself if she quit.

Taking a deep breath, she trekked up the last remaining flight of stairs. On the fifth-floor landing, the pickpocket was leaning against a small window inside a deep casement. He was staring out across the rooftops. Behind him was a single door, made of oak. Elaborate Manueline rope rigging had been carved into its surface. It looked at least two centuries old.

"If this is a torture chamber," she said, "you are in huge trouble."

He seemed curiously detached. "It's the home of O Paizão."

"You can knock," he said. "O Paizão never leaves."

Ainsley smoothed her coat, tipped her chin into the air, and rapped loudly on the door.

There was a scuffling sound from within, like a pair of chairs being scooted out. She heard voices arguing. There was no peephole, so he would have to open up—or else shout through the wood.

She heard footsteps approaching. It remained to be seen just how large Big Daddy was. Ainsley grabbed the pickpocket by the arm and pulled him over to her. "Stand next to me."

From behind the door, a muffled voice said, "*Quem é?*"

"*Sou eu.*" He glanced at Ainsley. "Carlos."

"Carlos?" said the voice.

"*Você me conhece. Eu trabalho para você. Abra a porta por favor.*"

The door swung open.

It was a young woman. She was short, in her twenties, decently curved, with a moon-shaped face and intelligent green Moorish eyes staring out intensely from beneath eyelashes thickened with mascara. A headset was affixed to her black hair with a tortoise-shell clip. She wore a white t-shirt, black leggings, and pink house slippers.

Ainsley was taken aback. She'd been expecting to meet a man.

The young woman recognized the pickpocket. "Ah," she said, with a wink, "Carlos."

When she saw Ainsley, however, a cloud immediately drew over her face. This was the moment to strike. Ainsley drew a deep breath. "*Estou procurando O Paizão. Você sabe onde ele está?*"

A ray of sunlight cracked through the girl's mask of suspicion. Maybe it was Ainsley's fumbling attempt at Portuguese. Maybe Ainsley was a welcome interruption in a difficult workday. Or maybe she was a cat that hadn't seen a mouse in a long time.

"*Sim*," she replied. "*O que você precisa?*" What do you need?

"*Para falar.*" To talk.

"*Sobre o que?*" About what?

"*Estou à procura de um azulejo. Eu não estou com a polícia.*" I'm looking for a tile. I'm not with the police.

The girl held very still, but her green eyes whipped over to the pickpocket. He nodded. Ainsley guessed the questions running through her head—who is this visitor, is she dangerous, how did she persuade him to guide her to my house, now she knows where I live.

The pickpocket nodded. Still, the girl with the green eyes shook her head.

"*Não*," she said, "*eu não confio em você.*" Then she repeated in English: "I don't trust you."

Her accent was invisible. Ainsley wasn't surprised any

more. She was growing accustomed to young Lisboetas having flawless English.

"Same here," replied Ainsley. She yanked out her phone and opened up the contacts list. "That is why I have Inspector Augusto's phone number. The police officer in charge of the azulejo recovery task force. He would be very interested in learning where you live—and asking more about O Paizão."

To her surprise, the girl said nothing. Her green eyes pinged between Ainsley's phone and Ainsley's face.

"I might have a few minutes," she finally said.

"That's good. But please don't waste my time."

"I won't."

"Are you sure?

The girl's green eyes flashed with an orange fire. "Of course I'm sure."

"I'm serious," said Ainsley. "I need to speak with him. I'm investigating a theft."

The girl waved away her concern. "It's no problem."

"When is O Paizão coming here?"

"Soon."

"When?"

The girl's patience broke like water through a dam. Her angry eyes were glinting as they caught and held Ainsley's eyes.

"I am O Paizão."

CHAPTER TWENTY-NINE

Ainsley stood there in the hallway, gaping.

O Paizão, the person who Augusto had identified as the lord of the underworld, the huge brain of azulejo thieves, this grand schemer ... was a young woman who was barely old enough to drink.

Ainsley turned to the pickpocket. "You could've told me."

The pickpocket's expression was blank. His default, the same game face he'd worn on the tram. "It was more fun to watch your reaction." His eyes darted to Ainsley's purse. "You promised money."

"I did." Ainsley rolled her eyes as she dug into her wallet, removed two twenty-euro notes, and tossed them at him. "I hope to never see you again."

He turned to his boss. "*Amanhã*."

"*Talvez*," she answered.

"*Tchau*."

The pickpocket turned and slinked down the staircase, smoothly and silently, like a cat evading detection.

Ainsley watched him go. "He tried to steal my wallet and

camera on the tram," she said. "I chased him down and took it back."

"You're the first to catch him," she replied. "Congratulations. Did he try to force you into an ATM?"

"Yes. Using a pen. He didn't get anything."

She looked impressed. "Another first."

This irked Ainsley. For some reason, she'd expected something less sardonic, more empathetic.

She stuck out her hand. "My name is Ainsley Walker," she said, "and I'm a private gemstone investigator."

The girl looked at her hand as though it'd been hacked off a plague victim. "You can call me Bia."

Ainsley dropped the hand. "It's a pleasure."

"You look like a tourist."

"I'm not."

"That's too bad. Lisbon is a beautiful city, with many azulejos, but you need to look for them."

"May I come in?"

The girl was still propping open the door with her right slipper. She crossed her arms tightly. "I don't know you."

"So we're going to talk like this?"

"We don't have to talk at all. Besides, I only have five minutes."

Ainsley looked over her shoulder into her apartment. It was roomy, with tall ceilings, modern furniture. Behind that was a large workspace, with a large wraparound desk, an Aeron swivel chair, and two large flatscreen monitors. The desktop was cluttered with azulejos.

Bia tapped a pink slipper. "What is your question?"

"I'm looking for an azulejo with a sapphire."

The girl tilted her head curiously. "A gemstone?"

"Yes. It's baked into the tile. Very historic."

The young mogul scrunched up her nose. She looked

genuinely confused. "Well, they're all historic. But no, I don't know about it."

"Are you sure?"

"Yes. It's surprising that I didn't hear about it."

A look of distress came across her face. Ainsley searched her features for a sign of disingenuousness. There wasn't any. Either that, or Bia was well-versed in the art of evasion.

From inside the apartment came a sound like an angry seagull. It was a woman.

"Who is that?" said Ainsley.

"My grandmother is cooking. She can't lift the *cataplana*."

Ainsley craned her neck and peered around Bia. At the rear of the apartment was a modest kitchen whose walls were covered in a flurry of blue-and-white azulejos. At the stove stood a tiny old woman, dressed head-to-toe in black. She was struggling with a large copper pot.

"You live with your grandmother?" Ainsley said.

Bia looked nonplussed. "We Portuguese all live at home after college."

"You went to college?"

"Of course."

She shrugged, looking at Ainsley matter-of-factly. It occurred to Ainsley that this was how master criminals got started all over the world: intelligence coupled with lack of opportunity in legitimate enterprises.

"Is there anything else you need?"

Ainsley felt panicked. This conversation couldn't end so quickly. "Could you to inquire about the tile? It was stolen from a property in Sintra."

A cunning look grew on Bia's face. "Maybe. What do I get for my trouble?"

Ainsley laid out the offer. "I have information about Augusto. He's planning to raid the Feria da Ladra."

"Really?"

Ainsley nodded. "Here's the deal. If you learn anything about the stolen sapphire azulejo, I will tell you exactly when the raid is going to happen."

Bia chewed on her lip. "Okay."

Ainsley shoved her business card into the girl's hand. She'd already scrawled her Portuguese phone number on the back. "Call me."

Bia took the card, but her attention was on Ainsley's feet. "I really like those boots."

"Great."

"Where did you get them? Are they American?"

They were ordinary brown Frye boots, the ones Ainsley had yanked out of her closet minutes before departure, but she wasn't going to reveal that. "I'll tell you when you get me the information."

Then she winked, swiveled on a boot, and clacked down the stairs. It was always better, she knew, to leave them wanting more.

CHAPTER THIRTY

That night, Ainsley uncorked a cheap bottle of port wine that she's purchased at a corner shop, sat down in her hotel room's only chair, and propped her feet on the edge of her bed.

Running through her mind was a replay of the events of the last three days. She'd inserted herself into so many places, found herself with so many tantalizing clues—

—and yet she didn't feel like she was getting any closer.

A strange clanging sound drew her out of her reverie. Ainsley realized that it was her phone. Or, rather, Joaquim's phone, which was inside her purse.

She ran across the room and retrieved it. "Hello?"

It was a man's voice, velvety yet rough. "You haven't lost my phone yet."

Ainsley's stomach plunged to her feet. "Joaquim."

"Everything is going well?"

"Sort of."

"You have made progress?"

"Some. I have three good leads."

"Tell me."

She replayed for him everything that had happened, the

meeting with Rita in Sintra, the failed lunch at A Caverna, the failed visit to the Polícia Judiciára, the backfired lure of Catherine Hampstead, the stalking of Augusto at his church, her failure to learn anything at Feria do Ladra, the ride on Tram 28, the pursuit of the pickpocket, the impromptu handcuff, the grand meeting with the azulejo gangster in pink house slippers.

Joaquim laughed. "We have to get some money for you."

"That would be nice," she said.

"We'll work it out. Trust me." His voice sounded confident and comfortable. "So it's eight o'clock your time," he said. "What are you doing tonight?"

"Waiting for a phone call," said Ainsley. That sounded more flirtatious than she'd meant it to be.

"What's his name?"

"Bia."

"Thank God it's not a man."

"Why do you care?" she said, twisting her hair around a finger.

"Portugal is full of many distractions for an attractive woman."

Ah. The first wall had been breached. Joaquim had admitted the existence of a physical attraction.

"Joaquim," she said, "has it ever occurred to you that I might actually be able to handle myself around foreign men?"

"I hope so. My San Francisco clients are still helpless. I won't be able to leave here for another week."

"So King Sebastião isn't going to return," she said sadly.

"You're screwing up the story. But he has some making up to do."

Ainsley sighed. "It would've been nice to have a native speaker as a guide."

"Well, I'm only part native. Besides, Rita said that you're doing well."

"Not well enough. I don't understand fifty percent of what's being said."

"Neither do I. Portuguese people mumble."

"It's been sweet of you to call," she said. "Should I touch base more often?"

"We would appreciate it."

"Guess what I would appreciate?"

"A retainer," Joaquim answered. "I'm working on it. Stay tuned."

"All right."

Ainsley disconnected and poured herself more cheap port wine. This was her evening—alone in a foreign country, with a four-euro bottle of wine, in a hotel room.

It didn't feel that much different from life at home.

The clanging sound burst out of her purse again. An ugly ring. Ainsley stood up. Maybe that was Joaquim, calling to say that he'd been playing a joke, that he was actually across the street.

Ainsley crossed the room again and looked at the phone. No luck: The caller ID was a number she didn't recognize.

She picked up. "Hello."

"It's Bia."

Ainsley was instantly at attention. She must've spooked the girl with news of the upcoming bust at the Feira da Ladra.

"Talk to me."

"So I learned some information."

"What"

On the other end of the line, a sound like an angry seagull began squawking. The girl argued with the voice in rapid, distorted Portuguese.

Then she returned to the phone. "I'm sorry, my grandmother is crazy and I can't talk now. Can you meet me tonight?"

"Yes."

"Come to A Brasiliera. At the top of the Baixa-Chiado Metro stop. I'll be next to Pessoa."

"Who?"

"Just come right now. It's urgent."

They disconnected. Ainsley sighed. She could sleep later. She swallowed her wine, changed tops, fixed her makeup in the bathroom mirror, and strapped on her boots.

CHAPTER THIRTY-ONE

Pessoa turned out to be a bronze statue of a man reading a newspaper. He was sitting on a park bench outside the café. Ainsley remembered that he was also Portugal's most famous poet.

Bia was sitting next to the statue, furiously tapping on her phone. She wore a black top with black leggings, one leg crossed over the other. She was also wearing a pair of boots.

They were brown leather. The heels were wide and chunky, and not too tall. They looked like Frye.

Ainsley blinked twice. Those were her own boots. Exactly.

"You've got to be kidding me," she said.

"Surprise," said Bia. "Do you know how hard it was for me to find an American brand on such short notice?"

Impressed, Ainsley found herself in a rare speechless moment. Quickly recovering, Ainsley sat down next to her. "Should we go into the café?"

Bia stowed her phone away. "A Brasiliera? No, it's over-priced and touristic. I chose it just because it's easy to find at the top of the Metro stairs. Why are you late?"

"It's my second day in the country. Give me a break."

A look of mischief lit up Bia's moon-shaped face. Her green eyes danced inside her skull. "You made me angry this afternoon."

"Why?"

"Because you told me that someone stole an azulejo without consulting me."

"I'm just the messenger."

"Come walk with me," said Bia abruptly. She stood up.

Ainsley followed her, strolling through the streets of Chiado. Ainsley walked slightly behind the tiny tile gangster, their four brown leather boots clacking on the ground in sync.

"I spent all afternoon making calls," said Bia. "The sapphire azulejo wasn't stolen by anyone in my network."

"How many thieves are in your network?" asked Ainsley.

"About seventy. They're independent contractors. I provide them with protection."

Ainsley looked at the girl. This was the shortest, youngest racketeer in the history of organized crime. "Protection from who?"

"The police. So they can sell at the Feira da Ladra."

"You've done a good job disciplining them," Ainsley replied. "None of those vendors would tell me anything. One even chirped like a bird."

Bia laughed again. "Oh, that guy. He makes those sounds when someone starts asking too many questions. It's a warning to the others."

Ainsley felt humbled. The bizarre birdman had been more clever than he'd seemed.

"So you must know Augusto? The officer?" she said.

"We've never met," Bia replied.

"He sure knows you. He couldn't stop talking about O Paizão. He made you sound like you grilled babies for lunch."

Bia laughed. "Excellent. I have good public relations."

For the first time, Ainsley caught a scent of this girl's accomplishment. In a country with a plummeting economy, she'd managed to carve out a niche for herself. And though it was criminal, nobody was getting hurt. It was a better than sliding into purposelessness.

She was resourceful.

"You don't have to answer," said Ainsley, "but I need to ask how you got into the protection racket."

Bia grew evasive. "I have connections. Let's save those details for another time."

For another time. Ainsley's imagination ran wild. How did someone establish a racket over a group of tile thieves? Maybe she'd been born into a family of police officers. Maybe she'd figured out the thieves' weakness. Or maybe she was just lying.

Bia led her into a small park in the Bairro Alto. They moved alongside a railing, beyond which was a steep slope, partly cemented, that tumbled into the Rossio train station. The Baixa lay beyond that.

"So," said Ainsley, "what's the news?"

"One of my thieves," replied Bia, "told me that he was asked to steal an azulejo from an estate in Sintra last month. It had a gemstone in it."

Ainsley's eyes widened. She felt beads of moisture spring onto her palms. How many different thefts like that could have occurred? How many tiles even had gemstones? This could very well be the break she'd been looking for.

"He turned it down?"

Bia nodded. "He said that he was too busy. It also sounded a little dangerous. So he recommended another man for the job."

"Who?"

"An older man, with many years of experience. He's not

part of my network."

"What's his name?"

"On the street, his name is Vasco the Italiano. He's not Portuguese."

Ainsley whipped out her notebook and scribbled it down. "How can I find him?"

"I don't know. But he doesn't live in Lisbon."

"Where does he live?"

Bia glanced at her. "I knew you were going to ask that, so I placed a few more calls."

"And?"

"He lives in Évora."

Ainsley's eyes frantically searched the horizon. "Where is that?"

"About two hours to the east. In the Alentejo. Vasco says he is retired, so I don't know if he took the job. But he's very skilled in stonework. He does legitimate work too, under a different name."

Ainsley thought back to the clean, professional theft from the chapel. That would fit the story well. "Do you have his address or phone number?"

"No. And I don't think his services are available online or in a phone book."

Ainsley nodded and flipped her notepad closed. "I'm going to have to find him."

Suddenly Bia pulled herself back. She had a very indignant childlike look on her face. "Now it's your turn."

"For what?"

"The information you promised me."

Ainsley remembered. "Yes—Augusto is planning a raid next week on the Feira da Ladra."

"What kind of raid?"

"I don't know. But he said that there will not be a single azulejo for sale there after next Tuesday."

All the color drained from Bia's face, and she muttered something like a curse to herself. Ainsley watched her small hand clench into a tight ball.

At last, the Portuguese girl exhaled, and her body seemed to fold forward. She leaned across the railing for support.

"I'm tired of this game," she said sadly. "I want to find a real job. You know, I studied anthropology at university. And everybody I know from school has already left the country to find work. My class reunion is probably going to be in Brazil."

"There are jobs in the U.S.," Ainsley replied. "Not many, but more than here."

"I would love to go to the States," replied Bia. "I want to see California, New York, Florida."

The two women faced one another at the overlook, the city lights of Lisbon twinkling below and around them.

"I have an idea," said Ainsley.

"I do too," said Bia.

"What is it?"

"You go first."

"No, you go first."

Bia took a deep breath. "If I help you find the azulejo—"

"—then I will help you get a legitimate job in the States," finished Ainsley.

"With who?"

Ainsley thought of Fatima leaving her job. "My boss Joaquim is looking for a new assistant. Portuguese fluency is a must."

The two women stood there, hearts beating wildly, searching one another for signs of disingenuousness. Ainsley couldn't find any. She hoped that Bia couldn't either.

Overhead, a pair of white points of light glowed against the darkening sky. "Is this really happening?" said Bia.

"It is."

Bia clapped her hands. "Then let's do it."

Ainsley stuck her hand out. Bia held hers out. They shook formally, then looked at one another, holding in their breath. A dam of emotion seemed to break inside of the short racketeer, and she flung her arms around Ainsley's neck.

"You are a great accident," she said, "maybe the best that has ever happened to me."

"It's a good thing I chased your pickpocket," Ainsley replied.

"He's not my pickpocket," said Bia. "He doesn't even steal azulejos, he only repairs them for me sometimes. Mostly he steals wallets from tourists. I don't want to be involved in that. Tourists are keeping this economy alive."

Suddenly the Portuguese girl stopped talking. "So when do you want to leave?"

"To where?"

"Évora," she replied. "We have to find Vasco the Italiano."

Ainsley didn't quite know what to say. She didn't really believe any of this was going to happen. This girl, however, seemed serious about joining forces, which meant that Ainsley would be required to reciprocate. That would be difficult. How could she help a stranger move to the United States? How could she handle all the different bureaucratic problems that came with that? Ainsley fast-forwarded through all the possible scenarios that could arise. There were so many.

"It would be a lot of work," said Ainsley.

"I don't care," Bia answered. "I have to get out of this country. My grandmother is driving me crazy. I'm trapped in this stupid job."

"I guess we can leave in the morning."

The rest of the evening seemed like a dream, their boots striding over the cobblestones as the two women flew out of the park, down the steep steps of the Bairro Alto, and back towards the Baixa, chattering all the way.

ÉVORA

CHAPTER THIRTY-TWO

The next morning, as the traffic light turned green, Ainsley squeezed her fingers on the steering wheel of the rented Toyota ... and stamped her foot on the accelerator.

Next to her was Bia, dressed in a modish white jean jacket with a ruffled black silk top underneath. She wore a pair of tight jeans beneath that, and the same brown boots that she'd worn the night before. She'd done her makeup and was tapping on her phone.

In the backseat were their two bags, both white leather. At some level, Ainsley thought, they were like lost souls reunited.

A half hour earlier, Ainsley had stood at the rental car counter, silently crossing her fingers as the clerk slid her debit card through the reader. He was attempting to run an authorization of five hundred euros. Ainsley had read all her receipts the previous night, called her bank overseas, done the math. There should be enough, but the process still made her nervous. When the machine beeped, and the small slip of paper curled out, she felt a sweet relief.

Before leaving Lisbon, she'd called Rita and left a message

about the latest developments. She was sure that the property manager would be ecstatic, not the least for the fact that she wouldn't be paying for Ainsley's room at the hotel any longer.

Now she was accelerating down a long entrance ramp onto the autostrada. She checked her rearview mirror, preparing to merge. The four lanes of concrete were almost totally empty of vehicles.

"There is nobody on this freeway," said Ainsley.

"It's because nobody is working," answered Bia.

Ainsley watched the speedometer needle reach 100 km/hr. Then she hit cruise control and let her foot off the pedal. She relaxed and sat back.

"So," said Bia, reading her phone, "someone in my network says that Vasco the Italiano likes to go to Praça do Giraldo in the afternoons."

"Have you been there before?"

"Of course. It's where everybody goes in Évora."

"How will we find him?"

"We dress well, and people tell us things."

The freeway crossed a long bridge over the River Tagus, swung left, and within half an hour they were crossing into the countryside.

This was the Alentejo. As they barreled along the autostrada, Bia described the region. It had derived its name from the Latin phrase *alem Tejo*, which meant "beyond the Tagus", and even from the freeway, it felt like a different world here. It was agricultural.

After an hour, they pulled off the highway to take the surface roads to Évora. As they zipped through the fields, the air smelled rich and fertile, the scent of clover and orange blossom wafting into the car. Cows placidly chewed their cud in the green fields. When they slowed at an intersection, Ainsley caught the sound of wild boars grunting in the field somewhere nearby.

A gaggle of women stooped over in a wheat field. Each wore a black felt hat on top of a headscarf. One stood up and fixed the passersby with an intense gaze that seemed to come from centuries past.

"These people look very conservative," said Ainsley.

"Tradition is everything in the Alentejo," said Bia. "They don't like anything new. Especially not jokes. Don't try to make them laugh."

A half-hour later, and they passed the first sign: *Évora, 12 km*.

"That didn't take long at all," said Ainsley.

"Portugal is a small country." She looked out the window. "I should've told my father that we were going. He says he wants to retire there."

"You can call him."

Bia shrugged. "We aren't speaking right now."

Ainsley thought about that. This explained why she was living with her grandmother, maybe even why she wanted to leave the country.

"Lot of people retire there," continued Bia. "The town is very historical and very slow. Everyone is old, except for the university students."

At last the two-lane blacktop came over a small rise and there, on a hilltop, was a sizable sprinkling of orange roofs. Évora looked about the size of a college town in the States. The difference was the old wall encircling the town. It looked to be thousands of years old.

"It's beautiful," said Ainsley.

"That's built by the Romans," replied Bia. "You can park the car in the lot just outside it. Go that way."

Ainsley followed her direction, taking the circular road around the town, spotted a dusty parking lot, and pulled in, stopping the front of the Toyota at the edge of the ancient Roman wall. It was ten meters high at least.

Ainsley stepped out of the car and used her hand to shield her eyes from the sun. She gazed up at the sheer ramparts. "All these centuries. Just like this."

"Tradition," said Bia.

Ainsley nodded. Then she glanced in her backseat. "Should we bring the bags with us?"

"No, it's okay," said Bia, "we can leave them. It's safe."

"Are you sure?"

Bia nodded. "There is no crime in Évora. The people here are so lazy, they keep a stool by their beds so that they can sit down to rest after they wake up."

Ainsley laughed. She slung her purse over her shoulder, closed the door, and locked the car. "Lead the way," she said.

"Okay."

She followed Bia along the shadow of the dark Roman wall until they came to a steep cobblestone street. The little Portuguese woman pointed to the left. "We will go this way. What you will see at the top of this street is the most special place in my heart."

The excitement in Bia's eyes said everything. Ainsley took a deep breath and followed her, trekking up the sidewalk, alongside another tall wall that seemed to be the side of a palace, on top of which stood an authentic tower. She began to feel something odd, something mystical, as though ancient spirits were whirling around the air.

Then she saw it.

The ruins of an old Roman temple. Fourteen white fluted granite columns, capped by the sprouting acanthus leaves of Corinthian capitals, over which remained a thin horizontal architrave. The base was a mess of hewn rocks and smooth granite blocks. The entire structure had been roped off from the public.

"The Templo Romano," Bia said.

Ainsley stood staring, utterly transfixed. The Roman

Temple. She was only halfway listening as Bia described its construction in the first century, its partial destruction by German tribes during the fall of Rome. She barely heard Bia say that it had been used as a slaughterhouse for nearly five hundred years.

It was that haunting.

Bia sighed. "I remember my first time seeing it. I looked at it for two hours."

"I feel strange," Ainsley said.

"How?"

"Like there are ... spirits here, or something." Ainsley had never liked having these feelings, not since her father had passed away when she'd been twelve years old, and definitely not since she had occasionally seen him after that—materializing at the foot of her bed, in the corner of the dining room.

Bia arched an eyebrow. "Then let's keep walking. Praça do Giraldo is just five minutes away."

Ainsley followed her out of the square, and as the ruins of the Roman temple receded, she wondered if dead spirits might help her find the sapphire azulejo.

CHAPTER THIRTY-THREE

As the glass carafe of white wine threw rays of golden light across the table, Ainsley wondered if she'd ordered too much.

It was called *vinho verde*, and the carafe was resting inside a glass bowl of ice, which was slowly melting. The temperature was much higher here than it'd been in Lisbon. Ainsley had already taken off her coat.

She was sitting in a chair at a silver table, one of many massed in the middle of the large Praça do Giraldo. Shaped like a football field, the plaza was bordered on the near end by a high, flat, white church façade. On the long sides were three- and four-story buildings, the doors and windows painted bright yellow. She'd seen the same color through the alleys of Évora.

"You know," said Ainsley, "I feel like someone is watching us."

"That's probably the spirits," answered Bia. "It's why there is so much yellow trim here. It's to scare away evil ones."

"Why are there so many upset spirits?"

Bia grew quieter. "Many people were killed in this plaza."

"When?"

"During the Inquisition. *Auto-da-fé*."

Ainsley didn't know that word. Bia lowered her voice and explained in two brief words.

"Public burning."

Ainsley felt her stomach sink. "Oh."

"Even today, there's still a board announcing the local deaths." She pointed to a small board mounted on the pillar of an arcade. The word CME was etched above it.

"That's macabre," said Ainsley.

"It's better not to talk about these things," agreed Bia.

Ainsley wrestled her imagination to the ground and forced it to behave. Then she looked around the square.

Nearby, a group of three old men with tanned faces sat quietly in the shade of a Moorish arcade, their gnarled hands resting on the knobs of their canes. They were completely still in the way that only rural people can be. Ainsley guessed that they were retired farmers who'd come into town to occupy benches and stare at their shoes.

"So what do we do now?" said Ainsley.

"Wait for Vasco," answered Bia.

"How will we know who he is?"

"One of these old farmers will tell us."

Bia nodded and waved at the three tanned elderly men beneath the arcade. One of them attempted to respond. The wrinkles on his face rearranged themselves into a grotesque smile. The fingers of his left hand lifted slightly.

"See," said Bia, "there's the one to talk to. He'll tell us everything."

"I don't know," said Ainsley. "They look like they use less than ten words a day."

"They're frugal people," agreed Bia. "But they'll talk to me. We used to flirt with the old farmers when we were in college here."

"Why?"

"We were bored. There's nothing to do here. Watch."

Bia adjusted her makeup in the mirror of her compact, then stood up and walked over. Ainsley noticed that she poured some extra sauce into her hips. The farmers noticeably brightened as she approached.

Soon Bia was animatedly trying to goad the farmers into conversation. As soon as she touched their hands, the men's eyes looked down embarrassedly. Occasionally their mouths moved. One farmer even lifted his cane and gestured across the plaza.

It was a blessing to have met Bia. Engaging in conversation with sophisticated city people was challenging enough for a foreign traveller. No way could Ainsley have spoken with such rural people, with their clipped words, their regional dialects, their taciturnity.

Bia came striding back across the cobblestone plaza, her boots clopping loudly, a smile on her face. "They said Vasco should be here soon," she said. "He always comes in the mid-afternoon."

"Are they friends?"

"It's hard to say. Country people are different. But they know him." She sat down with fierce pride. "See, Bia knows this town."

Ainsley smiled at the third-person reference. She poured more wine for the two of them. "Then I guess we wait. For someone who may never come. Like King Sebastião."

Bia's eyes lit up. "You know about that?"

Ainsley nodded. She poured more wine and explained Joaquim. Soon the wine had gone to her head and she'd heard herself explaining how she'd come to get the gemstone assignment, who had hired her, her lack of a contract, her adventures with Rita, Catherine Hampstead, and Augusto.

"You are a brave woman," said Bia.

"I don't feel like it. I feel stupid for taking such a risk."

"Maybe," said Bia, "but nobody in Portugal takes risks. That's why we've been stagnant for five hundred years." She paused. "That's why I want to move to America. I want to be like you."

"No, you don't."

"Yes, I do."

"Then help me find that azulejo," said Ainsley, "and I'll do everything I can to help you."

"You'd better."

They clinked glasses and drank again. Ainsley looked at the carafe glinting white in the afternoon sunlight. It was nearly empty now. It hadn't been enough wine after all.

She lifted her arm and signaled the waiter for another.

CHAPTER THIRTY-FOUR

Two hours later, after finishing the second carafe of vinho verde, Ainsley was stretched out in her chair, feeling the spirits that were very much alive. They were whirling through her head.

The sun had tracked across the sky, the shadow of the church façade lengthening across the old cobblestones. An invisible black crow cawed from a nearby rooftop. She was trying not to think about the events that had occurred upon these stones, but her imagination couldn't be contained anymore.

Five centuries ago … she heard the apologies, the prayers, the screams. The crackle of burning wood, the smell of charred flesh. The blade of the axe slicing through the ropes. The heavy thud upon the cobblestones.

People had been killed here. Many people.

She looked over at her Portuguese guide. The girl seemed to be feeling equally tipsy. She was twinkling her fingers at passing children and laughing. Bia was used to this town, this plaza, the slow passage of rural life. She'd lived here.

To Ainsley, however, the afternoon was moving slower than a river of frozen syrup.

Suddenly Bia put down her wine glass. "I think he's here."

Ainsley glanced at the arcade. The farmers were shaking hands with a newly-arrived fourth man.

In his sixties, the man was dressed in a red shirt with a popped collar and an eggshell-white sweater tied around his neck. His orange leather shoes were thin-soled. She studied his face—the small eyes, the flattened nose, the full mop of gray curls that still sprouted from his head.

Ainsley paid attention to his body language. He moved slowly, with great deliberation. Like someone who worked with materials.

Then she saw something that sealed the identification. He made a very distinctively hand gesture, fingers steepled together and pointing upwards. It gave away his ethnicity.

"That," said Ainsley, "is an Italian."

"Are you sure?"

"I'd bet my paycheck."

"You don't have a paycheck."

"So what should we do?"

"We have to find a way to talk to him."

The girls looked at one another, trying to figure out the next step. The wine was slowing down their thoughts. Then one of the farmers was pointing at them with his cane. The Italian was staring at them.

"He sees us," said Ainsley.

"And now he's coming over."

It was true. The man was strolling across the plaza, his gait slightly sideways, his shoulders stooped. In his eye was a wicked glint.

"He's definitely Italian," said Ainsley. "He's got enough testosterone to choke a bull."

"But he's so old—"

"It gets stronger as they age. Don't you know any Italian men?"

"I've never left Portugal."

Ainsley drained her wine. "Then let me do the talking."

The Italian man arrived at the table. In accented Portuguese he said to Bia, "You're older than most of the girls who come looking for me."

"Really," she replied.

"Oh yes," he answered, then he took Ainsley's hand and kissed it. He studied her face. "My name is Vasco. You're American?"

It wasn't a surprise. Ainsley had learned on other gemstone assignments that people could guess her nationality. It was in her posture, her teeth, her eye contact, her height, the cut of her clothing.

She nodded. "And you're the man I've been hoping to meet."

The sound of a ringing telephone came from the man's pants. He removed a mobile phone and looked at the screen. He punched a button and slipped it back into the front pocket of his red shirt.

"See," he said, "that one bores me, so she has to wait. The lesson is this. Don't bore me, girls. Tell me something different, bella."

Ainsley smirked. "Are you sure you want me to tell you something different?"

"It's a beautiful afternoon," he said, "and you are beautiful women. I want to fill my life with beauty."

"Okay." She leaned forward. "Here's something you probably don't hear every day."

"Go ahead."

Ainsley leaned forward. "I know what you did in Sintra two weeks ago."

She watched his face carefully for a reaction. An expression of fear flashed across Vasco's eyes, and his eyebrows lifted momentarily. Then the machismo returned.

"Do you know," he answered slowly, "that I have never been to Sintra? It is supposed to be beautiful."

"You're lying," she said, "but fortunately we're not with the police."

Vasco appraised her coolly. "What do you really want?"

"I want to know who hired you for the theft," said Ainsley. "And I want to know what you did with the sapphire azulejo."

Vasco stood frozen now, his nostrils flaring in his broad nose. His face showed a mixture of suspicion and relief.

"No," he said flatly.

"I will pay you for your information."

Vasco paused. "How much?"

Ainsley smiled. Everybody had their price. "You tell me."

"My price is very high."

"That's fine," Ainsley lied.

He stroked his chin and stepped away from their table. He paced back and forth. "I have no idea how you found me."

"Let's keep it that way."

"I also want to think about your offer."

"That's wise." Ainsley fished around for the best response. "Here's an idea, Vasco. Let's meet for dinner tonight. You can tell us your decision then."

There was a method to Ainsley's madness. If he said yes, then all was good. If he said no, then he still needed to share a meal with them—at which point she would start buying the wine, and hope the truth spilled out.

Vasco's eyes met hers. There was a veil of secrecy drawn across them. "I don't like being asked somewhere by a woman. It's not typical."

"This isn't a typical situation. I'm investigating a theft."

He fixed her with a shrewd eye. "Meet me at Tasquinha

do Oliveira at seven o'clock. It's the best restaurant in town. Only four tables. Manuel always has a table waiting for me."

Ainsley couldn't tell how much was bluster and how much was truth. She made a mental note to call for reservations anyways.

The Italian stonemason rapped his knuckles on the table, winked, and strolled off, across the plaza, without a care in the world.

CHAPTER THIRTY-FIVE

Hours later, as the sizzling partridge landed on her plate, Ainsley felt her anxiety worsen.

She and Bia were seated at a table inside Tasquinha da Oliveira, which they'd found without much effort. It was a tiny restaurant, only fourteen seats, and the owner, Manuel, a rotund man in his sixties, had approached them skeptically.

As soon as she'd mentioned Vasco, however, the owner had changed his tune. They'd found themselves escorted to the window table. Napkins had been theatrically delivered onto their laps.

There were two problems. The first was that there was no menu. The kitchen cooked whatever the kitchen cooked, and you paid however much Manuel asked.

It seemed that Manuel had wrongly guessed that she and Bia were wealthy, maybe from the way they were dressed. Almost from the moment they'd sat down, he'd begun plying them with plates of succulent food. Olives and bread. Thin slices of meat and cheese. Bacalhau fritters. A copper pot filled with pork and clams. Ainsley, ravenous, had been unable to say no, and Bia had been vacuuming up plates of food like a teenage athlete.

In fact, Ainsley didn't have the faintest idea how she was going to pay Vasco either. If he asked for money up front, she would have to leave the restaurant, run to the nearest Multibanco kiosk, punch in her PIN number, and pray for the best.

The second problem was even more vexing: Vasco hadn't shown up yet.

"It's eight thirty," said Ainsley.

"The Alentejo is slow," replied Bia. "Plus Vasco is Italian. They're never on time."

"But he's an hour and a half late."

"Watch. He'll show up when we're having dessert."

Ainsley sliced into the partridge with a fork. It'd been cooked perfectly, the white meat juicy, the seasoning expertly applied. She put a forkful into her mouth. If this meal broke the bank, it would be worth it. In less than five minutes, she'd picked the small bird clean.

Manuel approached the table. "Ladies, are you full yet?" he said.

"Everything was delicious," Ainsley answered.

"I know," he said. "I asked if you were full. We only have four desserts left and the table of three over there wants some too."

"No dessert for me," said Ainsley.

"I want some," said Bia.

Manuel smiled. "Wait one moment."

He disappeared into the kitchen. Ainsley craned her neck. There was only one other person, an older woman, back there. This was literally a mom-and-pop operation.

"This is going to be an expensive meal," Ainsley said.

"No," said Bia, "I remember this restaurant from college. Manuel doesn't charge too much."

"Are you sure? He doesn't have a menu."

"It's just the way things are done here."

Manuel returned with a small crème brûleé for Bia. "The cream is fresh. We made it today." In his other hand was a small cordial, which he handed to Ainsley. "On the house," he said. "I don't want to take too much advantage of you."

Bia gave her a look that said *See, it won't be too expensive.* Ainsley relaxed a little.

"Thank you," she said. "You're very nice."

"Not really," he replied. The chef locked the front door and began gathering plates from an empty table.

Ainsley sipped the cordial. It was a thick cherry liquor. "You were wrong, Bia."

"About what?"

"Vasco. He never showed up. We waited, and he never came. Like King Sebastião."

Bia rolled her eyes. "Your favorite reference again. We have other history in Portugal."

True, but that other history didn't make her think of an oddly poignant farewell on an airport curb. Ainsley cleared her throat and waved to the owner. "Manuel, we were supposed to meet Vasco here. He recommended you. Do you know where he is?"

Manuel turned. He was holding several dirty plates in both hands, and lifted all of it towards the ceiling, shrugging his shoulders. "Vasco is my favorite. He's a good man. But sometimes he makes a reservation, then falls asleep on his couch."

"So he's at home."

"Probably."

"Do you know where he lives?"

The chef nodded towards the north. "Three streets away."

"Can you tell me the address? We really need to talk to him."

Manuel looked annoyed. "I don't know the number. But he lives on Rua dos Ossos. Under the mother of water."

Ainsley was puzzled. "What is the mother of water?"

"The aqueduct," Bia replied, in English. "It's the local term."

Manuel brought the bill and laid it upon the table. "It's been a pleasure."

He disappeared quickly. Ainsley tried not to wrinkle her nose as she opened the slim black case. Inside, the white slip of paper lay waiting like a terrible prize.

Her eyes widened. It was even worse than expected. "It's almost two hundred euros." She looked at Bia. "Two hundred? I thought you said this wasn't going to be that expensive."

"I don't understand," said Bia. "He must have raised his prices."

"Jesus."

"Don't worry. It's only money."

"Can we at least split the bill?"

"I left my credit card in the car."

"You're joking."

Bia looked apologetic. "I don't have it. You can look through my purse." She shrugged. "I can pay for the next one."

Her eyes looked imploringly at Ainsley. There was no way out of this, short of a dine-and-dash.

Sighing, Ainsley opened her bag and reached into her wallet, slowly, reluctantly, as though every joint in her arms were inflamed with arthritis.

She laid her debit card inside the booklet. Manuel casually came out from the kitchen, swept it off the table, and disappeared into the back. Ainsley sensed how valuable tourists like her were to the local economy.

"I thought you had plenty of money," said Bia.

"Oh, I do," replied Ainsley. "No worries."

She forced a happy grin onto her face. Under the table, however, her hands twisted the tablecloth into a small ball. When Manuel returned the receipt, she signed it quickly and stood up from the table.

"Now," she announced, "let's find Vasco's house."

CHAPTER THIRTY-SIX

As they stepped out of the restaurant, the darkness had fallen upon the hilltop town, cloaking the alleys in an odd silence. Ainsley sensed the presence of something ancient and terrible around her.

Behind her were the ruins of the Roman temple. Above her towered the ruins of a centuries-old Roman aqueduct. Ahead of her was a maze of twisting, ancient alleyways.

There was no escape. This feeling was enveloping her.

As she walked, the uneven cobblestones hard under her boots, she felt the presence of unsettled spirits, souls who were dead but not yet departed. Entities who had been murdered in life, and who now whooshed unseen through the dark streets.

Alongside her walked Bia, cheerfully describing her alma mater, the University of Évora, which lay on the other side of town. It had been closed, she'd said, in the mid-seventeen-hundreds by the Marquês de Pombal, who'd felt threatened by the power of the Jesuits to manipulate young minds. The university had only reopened in the nineteen-sixties.

The Portuguese girl didn't seem frightened. Maybe she

couldn't feel the spirits. Or maybe she'd already grown used to the feeling. Either way, Ainsley was too preoccupied with the oddly hollow feeling in her own otherwise full stomach to pay much attention to Bia.

The overhead aqueduct stretched away towards the outskirts of town, but soon the girls happened upon another alley. A small plaque embedded into the building at the corner read Rua dos Ossos.

Vasco lived here.

Ainsley stood in the dark intersection, the only illumination a small distant streetlight. She swiveled around, studying each structure on each of the four corners. They were whitewashed, two stories high, with black balconies and yellow trim.

"It's probably that one," said Bia.

"Where?"

"There. Look in the window."

Bia pointed. Ainsley stepped closer to the dwelling and squinted. Inside, orange light from an unseen candle was reflecting off the living room wall. In the wall was a ghostly series of blue geometric tiles.

They were azulejos.

"Maybe we should steal one from his house. See how he likes it."

Bia laughed. "If you get him to confess, you will be a hero to the Souza family."

"They're not supposed to find out," Ainsley said. "That's the whole point of my assignment."

"Oh, I'll tell them about you someday. Long after you're gone."

That sounded ominous. Bia probably hadn't meant it to, but Ainsley looked at her tiny guide again with suspicion. It was easy to forget how cunning she could be. She wondered if it'd been wise to trust her.

Ainsley led the way to the front stoop. She cleared her throat, lifted her arm, and rapped her knuckles on the heavy wooden door. Then the two women stood still, listening. Inside, the sound of her knocking echoed briefly and died.

They stood still a moment longer. Finally, Bia punched a small hand onto her hip. "He's not home."

"Maybe he left town," said Ainsley. "Maybe he's hiding in his bedroom."

"From a couple of girls?"

"Italians have strange tempers. You never know how they will react."

Then a sneaky look crossed Bia's face. "Let me turn the doorknob."

"Bia—"

The Portuguese girl waved off the protest, stepping past her. "It's fine. We're not stealing anything. Nobody locks their doors in the Alentejo. There is no crime here. The last murder was fifty years ago."

"Well, I can't stop you," said Ainsley.

The small racketeer placed a hand on the doorknob and tried to turn it. It didn't budge. She stepped back, flinging her wrist in pain. "It's too heavy. Help me."

"No."

"It's hard to turn. I can't do it alone."

"This isn't right."

She fixed Ainsley with a withering glance. "We have a deal, remember? I help you, you help me."

Ainsley said nothing but glanced around. The alleys were empty of life, no sounds of approaching feet. The surrounding windows were as black as tombs.

"Fine," she said.

Ainsley slung her bag under her armpit, pressed her shoulder against the door, and braced her boot on the cobblestones.

"On three," said Ainsley. "One—"

"Two—" said Bia.

And together: "—three."

Ainsley tensed her abdomen and drove her shoulder into the wood with all her force. Bia wrenched the knob. A loud crack sounded as a mechanism popped—

—and the door swung open. Ainsley found herself tumbling into the doorway, powerless to stop the fall, sprawling across the burnished hardwood floor, her arms flung out.

Bia giggled. "That was great."

"I've made better entrances," she admitted.

The girl helped Ainsley to her knees and brushed off her coat. Ainsley gently closed the door, then surveyed the living room.

The room was spartan, as though its inhabitant either hadn't been there long or hadn't accumulated much. A blue Queen Anne chair occupied one corner. A stack of hardcover books had been piled on the floor, Italian words gilded on their spines. Over the chair arched a reading lamp, which cast a small cone of white light onto the seat.

Ainsley felt a cold shiver zip down her spine. The light was on.

Someone was home.

To her right was the azulejo mural. She admired it, running her fingers across the tiles. It wasn't figurative, like the Souza masterpiece, but geometric instead—a kaleidoscope of green whorls, blue diamonds, and golden accent lines. More importantly, it was new, the cement looking fresh, the surface glossy and spotless.

On the floor, a single candle sat burning, its warm orange light casting onto the wall. Something about the scene felt a little off to Ainsley. Then she figured out what.

The tray below the candle was clean. No drippings.

"Vasco?" said Bia. "Are you here?"

They stood still, listening for a sign of life.

"I want to talk about the theft," said Ainsley. "I can give you money. How much do you want?"

No answer. Ainsley's hand quietly snaked into her bag, found her pepper spray, and flipped off the safety.

"We should go into the kitchen."

"You go," said Bia.

"This was your idea."

The racketeer crossed her arms. "No, it's your mystery. I'm just a sidekick."

"Bullshit. We're coworkers now."

But the girl wouldn't budge. "You first."

Ainsley lifted her face to the ceiling, inhaled deeply, then took a few tentative steps across the hardwood floor. Her boots sounded like gunshots cracking through the rooms.

"Vasco, I'm coming into the kitchen. We need to talk."

She turned the corner. The kitchen was empty of virtually everything. On the counter, a half-eaten block of cheese lay on a cutting board, the knife laying next to it.

A glint on the floor caught Ainsley's eye. It was a case of wine. She pulled out one of the bottles and tilted the label towards the faint light from the window over the sink. It read Quinta do Navalho.

It was port wine. No surprise. Everybody drank it.

"Vasco," she said, "if you're here, please make a sound."

Silence.

From the living room, Bia said, "This is scary."

Ainsley ignored her. "Vasco, I'm coming around the corner."

She put the bottle back in the case, then stepped through the kitchen and turned into a pitch-dark hallway. Her heart was pumping in her chest. She understood how people suffered cardiac arrest at critical moments.

"Vasco, I know you're here," she said.

No response. She stretched her arms out to either side. She touched plaster with both fingertips. The hallway was a little more than a meter wide.

What she needed most was a light switch.

She felt along the walls, a blind woman in a stranger's dark hallway, fumbling for something.

Then the toe of her boot touched something. It was shaped like a log and was wrapped in fabric. She stepped back, then gingerly nudged it again with the toe of her boot. It felt fleshy.

From far away, she heard Bia say, "Ainsley, come back."

But Ainsley was in too deep. She fumbled around the walls like a mime. She felt something vertical and smooth. A doorway. Her fingers ran up and down the trim. She leaned into the strange room, not moving her feet at all, lengthening out, her long arm straining to find a light switch—all to avoid the fabric-swaddled log at her feet.

Then she felt it. A hard plastic toggle.

She flipped it up. Light exploded into her eyes, and Ainsley instinctively lifted her arm over her face. Then, as her eyes grew accustomed to the light, she gradually lowered her arm.

Ainsley was looking into the haggard face of a young woman.

A moment later, she realized that it was a mirror. She was in the doorway of a bathroom, and above the mirror was mounted a ceramic light fixture that shone like the eye of God.

Then Ainsley looked down. The fabric-swaddled log wasn't a log at all.

It was a leg.

There were two legs, in fact. They were wrapped in a pair of brown pants. The legs were connected to a torso, which was wearing a red shirt. An eggshell-white sweater had been flung into a corner of the bathroom.

And the head was facedown in the toilet. A mass of gray curls, wet with toilet water, sticking out above the popped red collar.

Ainsley felt the room begin to spin. She wasn't going to be paying for any secrets from Vasco the Italiano, not tonight, not ever.

He was dead.

CHAPTER THIRTY-SEVEN

Ainsley staggered backwards, her shoulder blades into the other wall of the hallway. A loud scream began to rip out of her throat, but she clapped a hand over her mouth, stifling it.

The Portuguese girl's boots sounded hard on the floorboards. She was running through the kitchen. When she arrived in the hallway, she halted.

"I almost stepped on him," said Ainsley.

Bia quickly made the sign of the cross. "*Deus o abençoe.*"

"I thought you said that there is no crime in Évora."

"There isn't."

Ainsley let that comment stand. The two women stood beside one another. Bia's hand quietly sought out her own and gripped it. It felt small, tight, and strong.

"I hope he didn't suffer," said Ainsley.

"He probably did. Look."

Bia pointed at the upturned palm alongside the body. The reddened fingertips were scraped and raw.

"He was resisting," said Ainsley.

"But who could've wanted to kill him?"

Ainsley shrugged. "Did he have many enemies?"

"I don't know."

"Maybe someone knew he was going to talk to us."

As soon as she said it, a shiver zipped down her spine like a frightened little animal, sensing large, impending danger. Then Ainsley felt shame. It was egotistic to believe that she herself was important enough to warrant someone's death.

Still, it was possible that Vasco the Italiano had had some knowledge important enough to be murdered.

Bia disagreed. "Who are we to cause this crime? You are unknown in this country. I am barely one step higher. No, this is just a terrible coincidence." She backed up a few feet. "We should just leave."

"No," replied Ainsley.

"Come on," Bia said, yanking Ainsley's arm.

"I want to investigate."

"Let's just go."

Ainsley turned towards her. "You can go. I'll meet you later at the Roman Temple or something. Right now I need to investigate."

"But we've left our fingerprints all over this house," said Bia.

"Another reason to stay. I have to wipe everything down."

"You've seen too many American movies. You don't know how to do that."

"I have to try."

Bia crossed her arms. Her eyes glanced at the dead man on the floor. Then she turned on her heel and walked through the kitchen into the living room. Ainsley listened for the door opening. It didn't.

"I will wait for you," came Bia's voice from the main room, "but only because I don't want you to be alone right now."

"Okay."

"Please be fast. I don't like it here."

Ainsley would make this quick. Cavorting with a corpse that had been drowned in a toilet wasn't her idea of a pleasant evening.

She reached into her purse and withdrew her thin black leather gloves and slipped her hands inside them. Though she'd never been trained as a professional investigator, Ainsley could guess some of the basics.

She lowered herself onto her knees and gingerly patted along the sides of his body. She ran her hands along the narrow line where the soft fabric of his front pants pockets met the hardwood floor.

Ainsley wanted Vasco's phone.

She wedged her fingers further beneath the body, first on the right side, then on the left. Her fingertips discovered some keys, a pile of coins.

There: a thin, hard line in the left pocket. She rolled the corpse over with her right hand, slid the fingers of her left hand into the pocket, and pulled out the object.

It was a pocketknife. Vasco hadn't even opened it. Somebody really had surprised him.

Disappointed, Ainsley slipped the knife back into his pants pocket. She remembered him standing over the table, hanging up on the girl who bored him, then slipping the phone into a pocket.

His shirt pocket. On the front of his facedown body.

Another rule about crime scenes was to avoid disturbing the body. She decided to ignore that rule.

After all, Ainsley was easily traceable to this crime already. That afternoon, in the Praça do Giraldo, she'd asked three farmers to speak with Vasco. That evening, she'd had an entire conversation with the Manuel at Tasquinha da Oliveira about him. Then she'd paid with a debit card. That had been stupid, in retrospect. The police, if they were competent, were sure to find her. She'd left a trail of breadcrumbs long enough to feed a stadium of people.

But the police weren't necessarily competent.

She decided that there wasn't much harm in moving the body. Ainsley knew she was justifying it to herself.

Inhaling deeply, still on her knees alongside the corpse, she shoved her arms beneath the torso and rolled it halfway over. The left half of the face floated up to view, and she gasped. The awful grayish-purple discoloration had already begun. The bloating.

Gasping, she plunged a hand into the front shirt pocket. There: Vasco's phone. She pulled it out and quickly let go of the corpse. It rolled back to its original facedown position, the right arm thudding heavily onto her thighs and leaving a greasy stripe across her pants. Appalled, Ainsley knocked it back onto the floor.

Ainsley stood up, flipped open the phone, and found the recent calls log. There'd been seven outgoing phone calls that day, and three incoming. One of the numbers had been dialed three times.

She pulled out her own phone from her bag, turned on the camera, and snapped two pictures of the screen of Vasco's phone. She would check the numbers later.

She closed Vasco's phone and replaced it in the shirt pocket. Then she stood up, pulled a tissue from her bag, and began to methodically retrace her steps. First, she wiped down the trimwork on the door and the light switch in the bathroom. She shut the light off and returned to the kitchen.

There, she picked up the bottle of port from the box and wiped it down. Briefly, she thought it odd that an Italian would drink port wine.

In the living room, Bia was standing by the door, arms

crossed, a tight expression on her face. Maybe she was only used to financial crime. Or maybe she was hiding something.

"What did you find?" said Bia.

Ainsley wiped the azulejo mural, swabbing the surface with a new tissue. "His phone."

"Are you keeping it?"

Ainsley moved her aside like a piece of furniture and wiped the inner doorknob. "Of course not. I just wanted to see the recent calls."

"We're screwed."

"Not necessarily."

"We don't have an alibi."

"That's okay."

"They can find us. They have advanced crime units. They identify people from fibers."

"Yes, that's true."

"So we're screwed. I want to go back to Lisbon."

Ainsley grew impatient. This girl was useless in an emergency. "Bia, the worst thing that can happen is that the police find us, and we tell them everything. We tell them my assignment, your job, why we came to Évora. Minute by minute. We have nothing to be afraid of."

Bia grimaced. "But that will be the end of my income."

"You want to quit anyways."

"Only when it's under my control."

Ainsley opened the front door and gestured out. "It's already out of our control, Bia. Now, let's go—and don't touch anything."

The Portuguese girl moved outside and quickly ran into the shadows. Ainsley followed, pausing to wipe the front doorknob with her last tissue. She pulled the door securely shut. Then she turned and followed, hoping nobody had seen them enter or exit.

As she crossed the alleyways, clinging to the shadows like

a wraith, Ainsley remembered the CME board, the list of recently deceased locals. Vasco's name would soon appear on that board.

And a stronger whispering, in the back of her mind, that Vasco's murder, and her own arrival, wasn't a coincidence.

CHAPTER THIRTY-EIGHT

Standing in a telephone booth, Ainsley clutched the receiver to her ear and tried to ignore the rising puddle of cold water that was seeping into her brown leather boots.

It was eight o'clock in the morning. The sky had opened up just before dawn.

She and Bia had spent an awkward, restless night in a midrange hotel on the modern outskirts of Évora. They'd bought a bottle of wine, locked the door of the room, showered, and reviewed every detail of the day.

As someone who worked outside of the law, Bia said, Vasco had probably made a lot of enemies over the years. Ainsley had played devil's advocate and noted that there just weren't many reasons to kill a retired stonemason, legal or not.

They ran circles around these two ideas until the bottle was empty. Neither could figure out anything more. There wasn't enough information. They'd passed out well past midnight, and Ainsley had dreamed of wet gray curls and bloated faces.

In the morning, she'd woken early and paid cash for the

room. She'd resolved to avoid leaving any further electronic trace of her travels. The problem was that there was only twenty euros left in her pocketbook, and just under two hundred in her bank account.

After a quick breakfast of coffee and sweets at a petrol station, Ainsley had set out in search of a pay phone. She'd found one quickly, less than a block away, an old-fashioned kiosk with the letters PT above the door.

The problem was that the booth wasn't draining. The runoff from the curb was flowing directly into the booth, creating a swirling pond of rainwater directly under the telephone. The cord only stretched a short distance.

There was no solution except to stand in ankle-deep rainwater and place her phone calls. Ainsley had plunged in. Now, in one hand lay her phone, opened to a picture of Vasco's missed calls log. In the other hand was clutched several one-euro coins. The pay phone receiver was cradled between her ear and shoulder. This is how it would have to happen.

She plunked a coin into the slot and dialed the first number. A young woman's voice answered quickly.

"*Está,*" said Ainsley, "*posso falar com a Vasco?*"

Pause. Then: "*Vasco? Do Italiano?*"

"*Sem.*"

It was an intentional mistake. Ainsley could feign innocence, pretend that Vasco had given her the wrong number, and hope that the person would start gabbing.

"Oh no," the voice said, switching to English, "is he using me as testimonial?"

"Maybe. How do you know him?"

"I dated him." Then a pause: "Wait, do you know my mother?

"No—"

"Oh God, she checked my phone. Oh God. That bitch,

she did look at my phone. No, I can't talk. I have to go to class. Oh God—"

The line disconnected. Ainsley stared at the phone. It was probably better to forget that call. She plunked another coin into the slot and dialed the second number. It was a man whom Vasco owed money. He hadn't heard from the retired stonemason in weeks and asked Ainsley if she could plead his case. She hung up.

The phone calls went on like this for the better part of fifteen minutes. Ainsley knew that she was in fact expanding her electronic trail, that these phone calls could ultimately be traced back to this pay phone, but if Augusto was any example of the policework here, she would finishing a long, happy life back in the U.S. by the time they caught up to her.

She plunked her last coin into the slot. She was on the final number now. It'd dialed Vasco twice in the last day, and he'd dialed back once.

A man's voice answered: "Quinta do Navalho."

Ainsley felt her stomach drop. That was the port wine producer. A newly opened case of its product had been resting on Vasco's kitchen counter. Why would the quinta have been calling him?

She thought quickly. "I'm calling for a reference," she said in Portuguese, "about a man named Vasco. I want to hire him for his stonework."

The voice grew as cold as stone. "How did you get this number?"

"He gave it to me."

"Vasco?"

"Yes, last week. He said that you could give a reference. I'm sorry if I've gotten you confused with someone else."

It was a gamble, brassy and crude, and Ainsley fully expected to be hung up on. The temperature of the cold water in her boots seemed to drop ten degrees.

To her surprise, the man on the other end cleared his throat and said, "Vasco's a good man. He does a good job."

"Did you hire him?"

"Me personally, no. But I know him. We drank together. He does a good job. What do you need him for?"

"A retaining wall in my garden," Ainsley lied. "I just bought the house. What did you hire him for?"

There was a pause. "I cannot speak about that. But he'll do whatever you need. Again, he's a good man—even if he doesn't drink port."

"Thank you. What was your name?"

"Bernardo. He knows me."

They disconnected. Ainsley stood there, momentarily unaware of the numbness in her feet and ankles. Instead, her mind was running over the inconsistencies or unexplainable events in this situation.

Why did Vasco, a man who didn't drink port wine, possess a case of port wine? And why had the manufacturer of that very port wine called him three times on the day that he was killed? And why had a representative from that quinta just now refuse to discuss with her the specific task that Vasco had been hired for? And why had the murder happened on the day that she'd arrived in Évora?

Ainsley replaced the receiver on its cradle and looked down. The water had risen to her ankles. Her boots were probably ruined.

But this case, on the other hand, was beginning to come alive.

She ran back through the driving rain to the petrol station. She could see Bia inside, on a stool, sipping her coffee, tapping on her phone's screen. The small, crinkled V between her eyebrows told Ainsley that she was tangling with some of her criminals.

Ainsley walked inside. The rain had plastered her hair to

the sides of her head. Bia looked up at her. "I have to go back to Lisbon. I have business to look after."

"We're not going back to Lisbon."

Bia looked up, startled. "Why not?"

"Because I think I know who hired Vasco to steal the azulejo."

Ainsley set down her bag and told Bia everything about the phone call. When she'd finished, the little racketeer had raised a skeptical eyebrow. Her green eyes looked exceptionally bright and mischievous.

"So you want to go to Quinta do Navalho?"

"Absolutely."

"The Douro Valley isn't an easy place to travel. Tourists rarely go."

Ainsley shrugged. "If you want, I can put you on a bus back to Lisbon and then continue alone."

She delivered the words with conviction. The thought of separating wasn't inconceivable. Ainsley knew how to travel alone. True, Bia offered good companionship, and her occasional translation was appreciated, as was her fashion ... but the only practical value that Bia had added so far was in her connection to Vasco. And that was in the past. If necessary, Ainsley could roll solo.

"No," sighed Bia, "I'll come. I'll just worry too much about you."

"You're sweet."

"Not really. I'm interested in this case. And I want to move to the States." She powered off her phone and stowed it away. "My business can wait."

Ainsley tilted her head. "It's not really business."

"It's my work," said the girl sharply, "and it doesn't matter what you think of it."

"Sorry."

"Can I ask you a sensitive question?

"Of course."

"Why do you trust me?"

Ainsley stammered a response. "I don't really know."

"You know I'm a criminal, right? Technically? I protect criminals."

"Yes."

"So what makes you trust a person like me?"

Ainsley felt the answer intuitively. "I feel like … we're sisters. Maybe from another life."

Bia shrugged. "I wouldn't trust me, if I were you." She laughed to herself and drained her coffee. Then she peered outside. The rain had momentarily stopped. "We should leave now, while the weather is not so bad."

As they slipped back into the car and headed towards the highway, Ainsley tried not think about reasons to distrust Bia.

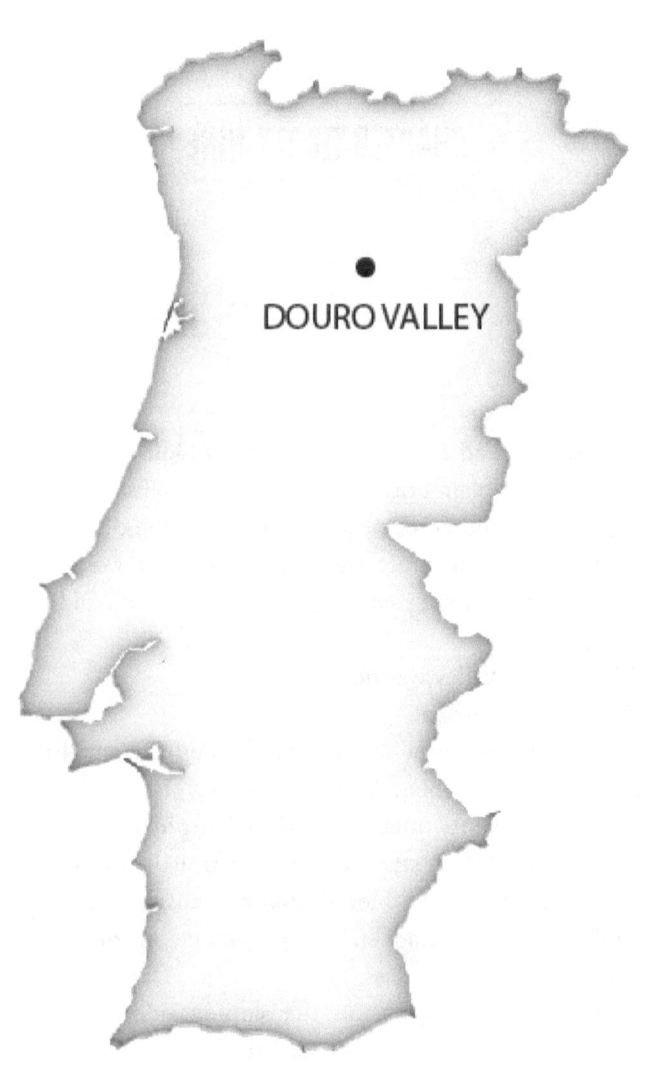

DOURO VALLEY

CHAPTER THIRTY-NINE

When Ainsley had first heard the words Douro Valley, she'd pictured a wide plain dotted with fat cows, rolling green hills, orange groves, and acres of gorgeous grapevines. She'd imagined the scent of jasmine. She'd seen courtly farmers tipping their hats to passing strangers. A place of Old-World gentility.

The Douro Valley was nothing like that.

First, it was vertical.

leaving the highway, Ainsley had guided the small rented Toyota down a switchbacked two-lane road. It was impossibly steep. Every twenty meters came a hairpin turn, and she quickly cranked the steering wheel through another one-hundred-eighty degrees. Her abdominal muscles were feeling the effect. Driving had suddenly become a core exercise better than any pilates class.

Outside the windows, on the sloping side of the road, were the bare terraces and crude stone retaining walls of a viniculture region. Long wires were stretched between posts and assisted wobbly grapevines in their attempt to stand upright on crooked trunks. Occasionally she glimpsed a large black sign reading Warre, or Fonseca, or Calém—the shippers who owned that particular set of terraces.

Not a single grape, leaf, or piece of greenery was to be found. It was the wrong season.

The storm had abated hours ago, and now a river gradually revealed itself at the bottom of the valley. It was a ribbon of green water that was as smooth as a sheet of vellum. This was the Douro, which Bia said became more dangerous further downriver, and which, before trucks, was used to transport the casks of port wine on flat barges to the ocean.

An hour later and two thousand meters lower, Ainsley had finally landed the car at the bottom of the valley. They were zipping along the coast of the river on a smooth two-lane road. As she came to a curve, Ainsley heard a honking ahead, and barely had time to hit the brakes and wheel inwards as a car came barreling towards her in her own lane. The vehicle's front left bumper flew by mere inches from her own.

"Holy shit," she said.

"We Portuguese are terrible drivers," replied Bia, "the worst in Europe."

She looked unfazed. Ainsley, meanwhile, was shaking. "Passing on a blind curve is suicidal."

"That's our way."

They started again, and a few minutes later, Ainsley caught sight of a small town on the opposite riverbank, a horizontal series of whitewashed balconies with orange roofs. It was built up the slope.

Soon the road led her onto a one-lane iron bridge that was headed for the very center of the settlement.

"This is the bridge to Pinhão," explained Bia, "which is the only town in the Douro Valley."

"What happens if another car enters from the other side of the bridge?"

"Then you must negotiate. There are a lot of situations like that here."

That was alarming. Ainsley jammed her foot on the accelerator and kept it there until they'd arrived at the other side safely. She didn't want to be trapped in a game of chicken.

Now she felt the cobblestones of the town of Pinhão humming and vibrating underneath the tires. A minute later, she was parking along the side of the street, emerging, and stretching. She'd been driving for nearly four hours, and the last hour had been absolutely harrowing.

"I need a drink," she said. "And lunch. In that order."

"Definitely," replied Bia. "But it has to be a place that takes credit cards. It's my turn."

That was a relief. Ainsley was running lower on cash than she ever had in her life—and travelling in a foreign country made the prospect of hitting zero even worse. It would be a miracle if she squeaked through this investigation without going utterly broke.

The first restaurant they visited was LBV 79, a two-story classy joint on the quay, a few steps down from the main street. A passerby had directed them there. A man behind the downstairs bar informed them that the restaurant upstairs was cash only.

"That is horribly disappointing," said Ainsley.

"We'll find another," said Bia.

"But this place smells really good."

"I know."

For the next twenty minutes, they walked door-to-door in the town of Pinhão. Not a single restaurant in town accepted credit cards. Apparently plastic was a liability. Ainsley contrasted this with certain merchants back home who didn't even keep cash registers anymore.

After the sixth rejection, they stepped out onto the street. Ainsley noticed that it didn't have a name. That's because it was basically the only road through the town. "We need to find an ATM," Bia said.

"We passed one back there."

Ainsley led her back to the ATM, which was built into the outside wall of the bank. She stood nearby on the sidewalk and watched the traffic zip past the hills on the opposite side of the river.

Bia cursed at the screen. "I don't believe it."

"What?" said Ainsley.

"It's out of order."

Ainsley walked over and looked. The screen read *Foro do funcionamento*.

She turned to Bia. "How much cash do you have?"

"Five, the same as before. What about you?"

"Twenty and some change."

"That's twenty-five together. Come on, let's share a good lunch. We can worry about what happens after, after."

"So you're an optimist," said Ainsley.

"No, I'm just in denial. Maybe the ATM will be fixed by this afternoon."

"You're definitely an optimist. This place probably won't see a repairman for a week. So where do you want to go?"

They looked at one another. They didn't even need to say anything.

As they headed back down to the quay, towards LBV 79, only one thought was passing through Ainsley's mind.

Eat, drink, and be merry, for tomorrow ... we die.

CHAPTER FORTY

As Ainsley sawed into the purple tentacle with her fork and knife, she tried to figure out a discreet way to throw the grilled octopus into the trash.

At LBV 79, the manager had apologized that the upstairs seating was full, since it was the height of the lunch hour. So he'd seated them in the downstairs bar, on two short wooden stools, with a wine cask as a table. He'd said the wait would be at least twenty minutes.

Then he'd sent the complimentary octopus. It was impolite to refuse. Still, Ainsley didn't relish the idea of putting suction cups, even cooked ones, anywhere near her tongue.

"Just taste it," said Bia. "You will like it."

"No."

"Trust me."

"You already told me that I shouldn't trust you."

"I was joking."

Ainsley sawed a sliver of octopus and gently set it in her mouth. She could taste the char of the grill, and it was appetizing. The texture wasn't rubbery either—in fact, the tentacle was tender and mouthwateringly good.

"See," said Bia.

Ainsley shot her a dark look. "So what?"

"One more thing. There is a man over there who keeps looking at you."

"Where?"

"At the bar."

Ainsley looked over. A paunchy workman in a white t-shirt and dirt-smudged jeans was perched on a stool, his hand wrapped around a glass of ruby red port wine. A brown flap-jack cap was tilted jauntily to one side of his head. He lifted the glass and winked.

It was a jarring sight. The man was some kind of laborer, and back in the States, laborers only drank one thing: beer. Usually from an aluminum can. But this place was different. Here, port wine was practically on tap, and everybody partook, it seemed.

The man slipped off his chair, hitching his jeans further up his prodigious belly. They immediately fell down again. He lifted his red wine glass by the stem, then slowly sauntered across the wood-shavings on the floor.

"Another man approaching us at lunch time," said Ainsley.

"Maybe we should tell him what happened to the last one," said Bia.

"We didn't ask for this one."

"Lucky for him."

He arrived at their table and stood proudly, feet splayed out. He seemed happy and confident and devil-may-care. Judging from the rosacea on his nose, and the way he was swaying in his shoes, Ainsley was pretty sure what was causing that.

"Do you know," he said slowly, in heavy Portuguese, "why two thousand ten was the best year for ruby port?"

"Why?" said Bia.

He paused. "I don't know either, but it's delicious." He

sipped his glass theatrically. "My family calls me Bruno. You can call me anything. Are you tourists?"

"No."

"Are you here for business?"

"Not really."

"Then why are you here? The quintas are closed to the public."

"All of them?"

"Most. They're working farms."

"We are planning to go to Quinta do Navalho," said Bia.

"That one is open. I'm passing by there later."

"Why?"

"To pick up a shipment from another quinta. I drive a truck." He pantomimed shifting a clutch and spinning a steering wheel.

"So you transport port wine?" said Bia.

He nodded. "All the way to Oporto. Four days a week. I drive up here in the morning, have lunch, drive back to the city in the afternoon." He threw the port wine down his throat and signaled to the bartender for another.

To Ainsley, that explained the roads around here. The locals were getting drunk on their own stuff in the middle of the day. Maybe it hadn't occurred to them that a bottle of wine wasn't the best prelude to driving these steep, twisting roads. Or maybe it had occurred to them—maybe a glass or two of port was customary before grabbing the keys. Maybe it took the edge off.

He seemed to read Ainsley's mind. "To survive these roads, we need to drink."

"I completely understand," said Ainsley.

"So what is so special about Quinta do Navalho?"

"We're looking for something."

"What?"

"Something special."

Bruno pulled up a stool and sat down at their table. "Tell me. I hear a lot of gossip."

The two women exchanged a glance, inside which a whole conversation occurred. That was one of the reasons that Ainsley felt she could trust Bia. She couldn't have that type of nonverbal communication with just anybody.

"It's an azulejo," said Ainsley, "with a sapphire baked into it."

"Here? At Quinta do Navalho?"

"Maybe, I don't know. But it's been stolen from Sintra, and I think it's here."

The bartender brought another ruby port to the drunken truck driver. He took it without acknowledging the service. He was probably LBV 79's most valued customer.

"You know," said Bruno, sipping the port, "I did hear about a delivery from Sintra. One of the other drivers said that he brought something up from there. I remembered that because nobody goes to Sintra."

Ainsley edged forward on her seat, her palms sweaty. "Do you know when?"

"Maybe two weeks ago."

That was the right time frame. "Who was the driver?"

Bruno grew demure. "Oh, I can't tell you that—unless you buy me another drink."

He threw the rest of his port wine down his throat. Ainsley signaled to the bartender and pointed at the truck driver. The bartender brought the bottle out and refilled the driver's glass.

The truck driver grew more expansive. "All of us," he said, "are contracted to different shippers. We get shared, depending on the time of year. My friend Filberto was being used by Framington's when they sent him to Sintra. It was out of the ordinary. They told him to go to an address where a man would be waiting with a packaged box. He was to drive very carefully, with that package on the seat next to him, not in the bed, and bring it back to the quinta."

Framington's. It must be one of the English-owned quintas. Ainsley remembered hearing that name. "Did Filberto get the package?"

"Yes."

"Did he open it?"

"Probably not. He is a good worker, obedient. He only does the things he's supposed to do. Not like me."

The truck driver grinned, revealing a row of small purplish teeth. Then he drained his glass again. It was the fourth one in twice as many minutes. She wondered if Bruno was going to have to sleep it off somewhere on the road.

She looked at Bia. "We should visit both."

"It's already two o'clock," replied her partner. "I think they close by four-thirty. We only have time to visit one. Unless we split up."

Ainsley nodded. The same thought had occurred to her. She needed to talk to the man at Quinta da Navalho, the one who'd hired Vasco. And now she needed to schmooze with people at Framington's too.

"You could drop me off."

The truck driver shook a finger. "The two are very distant. Also, it's very difficult to visit any quinta. Have you driven to one yet?"

Ainsley shook her head. "No, but how difficult can it be?"

A queer smile came over Bruno's face. "It's often difficult for outsiders. But you will have to discover that for yourself."

"Maybe I can take a taxi," said Bia, "as long as they take credit cards. We can meet back here at six pm."

Ainsley nodded. "We'll seem more vulnerable alone. Men love to help a vulnerable woman. So do a tasting, chat with the pourer, and see what you can learn."

"This is exciting," said Bia. "I'm going to solve this mystery for you, Ainsley."

"I hope you do. Then I can take all the credit."

"Never."

The two women grinned at one another.

Bruno set down his glass with a bit more force than necessary. He turned to Bia. "Don't take a taxi," he said. "I can drive you."

He had fixed his eyes on her chest, a drunken leer decorating his face like a grotesque mask. She instantly crossed her arms. "I would prefer to take a taxi."

"I have a comfortable truck. It smells good."

"You're drunk."

"No, I'm just relaxed."

The clumping of shoes sounded on the staircase, and suddenly the harried restaurant manager was at their side. "A table is ready, ladies."

Bia shot to her feet and followed him upstairs. Ainsley dallied a moment longer, shaking Bruno's hand. "You've been a big help."

"Maybe we'll meet again," he said.

She shrugged. "I hope you're not driving, if we do."

As Ainsley climbed the staircase towards the dining room, he hoisted another glass towards her, smiling broadly.

CHAPTER FORTY-ONE

An hour later, Ainsley was maneuvering through the backroads of the Douro Valley, alone in the rented Toyota, for the first time.

Over lunch, Ainsley had reviewed with Bia the details of the history of the sapphire azulejo. She would need it for Framington's. It occurred to Ainsley that Bia was now an equal partner in the investigation. There was virtually nothing that she hadn't told the tiny racketeer. She hoped that this decision wouldn't backfire on her. Bia's comment about trust had lodged itself in her head.

When they'd finished, Bia had called for a taxi, climbed inside, and sped off towards Framington's.

Here, in the car, the passenger seat was empty. In Bia's place was a single map, supplied by the helpful manager at LBV 79, with the two quintas marked by a pair of inkblots. They were indeed far apart, nearly an hour by road. Ainsley had to hand it to the Portuguese people—while they didn't seem very creative or efficient, they were always polite.

Following the map, she drove west out of Pinhão, across the bridge, and along the twisty riverside road on which she'd almost lost her life to the car passing around a blind curve. She made a left at the first intersection and began to climb into the hills.

Ten minutes later and a thousand meters higher, she saw a copper sign at the side of the road: Quinta do Navalho.

She turned into the gate and found herself on a steep but straightforward driveway. Ainsley floored the accelerator and pulled into the parking area less than a minute later. She wondered what the drunken truck driver had meant by quintas being difficult to visit.

Outside the car, she looked at the structure. It was a simple brown house, mostly granite construction, with small windows like a fort. A white shaggy dog slept in the gravel next to a stack of wooden pallets. Twigs and bits of brown leaves were stuck in its matted fur.

She shut the Toyota's door. At the sound, the dog lifted its head; its tail began sweeping wide arcs in the gravel.

Ainsley walked over and stroked the dog on the head. It licked her hand and then set its head back down on the ground. It wasn't much of a guard. There wasn't any need.

She straightened up and looked around. The quinta had been carved out of the side of the slope. To the left and right, up and down, were a series of narrow terraces, each with wire strung between posts, no grapes to be seen. They'd been harvested two months ago.

This is where the azulejo sapphire had been taken. Now Ainsley just needed to figure out a way to verify.

She checked her makeup in the outside rearview mirror of her car. Then she smoothed her dress, took a deep breath, and entered the quinta.

Inside was a single room with stone floors, wooden beams arrayed lengthwise across the ceiling. Near the door stood a polished wooden bar where a young couple stood with an array of empty wine glasses before them. At the far end of the room was a large granite hood supported by a pair of columns. Inside the fireplace, behind a grate, a small orange fire was quietly crackling. On either side of the fireplace was a wooden bench.

Standing behind the counter was a tall, thin man with a shock of white hair and a pair of black spectacles. He wore a grape-stained denim work shirt. He was uncorking a bottle of port.

"And for your grand finale," he said in English, "the forty-year-old colheita."

Uncorking a bottle with great care, he poured a small taste into the couple's dessert glass. Ainsley recognized the man's voice. She'd spoken to him on the phone.

He looked up at Ainsley. "Welcome to Quinta do Navalho. Are you alone?"

"Yes."

"Driving?"

"Of course."

He lifted an eyebrow. "Brave woman. "Where are you staying?"

"I don't know yet. Maybe Pinhão."

His nose wrinkled. "The three best things about Pinhão," he said, "are the roads leading out of it. Come over here, have some port."

He was a charmer. This would make Ainsley's job easier—or maybe harder.

Ainsley walked over to the bar. Feeling underneath the countertop, she found a hook for her bag. This was more modern and hospitable than she'd been expecting.

The man produced a glass and placed it on the polished mahogany. "My name is João. That's Joseph in English. And this"—he poured her a quick glass of a deep red wine—"is our ruby port. It's been matured in cask for only three years. The larger the cask, the redder the port. The smaller the cask, the browner the port. This explains the difference—"

"—between ruby and tawny port," said Ainsley.

He looked surprised. "You know port wine?"

"Sort of."

The couple had finished the tasting, left a ten euro note on the counter, and waved goodbye. The door swung shut behind them, and a moment later their car pulled away.

Ainsley was the only guest. João went over to the door and flipped the sign to *fechado*, or closed. "I don't want anybody else coming in today. You're my last guest." He sighed, then pulled another clean glass out and filled it with the same ruby port. "It's almost four o'clock. Time to relax."

Ainsley sipped the ruby port. It was rich and jammy, with note of tartness—and it left a deep, rich, sweet feeling in her mouth.

"What do you think?" he said.

"It's like fruit punch for adults."

He frowned. "What you call fruit punch was rated one of the top rubies in the world by the Instituto do Vinho do Porto."

Ashamed, Ainsley cast her eyes on the floor. "I'm just a beginner."

"Then let me teach you," he said. "Come sit on the *preguiçeiros*. The afternoon is getting cooler, and the fire will make everything nice."

He walked towards the wooden benches at either side of the massive granite fireplace. Ainsley unhooked her bag and hesitantly followed. Her guard was up. Out here, in the hills of Douro Valley, there would be nobody to rescue her if things went wrong.

CHAPTER FORTY-TWO

João sat on the left bench, his long arms spread across the back of the seat. Ainsley took the right bench. She arranged herself as primly as possible, legs crossed tightly, wrists crossed in lap.

"Is this your first tasting today?" he said.

"Yes."

"So you just arrived?"

"Yes."

"From where?"

"Évora."

Ainsley looked at him intently, wondering if he would recognize her voice from their phone call earlier in the day. His face registered no signs of understanding.

"That's interesting," he said. "I have never been there."

"It's spooky."

"Spirits?"

She nodded. "Many. It feels like they're following me."

The fire issued a sharp crack. It sounded like a tiny gunshot. João sipped his port. "A woman doesn't usually travel alone in the Douro."

"I'm different."

He sipped his port. "Or you're just an American."

"What does that mean?"

"You American women think you can go anywhere, do anything, that doors will open, that nobody will hurt you."

That was a jarring comment, but Ainsley decided to let it slide. "I'm definitely captain of my own fate."

"You would like to think so."

The quinta manager was looking sideways at her. Ainsley felt an odd disjointed sensation creeping through her upper back, as though she had just woken up in an unfamiliar room that she didn't remember falling asleep in.

She decided to change the subject. "How long has Quinta do Navalho been open?"

"Since nine o'clock."

It was a stupid joke, and Ainsley tried not to smile. "I mean, when was it founded."

"In eighteen sixty-three. Just before phylloxera."

"What's that?"

"The plant louse. It struck France first, then the Douro later, in eighteen sixty-eight. It destroyed fifty percent of our vineyards. Grafting from American root stock saved us." He lifted his glass, a silent toast to long-ago favors from across the Atlantic.

As the fire crackled, João went on, describing how vintage ports are declared as such by the quintas during exceptionally good years. He talked about the various important years in the history of port wine—how eighteen-fifteen is called the "Waterloo" vintage, how nineteen twenty-five was the peak of production, how production came to a halt during World War II, how France overtook England as the biggest importer of port wine in nineteen sixty-three, how nineteen ninety-three was almost totally washed out by rain, how brilliant the two thousand vintage was.

Ainsley listened intently. João was a walking encyclopedia of port wine knowledge, but the one thing she needed to know was the one thing she didn't quite know how to ask.

"Your glass is empty," he said. "Let's move on to the tawny."

He went to the bar, returned with a different bottle, and filled Ainsley's glass. This one was reddish-brown. "Our ten-year-old tawny. You should notice caramel."

Ainsley sipped the wine and fell instantly in love with it. It tasted like liquified *dulce de leche*.

"What do you think?"

"It's good."

"No metaphors?"

She shook her head. "You yelled at me last time."

He settled back. "There is nothing to be afraid of at Quinta do Navalho. Except the owner."

"I'm not scared of you."

João gave her a condescending look. "Do I look like a major force in wine production?"

"You talk like one."

He shrugged. "I've grown up in the industry, but I'm not the owner. Other people know much more than me."

"So who owns this quinta?" asked Ainsley.

"Until two years ago, my father. Since then, ConBev." He fixed her with a knowing stare. "My father sold out to them, just before he died." He shook his head sadly. "They're keeping me on ... as hired help."

"What is ConBev?"

"You really don't know?"

Ainsley shrugged.

"It's the world's largest producer of alcoholic beverages. A publicly traded corporation. Valued at twenty-four billion euros."

Ainsley tried to picture it. "That's enormous."

"It owns almost everything you've ever poured into a glass." He laughed suddenly, a sharp, nasty sound. "In this valley alone, ConBev controls forty different quintas. They love our advantages."

"Which are?"

João sighed. "Port wine is the most heavily regulated liquid in the world. The government only lets Douro Valley quintas use the word port wine on their product. Nobody else anywhere else in the country, in the world, can use those two words, even if it is made to our exact specifications."

"So the advantage to owning a quinta here is—"

"—exclusivity. And that means profit. If that government restriction is ever dropped, the port market will be flooded with cheap port from other regions of this country. And from other continents." He looked admiringly at the liquid in his glass. "All that would destroy our current standing. Lower our prices. Destroy our way of life."

"Could that happen?"

He raised a tentative eyebrow. "The European Union is trying. Since they began giving grant money to improve our roads and schools, they've also begun pressuring our government to drop these regulations." He shook his head again. "We appreciate the money, of course, but apparently these gifts came with, how do you say ... strings attached?"

Ainsley nodded. All of this was making her head spin. The politics of wine were staggeringly complex. There was so much more than simply bottling and selling.

João disappeared behind the bar. The fire at her feet seemed to have grown stronger, heating up her boots. That was welcome. They hadn't yet dried out from the pay phone debacle this morning. That felt like eons ago.

The manager reappeared with another glass of brownish wine. "This is our twenty-year," he said, handing it to her. "It's our best seller."

Ainsley tilted her head. "You poured it over there? But I already have a glass."

"The twenty-year port I always keep behind the bar. It's special. It requires its own glass."

Ainsley accepted the twenty-year but didn't taste it. Her intuition told her that something was amiss.

He poked the fire, then settled down on the left bench, one leg crossed casually over the other. "You're getting deep now," he said, nodding to the twenty-year.

"Really."

He was looking at her oddly. "So is this what you were looking for?"

"What do you mean?"

He paused, uncrossed his legs, and leaned forward. "I know why you're here, Ainsley."

She felt her stomach drop. She hadn't revealed her name to this man.

"How did you—"

João cut her off with a wave of his hand. "We spoke on the phone this morning."

"You recognized my voice?"

An ominous grin appeared on his face. "Even before you spoke. I knew you from the moment you walked in this door."

She edged further away on her seat. The word stuck in her throat. "How?"

"If I tell you that," he answered, "there will be a lot of problems."

Ainsley felt more than uncomfortable. She glanced behind her, at the long expanse of floor. She wondered how long it would take her to dash to the door.

She tilted her chin up. "Maybe you could try," she said.

"Or maybe you could try asking my brother Martim."

"If you told me where to find him."

His dark eyes seized her own. "Go to Framington's."

Ainsley remembered hearing about the Framington's. It was the quinta that Rita had mentioned, the one that carried an enormous grudge against the Souzas.

"Really."

João nodded. "He works there."

"My friend is at Framington's right now."

"I know."

Ainsley felt the panic now. This was feeling distinctly like a setup. She noticed that João wasn't sipping his port.

"I should probably go," she said.

"That might be wise," he answered.

She paused and stared at him. He was the most unreadable man she'd ever met.

"Are you trying to help me or hurt me?"

He opened his mouth to answer—then waved the question off, as though he'd said too much. Then he glanced at her new, untouched glass of port. "Are you going to taste the twenty-year?"

"No."

He laughed, shook his head, and stared at the ceiling. "You are just ... unbelievable." The quinta manager stood up and snatched the glass away from her. "That was the best decision you've ever made. Now go."

His eyes were burning with the things left unspoken. Ainsley was thoroughly confused. Had he been trying to poison her? Knock her unconscious? And why? There were far more questions than answers.

The only thing she knew for certain, however, was that this conversation was over. Ainsley slung her bag over her shoulder and stood up. In her boots, she faced him eye-to-eye.

"You know about the sapphire azulejo," she said. "Don't you?"

His nostrils flared and his lips tightened. "I know nothing about azulejos."

"You know that Vasco was hired to steal it."

"I know nothing about Vasco except that he worked for us briefly."

"Vasco was killed last night."

João's mouth dropped open. "No."

"Yes," said Ainsley. "He was murdered, drowned in his own toilet. But you probably already knew that too."

"No, on my word, I truly did not know that."

"I found him. And I found your number in his phone."

The manager muttered something in Portuguese. Then he removed a rosary from under his shirt, muttered again, and kissed the crucifix. His right hand made the sign of the cross.

"You also know why all of this is happening," said Ainsley.

João glanced up sharply. "Maybe. But you must find out on your own. I didn't want anything to do with it." He walked to the door and forcefully yanked it open. He stood there. The implication was clear.

As Ainsley left the quinta and peeled away down the drive, back towards the river, she felt her heartbeat growing faster in her chest.

CHAPTER FORTY-THREE

An hour later, spinning around what felt like the four hundredth curve in the riverside road, Ainsley finally spotted the Framington's sign. It was constructed of copper, featured block lettering, and projected a sense of warmth and ease.

The road up to the winery, however, looked like pure hell.

Ainsley pulled over to the shoulder of the main road and stepped out to get a better look. In this part of the Douro Valley, the slopes were steeper than ever, a forty-five-degree angle. The road to the quinta consisted of a single-lane gravel track winding up a steep series of switchbacks, through the terraces. It was exactly as wide as a single automobile.

Craning her neck, Ainsley peered at the switchbacks. They were hairpin turns, nearly one hundred and eighty degrees, with no guardrails of any sort. There was nothing to keep her Toyota from plunging over the edge.

That would never happen, not if she could help it. Still, any winery that honestly expected visitors to drive up such a devilish road was managed by either a pack of practical jokers or sheer misanthropes.

But this was the only road to Framington's.

She slid back behind the wheel and pulled onto the property. The car lurched off the pavement, the tires crunched on the gravel, and a moment later she was climbing the one-lane gravel track. To her right was a stone retaining wall; to her left, the edge of the road just at the edge of her tires.

Soon Ainsley's palms had moistened. Her heartbeat grew skittish. It was the same feeling as chink-chink-chinking up a favorite roller coaster.

The first hairpin turn appeared. Ainsley tensed her abdominal muscles and quickly cranked the steering wheel three full rotations to the right, then three full times to the left, all the while monitoring her mirrors.

There. She'd made it past the first one.

Breathing more easily now, she puttered up the steep grade in first gear, groaning to herself as she maneuvered around each hairpin turn. It was a miracle that any motor vehicle used this road. She wondered how Bia's taxi driver had managed it. She had probably been his most nightmarish fare.

That got her thinking about Bia. In just two short days, Ainsley's perception of her hand changed. She'd gone from feared stranger to close friend. Of course, those forty-eight hours had been packed with information, revelations, travel, adventure, laughter, fear, and murder—a white-hot crucible of experience. It had bonded them.

She trusted Bia—but she didn't know why she trusted her.

Comforted by this thought, Ainsley steered the Toyota to the top of the incline and found herself driving into what appeared to be a small but gleaming resort. She wheeled into a parking spot marked Visitor, stepped out of the Toyota, and shook the nerves out of her arms and legs.

Then she turned towards the building.

Framington's winery was a stucco beauty, ochre paint, white trim, and brown wooden accents. Its courtyard had been paved with glossy squares of polished schist, a grid of green grass blooming in the lines between the blocks. A bell tower loomed above the small complex, at the base of which was a wide glass door, welcoming visitors. From somewhere in the quinta floated the smell of burning hardwood and grilling meats.

This was unexpected. Though road had been unnerving and inhospitable, the winery here at the top appeared quite friendly.

She smoothed her clothing again, checked her makeup in the mirror for a second time, and walked to the door.

Inside was a modern tasting room. The décor was smooth surfaces, straight lines, and long, uninterrupted rectangles of polished cherry wood or white paint.

At a long countertop, fifteen visitors were standing, chatting, some French, some Portuguese, some English, all twiddling small glasses of port wine between their fingertips. Ainsley scanned the faces.

No Bia.

Frowning, she walked to the countertop and found a purse hook underneath the counter. She hung her purse on the hook, straightened up, and found the laminated wine list. It advertised five tastes for ten euros.

"Welcome to Framington's," said a man's voice. "Are you alone?"

She glanced up. A tall, thin man with a shock of white hair and a pair of black spectacles was uncorking a bottle of port. He wore a crisp white shirt.

It was João.

Ainsley was drowning in a sea of déjà vu. She scrambled for a response. "But ... how did you get over here so quickly? And change your shirt?"

He smiled. "Ah, you must have visited my brother at Quinta do Navalho," he said. "I'm Martim."

Ainsley absentmindedly shook his hand. "You're twins?"

He swept a theatrical hand down his body. "Indeed. Are you here to taste port wine?"

"And to meet a friend."

"Who?"

"Bia."

He thought for a moment. "What does she look like?"

"Short, green eyes, black hair. Good fashion. Portuguese."

Martim began polishing a wine glass with a white towel. It was casual. "Yes, I remember her. She was asking me about special item we've been storing in the back." He pointed over his shoulder with a finger, towards the rear of the complex.

"What was the object?" said Ainsley.

He smiled. "That's a secret."

That was the sapphire azulejo. It had to be. Ainsley felt her heartbeat speed up. This case was going to send her into cardiac arrest. "Do you know where she went?"

He shrugged. "All I know is that she went with Gonçalo to see the item."

"Who is Gonçalo?"

"Another worker."

"Can you find him for me?"

He frowned. "We're busy right now. Maybe your friend just left. Why don't you call her and find out?"

Ainsley had tried that already. "There's no phone reception on these roads."

"Try here. We have better reception."

She pulled her phone out of her purse. Zero bars.

"No," she said, "there's no reception." She stowed it in her pocket.

"Okay." The man set down the glass and sighed dramatically. "Come with me. Let's find Gonçalo."

He gestured with his head towards a side door. Ainsley quickly followed him, moving past the wine tasters, and around the counter. She noticed that they stopped their conversations and nudged one another.

She followed Martim down a long, dark hallway, towards a light.

"Gonçalo," he cried out, cupping his hands, "we are looking for you and your friend—"

"Bia," said Ainsley.

"—Bia. Gonçalo, where are you? Ah, here is the room."

He stopped before a glossy brown door. The handle was made of brushed steel. Martim fumbled in his pocket for a key, then inserted it, teeth down, into the lock. The handle clicked open. He used his shoulder to push inside.

Then he stopped. Ainsley peered around him.

It was a small room, but in the corner was a large man in a chair. He was wearing a Framington's polo shirt. His mouth had been gagged. His hands had been bound behind the chair, and his feet had been tied to the chair legs. His eyes were frightened and wide. The scent of something strong and pungent floated through the air.

"Gonçalo!" shouted Martim.

CHAPTER FORTY-FOUR

Martim ran in three quick steps across the room and untied the gag. Then he began to untie the man's hands. "What happened?"

"Jesus Christ," said Gonçalo in slurred Portuguese, "that little girl, she knocked me out."

"With what?"

"That."

The fat man nodded at a handkerchief on the floor. Martim picked it up and sniffed it. He turned to Ainsley. "Can you smell that?"

"Yes."

"Do you know what this is?"

"No."

"It's ether. Chloroform." He tossed it back onto the ground. "But why, Gonçalo?"

The fat man blinked twice. "I ... I don't know. I had just finished showing her the azulejo ..."

He nodded towards a cabinet. Ainsley bounded over and opened it.

It was empty.

Ainsley's heart was a caged animal trying to leap out of her chest. Bia had not only found the azulejo ... but she'd stolen it.

Her little Portuguese friend with the green eyes and the black hair. Brilliant and devious.

Ainsley tried to hide her elation. "This cabinet is empty," she said.

"Don't say that," said Martim.

"It can't be," said Gonçalo.

She nodded. "There's nothing here. See for yourself."

Martim finished cutting the last of the ropes off Gonçalo's feet. The fat man stood up. "It was right here," he said, "she was there, and then she came up behind me with a rag, she covered my face ... and then I remember waking up."

That was cutthroat. For the last two days, Bia had been painting herself as an innocent, unemployed college grad who humbly fell into a job of getting azulejo thieves to pay her for protection from the police. How she provided this protection hadn't ever been explained to Ainsley. It was entirely possible that Bia wasn't revealing everything about herself.

"So it was an azulejo?" said Ainsley.

Rubbing his wrists, Gonçalo traded glances with Martim, then said, "Yes, but that's all we can tell you."

Martim said, "How long ago did she leave?"

"I don't know. You would remember better. Maybe an hour?"

"That means she's already gone."

Ainsley nodded. That was long enough for Bia to call another taxi, or to leave in the one waiting for her. She felt the butterflies in her tummy. The Portuguese girl had done it. While Ainsley had been off having a puzzling fireside chat with João on the other side of the valley, Bia had found the azulejo.

Now, Ainsley's only remaining task was a bit more slippery. She had to convince these men that she really didn't know Bia very well. And then she had to get the hell out of there.

"I can't believe she would do something like that," said Ainsley. "Of course, I barely know her."

Martim turned to her. His head was reared back, nostrils flaring slightly. "How do you know her?"

"She's a friend of my cousin in Lisbon," answered Ainsley smoothly. "My cousin was too busy at college to travel. So this girl Bia volunteered to come with me. I don't even know what she does for a living."

It wasn't too far from the truth. Martim was buying it. "She's clearly a thief," he said. "Do you have her phone number? Her address?"

"I have her number," said Ainsley.

She showed them the contacts page on her phone, scrolled down to Bia. There was no harm in passing it along. Bia had told her earlier that she changed her number once a month, to stay ahead of the police.

Martim wrote it down. "Thank you," he said. "And can I have your number?"

"This phone?"

"Yes."

Ainsley's mind raced. She didn't want to turn over Joaquim's phone number to a total stranger who may demand the azulejo back. But he could always dump this number, if necessary. It was the cost of doing business.

"Sure," she said, then turned over the phone, to where the number had been taped onto the back. "It's right there."

Martim eyed her warily. "That's not a disposable phone."

"No," she admitted, "it's borrowed."

"From who?"

"My cousin."

"Ah. And what is your name?"

Gonçalo had collapsed onto the chair, his hands cradling his gut. "I don't feel good."

Ainsley's mind raced. She could turn over her real name and pay unforeseen consequences—or she could turn over an alias and pray they didn't ask for identification.

She chose the latter. It was riskier but more attractive. "I'm Karen Hall," she said. It'd been the name of her best friend in elementary school. Easy to remember.

"Miss Hall," said Martim, "my manager might want to talk to you. But first, let's get Gonçalo some medical attention."

"Absolutely," she said.

Martim wrapped his long arm around the other man's torso and hoisted the coworker to his feet. The duo left the room and shuffled down the hall, Gonçalo's feet moving slowly, still feeling the effects of the ether. She wondered if Bia had been carrying that stuff since the day they left Lisbon.

She followed the men outside into the courtyard. Martim accompanied his dizzy coworker across the polished schist floor and towards the small hotel opposite.

"You can wait here," he said. "I have more questions to ask you."

"Okay," said Ainsley.

They disappeared into another doorway. It whooshed shut silently behind them. Ainsley found herself alone in the glossy courtyard. A fountain burbled in the corner.

Then she had an epiphany.

She could leave.

The thought excited her. She could just scram, vamoose, hit the road. Nothing was stopping her. Nobody would be the wiser. Ainsley checked her watch. It was four thirty. If she left now, she could be back in Pinhào in thirty minutes. Bia was probably already waiting for her at LBV 79, glass of wine in hand.

Ainsley glanced around. Then she quickly scurried out of the courtyard, ran to her rental Toyota, and slipped inside the car.

CHAPTER FORTY-FIVE

Behind the wheel, she saw that she'd left the keys in the ignition. That was a godsend. She'd somehow sensed that she would be beating a hasty retreat from Framington's winery.

With trembling hands, Ainsley turned the key, and the small engine leaped to life. She threw the parking brake off, backed out of her spot, and pointed the nose of her rental car down the steep, twisty road through the vineyard.

Descending through the switchbacks, she discovered it was a lot tougher to control the car when gravity was behind her. Something always nudged her Toyota forward. Navigating one hairpin turn, she felt her tires begin to skid out, sending a shower of gravel spraying out across the terrace a few meters below. Ainsley hit the brakes and stopped the car. A moment of hyperventilation later, and she was ready to start moving again.

Ten minutes later, she finally reached the bottom of the switchbacks, straightened the steering, and drove onto the main road. She heaved a sigh of relief. This was the sweet feeling of success.

What she needed was a cigarette. Her nerves were frayed.

She reached onto the passenger seat for her bag, where she kept a spare pack of menthols that she liked to pretend she didn't have.

Her fingers met upholstery.

Alarmed, Ainsley glanced over. The seat was empty. Then she remembered why. She'd left her purse hanging on a hook at the tasting counter at Framington's.

At the top of the switchbacks.

Ainsley slammed on the brakes and shouted an obscenity that reverberated in her own ears. How could she have been so stupid? So negligent? Forgetting her purse was a rookie move. Getting it back would take another half an hour—if she could do it without being detected, which wasn't likely.

She didn't have a choice. All her most important items were in that purse.

Ainsley checked her rearview mirror. The road was hers alone. She closed her eyes and visualized success. She could do this. She'd pulled off more difficult tasks in the past. And she'd already navigated the ludicrously steep road, twice.

She executed a quick three-point turn and drove the few hundred meters back down the road to Framington's.

As she turned into the entrance gate and directed the hood of her car onto the narrow one-lane road, a wave of annoyance washed across Ainsley's body. Her arms cranked the steering wheel around the first switchback, and she took the first hairpin turn a bit more quickly than she should have. On the ascent, it wasn't a problem. She would be more careful on the descent.

She whipped around each successive hairpin turn at a faster and faster pace.

And then she saw it.

The aluminum grill of a small truck—and it was bearing down directly upon her.

Ainsley screamed and hit the brakes. The Toyota stopped

instantly. She could see the truck driver's knuckles whitening as they gripped the steering wheel. The front wheels locked up. Still, the truck's grill loomed larger.

Bits of gravel were spitting out from beneath the truck and bouncing off her windshield. Ainsley covered her face and twisted to the right and threw her body into the empty passenger seat and braced for the impact.

There was a grinding sound, the roar of displaced gravel— and then, finally, nothing except the idling of two engines. Ainsley peeked an eye over her arm.

The truck's grill had stopped less than a foot from her hood. Through the other windshield, the driver had covered his face with his hands. Then he dropped his hands from his face. Ainsley gazed in horror.

It was Bruno. The drunken truck driver from LBV 79.

She threw on her parking brake and popped open the door and leaped out of the car. He did the same.

"Hello," he said.

"What the hell are you driving so fast for?"

"It's downhill," he said. Then he jerked his thumb backwards. "Look in my truck. I have fifteen pipes. So much weight."

Holding onto the Toyota's antenna, Ainsley leaned out over the edge and peered at the rear of his truck. It was laden with several long wooden casks, probably filled with port wine.

Then she looked at their cars. They were nose-to-nose on a one-lane mountain road. No room to turn around. She couldn't imagine any way out of the situation, except for one: someone would have to drive backwards.

"What are we going to do?" she said.

Bruno thought for a moment. "It's a good question. Wait."

He reached into his cab and produced a bottle of port

wine and two dirty plastic cups. Wiping one on his sleeve, he filled it with ruby port and handed it over. "Quinta do Passadouro. An underrated winery."

Ainsley looked at the plastic cup. "Are you serious?"

"Yes," he said. "We must discuss the situation."

Rolling her eyes, Ainsley accepted the drink. "Fine."

"So," said the truck driver, sipping the port wine, "we have a problem."

"Yes, we do."

"Which you caused."

Ainsley heard the words blurt out of her own mouth: "No, the stupid designer of this stupid road caused it."

"Maybe," the truck driver said. "For locals, it's not much of a problem, of course. We enjoy discussing such situations for quite a while."

"I'd like to be more direct."

"There's no hurry," he said.

Ainsley felt her blood pressure rise. "This is an emergency. Who's going to back down. How?"

Bruno peered out casually towards the setting sun, swirling the wine in his hand. "See, usually we discuss our family history at this moment. Whose family owes which family what favor. Maybe there is a barter, an exchange. And then, eventually, we resolve the situation. But you're not one of us. So now maybe we're just having a drink together."

Ainsley felt herself grinding her molars in frustration. "I don't want a drink. I want to get my goddamned purse from the goddamned winery at the top of this goddamned road. And I want to get it now."

To emphasize her intent, Ainsley slammed her hand onto the hood of the truck. Underneath the metal, there was a loud clunk of a mechanism popping open—

—and the truck began slowly creeping forward.

Bruno's eyes went wide. "Oh no, no no no—"

He threw the plastic cup aside and scrambled for the door.

Ainsley listened in horror to the horrible crunch of the man's truck connecting with the hood of her Toyota. Then she watched, in even greater horror, as the man's truck began to push her own car backwards.

The wheels were locked, weren't turning, but it didn't matter—the loose gravel meant that the truck was pushing the sedan like a parent pushing a child on ice skates across a frozen lake. Her parking brake was useless against the force of fifteen pipes of port wine.

"Do something!" she shouted.

The driver had yanked open his door and was struggling to climb into a moving vehicle. It was harder than it seemed.

"Stop your truck!" she screamed.

With a grunt, the driver threw himself headfirst into the driver's seat, like a bellyflop, and scrambled to sit upright. Outside, Ainsley felt a yawning chasm where her stomach used to be. She couldn't even have run around the wine truck to help. She was a bystander.

A few seconds later, the back end of her Toyota had reached the hairpin bend. It dawned upon Ainsley that there might not be a happy ending to this story.

A second after that, the rear lights of the truck lit up a bright red. He'd found the brake. She breathed a sigh of relief.

Then Ainsley held her breath again. Twenty meters away, the front end of the Toyota lifted nearly straight up in the air, *Titanic* style, exposing its underbelly—

—and then disappeared completely from sight.

CHAPTER FORTY-SIX

There was a moment of silence while the miserable truth sank in. Her car had just fallen over the edge of a cliff.

Ainsley clutched her cheeks and screamed.

It was a long, horrid, painful sound that flew like a flame-eyed bat out from the fiery depths of her soul. It carried all the frustration, anger, fear, insecurity, and stress of this moment, of this assignment, of this life.

She squeezed herself along the left side of the port wine truck, out of which the drunken driver was scrambling, and then ran to the lip of the road. There, on the edge of the hairpin turn, she forced herself to look down.

A few meters below her, her rental car was laying on the narrow terrace.

Upside down.

The undercarriage was exposed to the late afternoon sunlight. It looked like a cat laying upon its back, lazy and content. She could hear the engine still running.

"Oh my God," she said. Then she spun towards the drunken truck driver. "You fool. You infant. You moron—"

He backed up, his hands held up protectively. "Senhora—"

"—you lazy pig, why didn't you set the parking brake?"

"I did—"

"You set the parking brake? Really? Then what was that pop when I hit the hood? When was the last time you checked your brakes?"

"I don't know," he admitted.

"Who fixes the truck?"

"I don't know," he said. "It's not mine."

"It's not yours?"

"I borrowed it."

"From who?"

"A friend."

"Where is your truck?"

"It's not working."

"Why?"

"I smashed it."

Ainsley's eyes flashed with massive rage. "You are an absolute menace. You are going to kill somebody."

Bruno's face fell. "Of course not. I am Christian. That is an unfair statement." He thought for a minute. "I demand an apology."

Ainsley clutched her hair in her hands and dropped into a crouch. "That was a rental car, Bruno—a *rental car*. Do you know what this means? Jesus!"

"Again, I am Christian, please don't say that—"

"Shut up."

The drunken truck driver finally clammed up. He wore a hangdog expression of guilt. "There is nothing we can do, the damage is committed—"

"You," she said, "can stop acting so sorry and fatalistic. I'm the one who is going to pay thousands of dollars to the rental company."

He gazed down at the wreck. "Maybe we can lift it."

"It's upside down!" shouted Ainsley. She was hopping

around the dirt now, kicking the air. "I don't even know how a tow truck is going to get up here to help. I am completely screwed."

The truck driver looked suitably upset. "It is a confusing situation, with no real answers." He leaned against his truck, lit a pipe, and took a long draw from the bowl.

Ainsley walked over, snatched the pipe from his hand, and threw it backwards over her shoulder. His jaw dropped open in surprise. "You," she said, "are going to help me."

He ruffled the back of his hair. She noticed that his fingers were stained purple with wine.

"I don't understand," he said.

"First," she said, "you drive me down to the gate. Then you turn around and go back up this road to the winery."

"Why?"

"I forgot my purse at the tasting room. You will get it for me."

Bruno looked pained but didn't complain. He had no right. "Okay," he said.

Ainsley climbed into the passenger seat of the delivery truck. As he started the engine and began maneuvering down the switchbacks, her fingers dug tightly into the flesh of her knees.

At the main road, she hopped out and watched him turn the truck around and rumble up the mountain. The shock was beginning to wear off. Her hands had stopped shaking. Now all that remained was a sick feeling in her stomach.

Back in Lisbon, at the rental car counter, Ainsley had turned down the insurance coverage. She'd assumed that her driver's insurance at home would apply overseas. This was the standard advice for most international travelers. She didn't know if it had been the right decision. If it hadn't been, this incident was going to absorb months of her life and thousands of dollars.

Twenty minutes later, the truck driver arrived back at the gate, the huge pipes of port rumbling ominously in the bed. She stood up as Bruno pulled alongside her.

Her purse was on the passenger seat.

Ainsley opened the door and slid inside and put her purse on her lap. She checked for her wallet, passport, everything. Nothing was missing.

"It pains me to say thank you," she said.

"That's what I do," said Bruno. "Always helping."

She rolled her eyes. "I'll figure everything else out when we get back to Pinhão."

He looked at her. "I'm not going to Pinhão."

"Yes, you are," she answered. "You pushed my rental car off a cliff."

"It was a small cliff," he said, "not very high. And I have already paid for my sin." He glanced at her bag.

Ainsley fixed him with her strongest glare. "You ... are taking me ... to Pinhão."

They held eye contact. It was a battle of wills.

Bruno was the first to break eye contact. He took off his flapjack hat, rubbed his hair, made a show of folding his hand-kerchief.

"It's a beautiful night," he said, "just right for a drive to Piñhao."

Then he reached under his seat, pulled out a new bottle of port wine, twisted off the cap, and tilted his head back.

Ainsley watched him guzzle part of the bottle and wipe his mouth.

"I really would like to know your last name," she said.

"That's not necessary."

"Yes, it is. For legal purposes."

"No."

She yanked the keys out of the ignition and held them out

of the passenger side window. Bruno looked at her. "Woman is born in hell."

"I think Portuguese drivers are."

Bruno laughed. "You win." He reached into his wallet and handed her his driver's license. She handed the keys back.

He started up the engine, popped the clutch, and put the vehicle into first gear. The truck slowly lumbered onto the main road.

As she jotted down his information into a notebook, Ainsley glanced in her rearview mirror. The Framington's sign had disappeared into the distance.

CHAPTER FORTY-SEVEN

Looking at the concrete between her shoes, with her head buried between her knees, Ainsley shut her eyes ... and prayed for a way out of this horrible situation.

In her left hand was a hank of her own hair, tightly wound around her fingers. In her right hand was her cell phone, grasped tightly enough to shatter the casing.

She was waiting for Bia.

It was almost seven-thirty pm. She was sitting on a bench in the small promenade along the Douro River, with a clear view of LBV 79. Their prearranged meeting place.

Ainsley had been here for almost two hours. It was now ninety minutes past their meeting time, and Bia still hadn't arrived. She hadn't even sent a single measly text message, and Pinhão, despite its bad reputation, had good phone reception.

This was unexplainable.

Or rather, there was an explanation—but it was unthinkable. Ainsley forced herself to consider it.

Maybe Bia had stolen the azulejo and vanished.

The suspicion had been tickling Ainsley in the back of her

mind. After all, Bia had nearly admitted that she was a bad seed, a rotten apple, when she'd mocked Ainsley for trusting her. But Ainsley had given her the benefit of the doubt. Maybe that had been a bad decision. Maybe Ainsley's own judgment had been clouded by the mystery and glamour of being with a tiny racketeer with a heart of gold.

But Ainsley had brought this upon herself. She'd sought out O Paizão, gone through extraordinary measures to find him, discovered that he was actually a she, a girl her own age, living with her grandmother—and then she'd been suckered in by the I-just-fell-into-this-racketeering-job-oh-poor-unemployed-me sob story.

Ainsley crinkled her nose. Now she could see that it'd been utter horseshit. A long trail of lies and fake empathy. It was clear now that Bia had been absolutely scheming to get her hands on the sapphire azulejo from the moment Ainsley had described it. In fact, the girl was probably in a train headed back to Lisbon right now, working the phones, playing vendors off one another, figuring out how to sell it for untold wealth.

Ainsley lifted her head. At least she would go down swinging. She'd wrangled the name, address, and phone number of Bruno the drunken truck driver. She hoped that someone at her insurance company would understand.

But the more pressing question, as the chill of springtime evening grew colder on her skin, was the question about which pillow she would lay her head this evening.

Getting a room wouldn't be cheap, and it seemed that cash was the modus operandi here. She prayed that the ATM was back in working order. She knew that she still had enough to afford a couple nights' room.

Resigned to her fate, Ainsley stood up and staggered back to the main road, to the ATM that had been *foro do funciona-*

mento. It was her only option for cash. She hoped that some-body had fixed it.

With traffic whizzing a few feet from her back, Ainsley faced the ATM. The screen welcomed her in Portuguese. She inserted her card, changed the language to English, and proceeded with the transaction.

It was working.

She heaved a sigh of relief. The screen asked the amount of withdrawal. She punched in 140 €. Then she watched the small cursor whirling, and a new message popped up.

Transaction denied. Insufficient funds.

Ainsley stood there, stunned. She read the words twice, then three times.

It made no sense. In her head, she ran down a list of all her expenditures. She should still have at least two hundred dollars. Maybe she'd miscalculated the exchange rate. Ainsley reinserted her bank card and went through the process again. This time, she punched in 100 €. A moment later, the message returned.

Transaction denied. Insufficient funds.

Ainsley tried twice more, with even smaller amounts. Same result. A hot wave of panic flashed through her face, head, and body. This couldn't be happening. A loud beeping pulled her out of her panic. The machine had spat her card back at her, reminding her to take it.

She stepped to the side of the machine and frantically ticked off, on her fingers, all the charges that could have hit her account in the last week. Then she added them up. It was fine. Two hundred dollars, at bare minimum, should be remaining.

Then she remembered.

There was a new charge. The automated repayment plan to David Madradis. They'd set it up on the website before she'd left the States. And today was the second of the month. It must've been debited yesterday. It was two hundred dollars.

Ainsley felt another wave of bittersweet agony. Bless David's heart for the emergency loan—but why couldn't the first payment have been delayed another week?

Ainsley walked back to the river in a daze, running over the tragedies of the last two hours. First, her rental car had been pushed over a cliff. Then she'd been betrayed and abandoned by Bia. Now she'd learned that she had exactly one euro to her name.

And the sapphire azulejo had almost been within reach.

She arrived back at LBV 79. Nobody was outside except the same beggar. His sad eyes looked up at Ainsley.

She reached into her bag and pulled out her wallet. Inside the wallet was her last euro. Ainsley held it between her fingers, studying it, feeling the metal embossment.

Then she flipped it at the beggar. "It's yours," she said.

It clattered on the concrete. The beggar's dirty fingers struggled to pick it up. "*Obrigado*," he mumbled.

Ainsley walked a few more steps to the waterfront. Down the way, a shop in the shape of a pair of large wooden casks had just closed its doors.

She stood at the railing, looking out over the river that looked like a sheet of green vellum. On the other bank, the orange sun had dropped and wedged itself tightly between a pair of purple peaks. Soon it would disappear completely in the mountains of the Douro Valley.

And so would Ainsley.

She dropped her bag on the concrete. Then she dropped herself, first on her knees, then to her hands, and finally facedown on the concrete, head to one side, arms and legs spread out, like a facedown starfish.

This was how it would end.

Her imagination ran wild, into farflung pastures. She

pictured somebody, a local man, finding her corpse in the morning, eyes open, one hand stiffened protectively around her bag. They would haul her corpse off to whatever passed for a coroner's office here. Then, she imagined, the local would steal her bag and bring it home to his wife, who would use it to store raw pork in a backyard refrigerator. There would be an autopsy. The official cause of death: bankruptcy.

And that would be all.

It wasn't a totally bad ending. She'd done her best in life. She'd squeezed everything she could out of it.

Her cheek against the cold concrete, Ainsley closed her eyes and waited for the darkness to swallow her—

—when a low sound from her purse reached her ears. She cracked an eyelid. It was her phone.

Her phone was ringing.

She wearily hoisted herself up, pulled it from her purse, and looked at it in disgust. It was an unknown number. She scowled. This caller was interrupting her victim's fantasy. She reluctantly picked up.

"What," she said.

"Ainsley, I'm trying to find you, but it's getting dark and I don't want to drive around this stupid little town anymore."

That voice was familiar. She could almost smell the cork, the masculinity.

It was Joaquim.

CHAPTER FORTY-EIGHT

Ainsley bolted straight up. Her mouth had gone dry. She felt her heart fluttering in her chest.

"Joaquim?"

"Yes."

"You're trying to find me?"

"Yes."

"And you're here? In Portugal?"

"Yes, I'm right here in Pinhão. Where are you?"

"I'm down by the river, alongside LBV 79. You weren't supposed to come."

He sighed. "San Francisco suddenly decided they could walk on their own two feet, so I used my frequent flyer miles and got a last-minute flight to Lisbon. I rented a car and drove here. Ah—I see you now."

The call ended. She looked up. A black sedan had pulled up alongside LBV 79. The door opened.

Joaquim stepped out, wearing a black t-shirt and fitted blue jeans. A leather jacket was draped across his shoulders, his white teeth gleaming in the twilight.

Seeing him had an odd effect: Ainsley felt herself crumple inside. She couldn't even summon the energy to stand up.

Joaquim crossed the pavement to the water's edge. He approached her and crouched down, his forearms resting on his thighs, his hands folded.

"I'm usually stronger than this," she said.

"It's okay to be weak. You've been through a lot."

"How did you know I was in Pinhão?"

"The same way I knew you were in Lisbon, Sintra, and Évora." He tapped her phone—the one he'd loaned her.

Her eyes widened. "You were tracking me?"

"Of course," he said. "The software is free." Then Joaquim placed a friendly arm across her shoulders. "Ainsley, you didn't think that I was going to let you run totally unsupervised in a foreign country, did you?"

Ainsley groped around for a response. There was none. It made good business sense. If she had died here, next to this river, he would've been open to civil lawsuits from her next-of-kin.

Or maybe he'd thought enough of her, personally, to track her whereabouts. A small glow of happiness lit up in her soul.

Joaquim helped her to her feet. "How did you like Évora?"

"I didn't," she said, leaning on him.

"Why? It's beautiful. The Templo Romano—"

"Someone was killed."

"Who?"

"A stonemason. He was an Italian. We were there to see him."

"We?"

Ainsley gestured towards the far distant mountains. "I met somebody who led me to him ... but I think she stole the azulejo."

He looked ecstatic. "Ah, the culprit! Fantastic! I knew you could—"

"No," said Ainsley, interrupting, "I mean that she stole it from the thieves."

Joaquim's eyes danced around. "So it's been stolen twice?"

"I think so. She was supposed to meet me here two hours ago." Ainsley paused: "And I wrecked my car."

"Your rental?"

Ainsley nodded. Joaquim looked crestfallen. "I'm going to need some food and wine to hear the rest of this."

She let Joaquim lead her into LBV 79. For the next hour and a half, over a carafe of wine and seven appetizers, she told Joaquim everything about the journey. Her suspicion of Lúcio, her complicated afternoon at the Kensington Club with Catherine Hampstead, her pursuit of Augusto, the dead end at the Feira da Ladra. Then the robbery on Tram 27, the blackmail that led her to O Paizão, Bia's real identity, their unexpected friendship, the trip to Évora to find Vasco the Italiano, his awful murder in the toilet. Then she outlined the speedy race up to the Douro Valley, the weird afternoon with João at Quinta do Navalho, the race to Framington's, the discovery of the drugged man in the back, the missing package from Sintra.

"So you missed it by twenty minutes," said Joaquim.

"An hour at most," she answered. "I can't believe Bia stole it. She probably knew all along exactly where she's going to sell it."

Joaquim nodded. "From what you said, it sounds like she was probably scheming from the moment you told her about it." He shook his head sadly. "You can't trust some people."

She remembered Bia's line. *I wouldn't trust me, if I were you.* That had been a subtle warning, but Ainsley had been too stubborn to listen.

Then her telephone rang. It was on the table between them. Joaquim and Ainsley both reached for it.

Joaquim stopped. "Sorry, force of habit. Go ahead."

Ainsley picked up. "Yes."

"I have some good news for you," said a man's slurred voice.

Her brow furrowed. It was Bruno, the drunken truck driver.

"Did you pull my car back onto the road and repair the damage?" she said.

"No—"

"Then why are you calling me?"

On the other end, a loud horn blared, and the drunken truck driver mumbled something. He was driving.

"I'm hanging up now," she said.

"But the package," he said, "the package you told me about, I learned about it."

"From who?"

"I called Filberto."

Ainsley grew cautious. "The same one who brought the package from Sintra to Framington's?"

"Yes, yes," said Bruno. "Today they sent him to deliver the same package to Oporto. He left at three o'clock."

That didn't make sense. As far as Ainsley could tell, Bia had stolen the azulejo. "Did he open the package this time?"

"Filberto is very obedient."

"You said that earlier. So he didn't look inside."

"But he is also curious. It's an unusual quality here in the Douro Valley."

"So?"

"He opened the package."

Ainsley sucked in her breath. "And?"

"He said it was an azulejo. With a hand. And a beautiful blue stone baked into it."

Ainsley nearly dropped the phone. After nearly a week of frenzied searching, she finally had a positive identification. If this drunken truck driver could be believed. Bruno probably could. He may be perpetually sloshed and irresponsible, but he didn't strike her as a liar.

"Did he say where he was taking it?"

"Yes, I asked him."

"Where?"

"Hold on."

She heard the pop of a wine bottle being opened. Then she heard him wiping his lips. "A place called ... the Factory House."

Ainsley saw a small bubble pop on the surface of her port wine. She looked up, staring at the horizon.

The Factory House, home to British port wine shippers. It was supposed to be off limits to outsiders. She could finally understand the size of this mystery.

Her throat went dry. "Did he say anything about my friend?"

"The cute one? The *lisboneta?*"

"Yes."

"No, he didn't mention her."

Her nose twitched. "Thank you, Bruno."

"It's my pleasure to help. You have had some unfortunate difficulties."

She ended the call. Joaquim was staring at her. "Your Portuguese is getting better," he said.

Ainsley slowly reached for her wine. The bubble had broken the surface. "Your azulejo," she said slowly, "is in Oporto. At the Factory House."

The statement sat between them like a side of roast beef, steaming. Joaquim was struck momentarily speechless. "Are you sure?"

"Pretty sure."

"That's three hours away."

Ainsley drained her wine, then checked her watch. "It's only nine o'clock. We can get there by midnight."

OPORTO

CHAPTER FORTY-NINE

With great reluctance, Ainsley sunk her knife into the most bizarre sandwich she'd seen in a long time.

It was lunchtime the next day, and much like LBV 79, she was sitting at a dockside table along the River Douro. Today, however, she was in the biggest metropolis of the northern part of the country, a city built by the port wine trade, the workhorse of the nation.

Oporto.

Next to her, Joaquim was enjoying his own dish of bacalhau and potatoes. "My faithful friend, bacalhau. You never disappoint." He looked at Ainsley. "Aren't you going to eat? That is Oporto's second-most famous dish."

"Maybe I should've ordered the most famous," she answered.

"It's tripe with cooked blood."

Ainsley crinkled her nose. That sounded even worse. She looked down at her sandwich. It was called a *francesinha*. Two pieces of thick bread, stacked high with four different meats, topped with a fried egg, and swimming in a weird red sauce.

"Here goes," she said.

Her knife sliced into the sandwich, the red sauce running everywhere. Ainsley cut a cross-section, speared it on her fork, and put it in her mouth. She chewed.

"The verdict?" said Joaquim.

"It's edible."

The previous night, they'd driven out of the Douro Valley and maneuvered through a couple of freeway interchanges. They'd slept at a simple roadside hotel on the outskirts of Oporto. Joaquim had chivalrously paid for two separate rooms. Ainsley had been too tired to indulge in any sexual fantasies about connecting doors and mistaken beds. She'd passed out for nine solid hours.

This morning, they'd slept late, left quickly, parked Joaquim's car on the outskirts of Oporto, taken the subway into the city center, hopped out at the São Bento train station, and walked south, down the narrow urban streets crammed with towering five-story structures towards the riverside.

Joaquim had led the way, Ainsley walking slightly behind him. She wasn't used to following, but she didn't resist. After all, Joaquim was both the quasi-native and the boss. And the sidewalks were so narrow that they didn't allow for side-by-side strolling.

Now, at the table, they were perched on the edge of the Douro, the same sheet of green vellum as she'd seen yesterday. Here, in the city, however, there were no purple mountains on the other side of the water.

Instead, there was a torrent of red-roofed warehouses tumbling down to the opposite bank. Each one had gray walls, matching the color of the dank sky overhead. Words had been written in large black font on the front of each structure: Graham's, Fonseca, Warre.

She recognized those names. "Those are the port wine shippers."

Joaquim nodded. "That's Vila Nova da Gaia. That's where the port wine lives."

"What do you mean?"

"Typically it spends two years in casks in the Douro Valley. Then it's brought here, to these lodges in the city, for several more years, even decades, where it sits in the cold, damp warehouses. Only then is it shipped out of the country to be sold."

To their right, an enormous steel bridge spanned the river. It was multileveled, with trams crossing the upper story and pedestrians crossing the lower.

"It looks like the Eiffel Tower," said Ainsley.

"It's the same architect. Gustav Eiffel."

Ainsley nodded. This was an interesting city. It felt less Mediterranean, more British—the gray skies, the perpetual mist, the heavy overcoats, the sense of workaday drudgery.

Joaquim glanced at her meal. "You might want to finish the sandwich. We probably won't eat again for quite a while."

"Why?"

"Because we have a tour booked at the Factory House."

Ainsley set down her fork. "Are you kidding?"

He grinned. "Rita called for us. They've arranged a private tour."

"So it's not off limits to the public."

"For those who have a way in."

He held up a warning finger. "That's the good news. Are you ready for the bad news?"

"Go ahead."

"They didn't want to admit you."

Ainsley thought back to her conversation in the exclusive British club in Lisbon. "I was afraid of that."

"The Factory House has been a men's club for centuries. They just welcomed their first female member a couple of years ago."

"That's horseshit," said Ainsley.

"No, that's tradition," corrected Joaquim. "But we figured out a way around that."

"How?"

"I am going to be a blind man," he said, "and you are going to be my girlfriend."

Ainsley felt her heart skip a beat. "That's ludicrous," she said.

"Why?"

"You can't pretend to be blind."

"Of course I can. I played an old man in a college production. I even played a Mexican off-Broadway." He sat back, confident, relaxed. "A pair of black glasses and a cane. It won't be that hard."

"Do you expect me to play your girlfriend?"

"And my lead. My eyes."

It sounded like a cockamamie idea, so farfetched that it just might work. And try as she might, she couldn't think of a better plan.

"I don't know what to think of you sometimes," said Ainsley.

"While you're trying to figure me out," he said, reaching for her plate, "I'm going to finish your sandwich."

CHAPTER FIFTY

As Ainsley walked slowly up the steps of the Factory House, she watched Joaquim tap his orange-tipped cane against every step. A wide pair of black glasses stretched across his face.

"You're trying too hard," she said.

"I honestly can't see these steps," he replied.

He was one step behind her, his fingers rested lightly on Ainsley's tricep.

"So just how are we going to do this?" she whispered. "Ransack the place? Take a hostage?"

"We'll figure that out," he said. "Just stay loose—and remember that blind men sometimes go wandering aimlessly."

Craning her neck, Ainsley studied the neo-Palladian mansion. It was made of stark and imposing granite blocks. It was a centuries-old signal to the Portuguese that the British, and British culture, were here to stay, whether the country liked it or not.

At the front door, a man in a navy-blue pinstriped suit and pink necktie had stepped outside to greet them. A furze of white hair stuck crazily up from the left side of his head, and his nose was blooming in tiny bits of broken blood vessels.

"Welcome to the British Association," he said in an accent as fluted as a champagne glass. "And may I have your names?"

Ainsley told him, and he checked the ledger at the podium. The British loved a good podium.

"Ah, there you are. Guests of Quinta da Souza." He eyed them suspiciously. "Have you been to the Factory House before?"

"Never," said Ainsley.

"The moderately good news is that you've been reserved for a personal tour of our historic building. The extremely good news is that yours truly is going to be the guide. My name is Simon Framington, and I'm the Factory House treasurer."

Her heart skipped a beat when she heard the name.

"Only the treasurer?" she joked. "When will they let you become the president?"

"I am," he answered. "There's nothing higher than treasurer."

"Brilliant," said Ainsley.

Simon nodded. "All right, let's head inside. Hand me your coats, I'll pass them to the little man in the closet, and we'll be off. Chop chop."

Ainsley held her breath as she followed Simon into the building. The entrance hall was floored and pillared in solid granite. In the center of the entryway, a cantilevered stairway ascended to the second floor. The air was noticeably cooler too. It was a gorgeous feat of engineering.

"I wish you could see," said Ainsley loudly, "because this place is spectacular."

"Well done," Joaquim whispered.

Simon Framington came over from the coat check. "The

temperature is quite constant because of the meter-thick walls. Now, point of order—there will be stairs. Many stairs. Will you be able to navigate them, Joaquim?"

He nodded. "As long as I have my guide dog, it should be fine. Bark for the man, Ainsley."

She stared daggers at him. "You first."

"Now now, children," said Simon, "let's behave. This way."

The three of them began to ascend the staircase, and Simon began a well-practiced narrative history of the Factory House. "You are currently climbing to the second floor of the British Association, which is in fact the most British institution in Portugal. Prior to the Napoleonic Wars, it was called the Factory House, but the Marquês de Pombal slaughtered twenty-six members of the group over a disagreement about trade policy. In 1811, a group of eleven British port wine companies reopened the building. They maintain it to this day." He paused. "You can ask for their names, but the list is quite tedious and won't add to your enjoyment of the evening."

Ainsley smiled, but her mind was racing. Where, in this massive mansion, could the sapphire azulejo be hidden? And how could she plausibly find a reason to snoop for it? The mind boggled. Joaquim had the answer—keep her eyes open, her mind quick, and be ready to improvise.

On the second floor, Simon led them into a ballroom. The blue walls were decorated with white garlands. The wooden floor was the color of a rich chocolate mousse. Overhead hung a pair of elaborate crystal chandeliers.

"I like the acoustics," said Joaquim, cocking his head.

"Oh, the balls here were legendary," said Simon. "In fact, the dance cards are on display over there. They're quite charming." He clucked. "We lose a lot when we abandon tradition." He paused. "Of course, I wouldn't know, being so newly hatched."

"Of course," said Ainsley. Her eyes scanned the room, but there wasn't a tile to be seen anywhere. "Can I ask about azulejos?"

A queer look grew on Simon's face. A frosty distance suddenly had opened between them. "If you would like."

"Are there any in the building?"

"No," he said, "we have never commissioned azulejos. They're Portuguese."

The implication was clear: This house was an outpost of England.

Ainsley left the question at that, and soon Simon had led them into the library. It was a suite of three rooms, the walls painted a rich pumpkin hue, arches between each room. The wooden shelving was laden with leatherbound books. The dim gray light of a winter sun fell through the windows on the right side of each room.

They stood at one end of the enfilade as Simon described the library. It was ironically the most valuable part of the property. While the British Association was running "low" on port wine—the cellar only carried a few hundred bottles—it did have twenty thousand rare books, mostly fiction, from the nineteenth century, worth millions.

"It makes sense," said Simon, "that the library would ultimately be worth more than the cellars."

"Why?" said Ainsley.

He crinkled a smile. "You can't drink a book, Miss Walker."

The tour twisted through the mansion, downstairs into the cellar. Joaquim clutched Ainsley's arm as they descended the stairs. He was really playing the part.

"We do need strong legs for this tour," said Simon.

"You could add an elevator," said Ainsley.

"That," replied Simon, "would be a bit like adding high-fructose corn syrup to a Dom Perignon." He winked. "They got it right the first time."

The cellar was a long, cool room lined with shelving. "Here it is," he said, "in all its splendor. Many people expect a wonderland of port wine. Perhaps in the past, but right now it's honestly a rather small wonderland. More like a wondrous walk-in closet."

His hand ran along the mostly empty cases. Ainsley saw that each cubbyhole was marked with a stenciled sign. Delaforce Vintage 1970. Croft Vintage 1981.

"Amazing," said Joaquim, "they're all vintage."

Simon turned around suspiciously. "Pardon me?"

Ainsley's heart caught in her throat. That was a major screw up. Joaquim wasn't supposed to be able to see to read the signs.

"We did our research before coming here," said Ainsley quickly.

It was a decent recovery. Simon's steely eyes studied them for a moment longer, then relaxed. "Yes, everything is vintage. When a merchant joins the association, it is required to donate a dozen cases of every declared vintage."

Ainsley remember what *declared* meant—a year in which the weather so perfect, the grapes so good, the port wine so powerful, that all the producers in the Douro Valley agreed to label their bottles "vintage port". It happened every three or four years. The trick was getting everyone to agree, a role usually played by the government.

"The problem," he said, "is that we hardly ever admit any new members. So we're running quite low. Look."

He pointed to a stenciled sign: Warre's Vintage 1985. Behind it lay an empty shelf. "All gone. It's not coming back either, not without a time machine."

Ainsley smelled the dankness, admired the musty bottles. She wasn't going to be cracking into any of them.

"We have one more stop on the tour," said Simon, "and it's not a place I usually take other guests. Since you're guests of the Souzas, however, all doors are open."

"Where is that?"

"The old kitchen."

They ascended four flights of stairs, to the third floor of the mansion. The distant sound of clinking glass and scraping porcelain told Ainsley that, somewhere in the mansion, the dinner setup had begun.

At a closed door, Simon turned around theatrically. "Nothing has changed for decades in this room, and people rarely enter. In fact, I have one of only two keys. Please don't touch anything."

He fished an ancient key from his pocket, twisted open the lock, and used his shoulder to push the door open. Then he gestured for them to enter.

Ainsley walked inside, Joaquim holding onto her arm, tapping his cane on the floor.

She found herself in a long, narrow, nineteenth-century kitchen. On the shelves were antique chafing dishes and pottery. A pair of black cast-iron stoves stood implacably against the walls, each at least three meters long. Each one weighed about as much as an automobile. Ainsley imagined how difficult it must've been, without modern machinery, to trundle them up four flights of stairs.

"This is nice," said Ainsley.

"Sturdy construction," said Simon. "It served us quite well for over six generations. I do think our modern kitchen sometimes pales in comparison."

"I would love to eat supper here," said Ainsley.

"Certainly it would be an experience. But tonight's dinner is being served in the dining room. Most of us old coots prefer cushioned seats."

Ainsley admired a chafing dish. "This crockery is beautiful."

"What type is it?" said Joaquim.

Simon lifted a dish, fondled it. "Spode. It's original, from eighteen sixteen. Truly fine design. Occasionally our chef will surprise the members, you know, serving the Wednesday luncheon in these dishes." He lifted a different piece. "This one is quite special. It was the Duke of Wellington's favorite soup tureen."

As Simon continued, relating the history of English crockery during the Napoleonic Wars, Ainsley was distracted by a pressure on her elbow. It was Joaquim's fingers, squeezing her tightly. She glanced at him. He tilted his head ever so slightly to the left. She followed the direction of the tilt.

On a shelf in the dark corner, nestled quietly alongside a mortar and pestle, was an azulejo.

On the azulejo was a hand—

—and in the hand was an emerald-cut sapphire.

CHAPTER FIFTY-ONE

Ainsley felt the wind knocked out of her.

That was it.

Someone, maybe Simon, had placed the sapphire azulejo here. In a room that was off-limits to the public, with only two keys. A very safe place.

"Let's move along," said Simon. He stood at the door, the stairs beckoning behind him. He was looking at Ainsley. There was no wiggle room—no way to casually cross the floor, linger at the shelf, and slip the azulejo into her bag.

But Ainsley couldn't move. Her legs were rooted to the floor.

"If you need some fine dining," said Simon, "I can recommend that you make a call at the Yeatman and ask for Rodrigo."

"That's kind of you," said Ainsley, "but it's so difficult to leave this room. Joaquim and I just love old vintage kitchens. Could we be left alone here for a minute?"

She was desperate. Simon's steely eyes peered out over his spectacles. "It is quite difficult to let go of the things we love. But do give it a try, my dear—hm?"

That was a diplomatic no. There was no dignified way to delay any longer. Ainsley trudged slowly over to the doorway. Joaquim, however, remained in the middle of the room.

"So you're deaf as well," said Simon.

"No," said Joaquim, "just in love with this room."

"Come on, sweetheart," said Ainsley, "the man says the tour is over."

Joaquim gradually shuffled over towards the door. Ainsley took his hand, glancing at the azulejo again before passing under the lintel.

Outside the old kitchen, Ainsley watched as Simon removed the key from his pocket, locked the door, and stowed the key in his pocket once again.

Ainsley followed him down the granite staircase. She was feeling electric. The sapphire azulejo was here, in the vintage kitchen of the Factory House. How and why it had arrived here didn't matter as much as getting back into that vintage kitchen.

On the second floor, she heard a low murmuring of male voices. She peeked into a doorway. In the room, a group of tall men were standing in small groups. They were wearing gray suits and holding small glasses of golden liquid that looked like sherry. On the walls were tattered, yellowing Mercator projections of the world. A large globe in a brass stand anchored the middle of the room.

"That's the map room," said Simon. "And those are the members, savoring their aperitifs before dinner. I need to join them shortly so let's not dawdle." He waved hello to one; the man waved back.

The trio began to walk down the staircase in a single-file line. Ainsley felt Joaquim release her arm and fall in behind her. As she descended to the entryway, her mind raced with possible ways to prolong the visit.

"You two have been splendid," said Simon, reaching the

bottom of the staircase, "and I wish you a very pleasant stay in Oporto."

"You've been very hospitable," she replied. "It's a beautiful mansion."

"Fortunately we have lovely sounds and smells and tastes here as well," added Simon. "I'm sure that Joaquim has noticed far more than we have, as regards to the other four senses?"

There was no response. As he reached the entryway, Simon turned to face them. His face fell. "Where has he gone to?"

Ainsley whirled. Joaquim had disappeared.

CHAPTER FIFTY-TWO

Ainsley and Simon Framington stood alone on the granite foyer, both equally shocked.

"I don't know," Ainsley said. "I wasn't watching him. He does tend to wander off. It's the prerogative of the blind."

Simon's face grew dark. "Slippery little seal, isn't he? Well, no time to play nursemaid. I'm needed at supper."

"You can go. I'll look for him."

Simon shook his head. "No, we can't have a blind man stumbling around this mansion alone. It's a recipe for disaster. We'll search together. Come along, back upstairs."

He gestured for her to follow. Ainsley and Simon climbed back up the spectacular staircase. She hoped that Joaquim had hidden himself well.

Ainsley followed Simon as he retraced the tour, from the ballroom to the cellar to the fourth floor. She watched him peek into other places too—a chapel, a linen closet, the men's bathroom.

After twenty minutes of roaming, his patience finally broke. "This is outrageous," he said. "I'm supposed to give the toasts in less than five minutes." He turned to Ainsley. "You'll have to find him yourself."

"But this house is so big," said Ainsley.

"Then you should've put him on a tighter leash," replied Simon. "If you have any more problems, head to the kitchen —the new one on the second floor—and ask for Nuno. He's the kitchen manager."

"No more help from you?"

"Heavens, no. I've got to entertain this evening. Big surprise planned."

Then Simon caught sight of a male servant moving through the passageway, his arms loaded with folded towels. "Peter," he said.

Startled, the servant stopped and turned. His head peeked out from the side of the stack of cotton. "Mister Framington?"

"Put down those towels. I have a new assignment for you."

Peter obediently stacked the towels in the hallway against the wall. Then he walked over to them. He blinked his eyelids and his mouth hung open a bit too far. Ainsley guessed that he was a bit dim.

"Please accompany Miss Walker as she searches for her missing boyfriend. He's in the house somewhere. And he's blind." Simon glanced at her. "And see both of them out when he's found."

"Yes, Mister Framington."

The treasurer smiled at Ainsley, revealing a grotesque set of teeth. "It's been a pleasure."

Simon turned on his heel and moved away, his stiff arms swinging. Ainsley stood there, nose twitching.

Then she turned to the servant. "Peter, I'm not feeling too well. Where is the ladies' toilet?"

He pointed a finger straight up into the air. "Third floor, ma'am."

"Thank you. Can I meet you back here in a few minutes?"

"Very good, ma'am." He bowed slightly.

Ainsley turned and climbed the staircase. That had been too easy, unlike these stairs. This mansion was killing her dream of living in a tall brownstone. It was hell on the thighs.

On the third floor, she beelined for the nineteen-century kitchen. She walked up to the locked door, turned the handle, and pushed hard.

It didn't budge. That was a secure room.

So close, yet so far.

For a moment she wasn't referring to the azulejo either—but about Joaquim. All day together, and they'd worked well. No impatience, no annoyance. They had the same energy levels. It felt natural.

But Joaquim was her employer.

At the other end of the hallway stood a green door. A ladies' symbol had been discreetly added to the wall next to it.

She entered the tiny toilet. It was quiet as a tomb, the meter-thick walls muffling and deadening all outside sound. She could practically hear the blood squirting in her veins.

She put her purse on the sink, dropped her pants, and sat down on the commode. Directly in front of her was a small closet, the type used to store mops and cleaning supplies. Her eyes landed on the doorknob. She noted its antique design, the flecks missing off its brass finish.

Then the doorknob began to turn—all by itself.

"Ainsley," said a voice from the closet.

"Jesus Christ," she said, leaping off the toilet. She yanked her pants up around her waist. "What are you doing in there?"

She opened the supply closet. Joaquim was standing

inside, arms at his sides, amidst a vertical bundle of broom sticks and mop handles. The black glasses were off his face. He wore an incredibly guilty look.

"I didn't see anything," he said, "I swear. Well, maybe the top of your head."

She punched him in the shoulder. "You asshole."

"It's a good hiding place, isn't it?"

"You're still an asshole."

"Why?"

"Just get out of there."

As he stepped out, she kicked the toilet lid shut and flushed. Then she turned to the sink and washed her hands. In the mirror, she saw him watching her, a smile on his face.

"What does that little smile mean?" she said.

"Nothing."

As she toweled off, she felt Joaquim's hands touch her spine, then begin to gently massage back and forth. He was rubbing her back.

Ainsley froze. "What are you doing?"

"It's the least I can do for scaring the life out of you."

She didn't say anything.

"Do you realize," he replied, "that you're almost done with the assignment? All your incredible effort—and now the azulejo is right next to us."

"I do realize. Now let's go get it."

The rubbing stopped. "Good luck with that."

Ainsley turned around. In this tiny bathroom, they were uncomfortably close, face to face. "What do you mean by that?"

"The lock is serious. The door is heavy. The construction was original."

"So?"

"So I don't think we can break in," he said.

"We have to try."

"I'm not a locksmith. Neither are you."

Ainsley leaned backward against the edge of the sink, putting a little space between them. The air was stifling. She nibbled on the edge of a cuticle.

"Maybe," she said, "we need to hatch another plan."

"You go first."

"There's very little chance we can get the key from Simon. He wants us out of here. But he did say there was a second one."

"Yes."

"Who would have the other?"

Simon shrugged. "We don't know anybody at the Factory House."

"My guess is that the chef might have it."

"Why?"

"It's a second kitchen. He might want to have a key to access it. Also, Simon mentioned that he occasionally uses the old crockery for the Wednesday luncheon."

"So we should talk to Nuno."

"Yes—but we need a plan to get the key from him."

They both thought for a moment.

"I know," said Ainsley.

CHAPTER FIFTY-THREE

With only a vertical sliver of her face peeking around the edge of the wainscoting, Ainsley Walker studied the men in gray suits seated in the dining room of the Factory House.

Thirteen men were gathered around a mahogany table, on which lay an impressive array of crystal goblets and bone-white china. These were the members of the British Association, all port wine shippers. Most were over sixty, though a few were middle-aged. All spoke in rich baritones. The air of the room felt charged with grandeur and arrogance.

It dawned on Ainsley that half of the port wine in the world was produced by the men at this table.

A stream of tuxedoed waiters glided silently out of a swinging door into the dining room. Each bore a pair of aluminum domes on plates. Ainsley watched the waiters place one in front of each diner, then whip the domes away. The plate below appeared to be a scallop in a wine sauce. It certainly wasn't bacalhau. The local passion for dried cod had been kept safely out of this bastion of British culture.

As the diners applauded—either the cooking or their own perceived excellence—Ainsley tiptoed away from the dining room. She crossed through the map room into the service hallway and entered the new kitchen from the rear.

There, she waited in the back doorway. It looked like most other service kitchens—large mixers, heavy-duty eight-burner stoves, white-aproned prep cooks furiously chopping and mixing and emulsifying. All for thirteen people.

Thirteen very important people.

Ainsley stood near the walk-in refrigerator, waiting to be noticed. It didn't take long. A young man in a white apron came running around the corner of the island, carrying a plastic-wrapped mixing bowl, when he saw her.

"Yes?" he said.

"I'm from the United States," she said.

"So?"

"I'm writing an article on British crockery. Simon was supposed to show me some examples, but my plane was late, and he didn't have time before dinner."

It was a good lie, well cooked, but it was wasted on the sous chef. "Okay," he said.

"He said that the china is upstairs in the old kitchen. Third floor."

"Okay."

"I need to get into the old kitchen."

"Okay."

"Do you know any words other than okay?"

"Maybe."

"Maybe you could find Nuno for me? The man who has the key?"

The sous chef blanched. He ran into the walk-in, tossed the bowl down, then returned and sped to the far end of the kitchen. He spoke urgently to a very fat man in apron whites and checked pants.

The fat man looked over his shoulder at Ainsley. His eyes

glanced up and down her body. A sneer emerged on his lips. He set down his mixing bowl and waddled over.

"You're a journalist?" he said.

Ainsley nodded. "Simon said he didn't have time to help me tonight. I'm doing an article on British crockery, and I need the key to the old kitchen. We need to photograph before the sun sets."

"It's a difficult request," said the chef. "I need to ask for Simon's approval, because that room is off limits."

"He's busy making toasts to the shippers. Then he'll be eating with them. Let's not disturb him."

Nuno leaned against the countertop, picking his teeth, and looked at Ainsley. "So you can't wait?"

"I have a photographer with me. He wants to use the golden hour." She tried to look vulnerable. "Please—he told me you could help."

The chef lifted a wary eyebrow. "How do I know I can trust you? There are some valuable pieces there."

Ainsley admitted to herself that his suspicion was one hundred percent correct. Unslinging her bag from her shoulder, she dropped her bag onto the marble countertop. "If you don't feel like you can trust me, then I will leave this bag here. It contains all my identification, my wallet, everything. When I come back with the key, you can return my bag."

This was only fair. Joaquim could take the azulejo and slip away while she returned to the kitchen.

Before Nuno could answer, a sous chef approached him with a ladle of broth. Nuno dipped a pinky finger, tasted it, then barked some orders in Portuguese. Then he turned back to Ainsley. "Okay," he said. "Just leave the bag somewhere here."

Ainsley glanced around. An upper shelf lined the kitchen, and at the far end, above the walk-in, it was stacked with clean plastic bins. If she placed the bag high, nobody would be likely to hunt through it, or spill food on it.

She moved down to the walk-in refrigerator, reached up on her tiptoes, and placed her bag above it.

"I really should talk to Simon about this," said Nuno.

"There's no need," she said. "He told me to come to you. How else would I know your name if he didn't send me to you? How else would I know where the old kitchen is if he didn't already take me there?"

Ainsley felt a bit like a little girl playing her two parents for permission to sleep over at a friend's house. Finally Nuno produced a skeleton key from his pocket. "Here. Make it fast."

"Absolutely," she said.

He turned back to the broth, and Ainsley took the key and scooted out of the kitchen.

A quick dash down the service hallway, crossing through the map room, up the staircase, and back to the third floor— and then Ainsley found herself at the door to the old kitchen.

"Joaquim," she said, over her shoulder.

At the far end of the hallway, the women's restroom opened. "You have it?"

"Come here and find out."

He ran down the hall, joined Ainsley at her side. "You have the magic touch."

"Don't be so sure of that," she said. She was fumbling with the key in the lock. Either she was too excited, or Nuno had given her the wrong key.

"I take that back."

"Help me."

"Fine—but you have to step aside."

Ainsley reluctantly moved aside. She watched Joaquim as he took the key, inserted it halfway into the lock, gently manipulated it, applied pressure on the base of the handle with his fingers, then turned the key with one hard thrust. The nineteenth-century mechanism clicked, and the door popped open.

Ainsley smiled. "You have the magic touch."

"I watched Simon."

"Why do blind people see so much?"

Together, they pushed into the kitchen and rushed to the shelf where the azulejo had been.

It was gone.

CHAPTER FIFTY-FOUR

Ainsley gaped in astonishment. Then she was subsumed in a torrent of anger. She watched her fists punch the air. She felt her boots stamping the floor.

When the red moment had passed, she noticed Joaquim. He was standing a safe distance away, watching her, a faintly amused smile on his mouth.

"What?" she said.

"You're funny when you're frustrated," he said.

"People have told me that my whole life."

"But I appreciate your dedication. You're for real."

Ainsley dropped onto a bench. "I bet Simon knew all about the azulejo. I bet he was storing it here, and figured that we, a couple of tourists, wouldn't pay any attention. He had something to do with the theft."

"You're probably right."

"So now what?"

"We can't confront him."

"Agreed. The timing is all wrong. There are too many people downstairs."

Joaquim placed a hand on her shoulder. "You've worked very hard, Ainsley."

"That's your way of saying we're finished, and that you can't pay me."

"I don't know yet," he replied. "I'm out of ideas right now. Maybe we just go home. Maybe we just disappear. Maybe my sister gets fired."

A wave of misery swept over Ainsley. She pushed her face into her hands and bent over between her legs.

"Come on," said Joaquim. "Let's change roles. You take my arm, and I'll lead us out of here."

"You're supposed to be the blind one," she mumbled.

"Who cares? The charade is over. We failed."

"No, I failed."

"No, you've succeeded."

"In what?"

"Impressing me."

She looked up. Joaquim was looking at her with intense eyes.

"Very reassuring," she said. "Help me up."

He lifted her by the arm. They left the vintage kitchen, Joaquim locking it securely behind them. Then they went down the staircase for the last time.

On the second floor, Ainsley said, "Hold on."

"What is it?"

"I have to get my bag. It's in the kitchen."

Suddenly Joaquim halted too. He was pointing towards the dining room. It was about fifteen meters away. The door was still open. The men were visible inside, drinking glasses of tawny port, talking boisterously. Ainsley heard someone sarcastically refer to it as mouthwash.

"What's wrong?" she said.

His mouth opened and closed. "It's Fernando."

"Who?"

"Fernando Souza. The owner of the Sintra property. My sister's boss."

He discreetly pointed to a large, fleshy, mound of a man, with an enormous bald head. He wore a bib over his suit and was stabbing a lobster with a fork.

Of course, Ainsley though. That was Rita's boss, the man whom needed to never learn that the sapphire azulejo had been stolen. And now the treasure was somewhere here, in the very same house.

A tickling sensation along her neck told Ainsley that it wasn't a coincidence.

"Why is he here? Isn't he Portuguese?"

"I don't know," said Joaquim.

"I was wondering why there were thirteen men. There are supposedly only twelve British members."

"This isn't good," he said.

"I still have to get my bag from the kitchen," she said.

"Hurry back," he said.

She crossed through the map room, into the service corridor, and back into the kitchen.

A row of thirteen aluminum serving platters lay on the long kitchen countertop. On each one was a plate with a piece of white cheese. Next to the cheese was a small snifter of light brown port. They were probably vintage. That's how port wine looked when it had aged.

On the thirteenth platter, however, there was no cheese and no wine. There was something else.

The sapphire azulejo.

And standing with one hand on the aluminum dome was Simon, the Factory House treasurer.

He was grinning wickedly at her.

CHAPTER FIFTY-FIVE

"Now, Miss Walker, don't get angry at me for the theft of this valuable item," Simon said. "I'm just the last stop in a very long chain of causation."

She scrambled for words. "You knew all along—"

"Of course I knew who you were," he said. "We've been following you for days."

"Who is we?"

"Concerned interests."

"Be more concrete."

He grew still. "The type of people who have enough money to make all their problems go away."

"Did they make Vasco the Italian go away?" she said.

"Quite unfortunate," he replied. "I did hear about it after the fact. Things never turn out the way you want them to."

"You have to tell me what's going on."

"You don't deserve to know what's going on."

"I think I do."

"You would have to have been born into a family, a British family, that has spent countless generations building a brand, a reputation, for excellence."

Ainsley was confused. Suddenly she felt the urge to flee. "I just came to get my bag and leave—"

She turned and looked above the walk-in refrigerator. Her bag was gone.

"You'll get it back," said Simon, "once dessert is finished."

That was unacceptable. In fact, she had a pretty good idea of where it'd been stashed. She flung open the walk-in refrigerator and saw her bag sitting next to a bowl of cold shrimp.

Ainsley dashed inside, snatched her bag, and dashed out.

"That was uncalled for," she said, cleaning it off with a towel.

"So was lying to me."

With a flourish, Simon clamped the aluminum dome onto the sapphire azulejo. The tuxedoed waiters covered the other trays. On a signal from Simon, they simultaneously hoisted the domes onto their arms and filed out of the kitchen.

Simon lifted the dome containing the sapphire azulejo. "And this one will be delivered by yours truly. We do appreciate the personal touch—even in blackmail."

He lifted his eyebrows, then took the domed platter and followed the wait staff out the swinging door. Nuno stood in front of it, crossed his arms, and glared at Ainsley.

The message was clear: Don't follow him.

No problem. Ainsley turned, ran down the service corridor, scurried into the map room, crossed it, and saw Joaquim, still waiting.

"I found it—"

"And?"

"They're serving it to Fernando, I don't know why, come on—"

She streaked around the edge of the open door, into the dining room, and shouted, "Stop!"

Screech. The dining room was empty.

Twelve chairs stood empty around the mahogany table, its

surface covered in used silverware, empty tureens, dirty plates, discarded cloth napkins, and stubbed-out cigar butts. The men were gone.

Joaquim arrived at her side. "They were just here a minute ago."

The sound of muted laughter sounded from behind them. Ainsley wheeled around. It was a plain wall, with a bookshelf.

Then she looked more closely. The bookshelf had been left slightly ajar. It was a hidden door.

"That's a secret room," said Ainsley.

Joaquim wiped his forehead in frustration. "Of course there's a secret room."

"And they're not going to appreciate us breaking into their treehouse."

"Especially not a girl."

"So?"

Ainsley thought. What was the worst that could happen? They couldn't arrest her. She'd blow the whistle on Simon, the theft, everything. The police, if they were dutiful, would have a field day connecting these dots.

"They won't do anything to me," said Ainsley.

"Because you know about Vasco the Italiano."

Ainsley nodded.

"Ladies first."

Ainsley pressed her shoulder against the hidden door and pushed. It swung open more easily than she had anticipated —the hinges were silent and well-oiled—and she stumbled inside, sprawling onto the floor.

She scrambled back to her feet, pushing the hair out of her face. It was another dining room, identical to the first, except lit only by candles. The thirteen men were sitting around another long mahogany table. Each man had an aluminum dome placed before him.

And all of the faces were looking at her.

Joaquim appeared at her side. He pointed to the far end of the table, where Fernando Souza sat, at the head of the table, an aluminum dome before him. Simon's hand was already on the handle.

"Fernando," shouted Joaquim, "wait, don't lift that—"

Simon's eyes flashed with a red wrath as he yanked away the dome.

CHAPTER FIFTY-SIX

For Ainsley, the moment seemed to telescope, stretching out just beyond her reach.

Ainsley watched the aluminum dome disappear behind Simon's back. She watched the sapphire azulejo, flat and small, glinting blue in the candlelight.

She didn't know Simon's intention, but she did know her feeling of failure. Ainsley had failed the assignment. True, she'd found the sapphire azulejo, but she'd been unable to keep its theft a secret from the man who would be most affected—its owner.

Fernando appeared to be in shock. He looked at the other twelve platters, the cheese, the small glasses of port wine. The faces of the other men looked back at him. They were strangely impassive.

Then he looked up at Ainsley, and their eyes locked. Seeing the surprise in his eyes, she now understood the subtext: He'd been set up. But the reason why remained to be seen.

"These two have to leave," said Simon, pointing at Ainsley and Joaquim.

"No," said Fernando, locking eyes with Ainsley, "they stay."

The treasurer grimaced. "But we are going to be speaking of sensitive matters, Senhor Souza."

"She knows a lot already," said Joaquim. "And besides, he hired this woman himself."

"I did?" said Fernando.

"Indirectly."

Fernando sat back in his chair and held his forehead with his hand. He opened and closed his mouth several times.

"How much did I pay?" he said.

Joaquim pushed aside the conversation. "Later, Senhor."

Simon pointed at Ainsley. "Fine. But you two, stay against the wall."

With Joaquim at her side, Ainsley melted back into the shadows of the nearest corner. She was happy for the anonymity, as she was still trying to absorb the moment.

All eyes returned to Fernando. "I don't understand," he said, picking up the azulejo. "This is my own property. From Sintra. Did you steal this?"

The twelve men didn't so much as blink. Nobody volunteered to explain.

"We're friends, yes?" said Simon.

Fernando shrugged. "Our families have had a complicated relationship."

"Almost like brothers, wouldn't you say?"

Fernando shrugged. "It is your view."

Simon inhaled. "And, in your family, you have a nephew? Lourenço?"

"Yes," replied Fernando.

Ainsley remembered meeting him at the Kensington Club. Lourenço was the short politician who loved his family's Sintra property more than anything, including the capela —and especially this sapphire azulejo.

"And Lourenço is a member of Portuguese Parliament?"

"Yes."

"And he chairs the committee that proposes trade regulations."

"Yes."

"And this chairperson can vote down proposals about trade regulations? Or cause them to be tabled before they're even voted upon?"

"Yes."

Simon circled the table and sat down in an empty seat at the opposite end. He steepled his fingers. "There is an important proposal coming up."

"About what?"

"Your nephew hasn't told you?"

A sad expression landed upon Fernando's face. "We don't speak very often. He is very busy, my wife doesn't like him—"

An expectant hush had settled over the table. Ainsley clutched Joaquim's arm.

"The bill is about something that could be quite tragic for everyone in this room. As well as for other interests in the Douro Valley."

Fernando dropped his head. "I know what you are going to say."

"Then say it for us."

Candlelight danced off the bald pates of all twelve Englishmen. They faced the Portuguese man like Pharisees in judgment.

"The exclusivity," said Fernando. "The bill is supposed to end the exclusivity."

"And we don't want that," said Simon. He stood again, circling the table, hands behind his back. "The Marquês de Pombal started the regulation of port wine two hundred and fifty years ago. That protectionism needs to be preserved. Tradition is all we have."

Around the table he went lecturing, explaining how the passage of this bill would allow people anywhere in Portugal, anywhere in the world, to label their product as port wine, and at substantially lower prices. Ainsley remembered hearing the same argument from João at the Quinta do Navalho, before things went downhill, literally.

Simon leaned in over Fernando. "It will dilute our product. It will cause severe loss of market share. Three hundred years of development, of history, will be flushed away." He had come up behind Fernando now. "They're voting next week. Deliver this to your nephew. To express our opinion."

A cunning look came across Fernando's face. "You stole this from my home—to give it back to me—to give to my nephew?"

Simon nodded. "We remember Lourenço's attempt to have the capela recognized. We, in this room, know of his passion for this azulejo."

Fernando looked at the other members of the room. They refused to meet his gaze.

"So this is blackmail?"

"No, not at all," said Simon, a sincere expression sliming across his face, "it's, shall we say, a sign of our commitment to our position. He should understand this."

In the shadows, Ainsley understood perfectly. The sapphire azulejo was the proverbial horse head in the bed.

Fernando heaved a massive sigh and covered his face with his hands. "I'll do it, if that's what you want."

"It is."

Joaquim tugged at Ainsley's sleeve. "Let's go."

There didn't seem to be a reason to stay any longer. Ainsley had no dog in this hunt, the azulejo had been found, the British Association had somehow taken it. Most of all, this was the worst time to ask Fernando Souza, a stranger, to give her thousands of dollars for a task that she hadn't quite successfully completed, one that he hadn't even asked to be done.

"Okay."

Ainsley slipped out of the secret candlelit room through the bookcase door, Joaquim behind her. They moved out of the first dining room, over to the staircase, and circled down to the spectacular entryway.

When her feet hit the granite floor, Joaquim whispered, "I hope you didn't forget anything, because we will not be welcome again here."

"I have everything."

They arrived at the front door, took their coats from the check, then pushed the front door open—

—and nearly collided with a woman rushing up the steps. She lifted her head.

It was Rita.

"Oh my God," said Ainsley.

"I thought I missed you," said the Portuguese woman. She hugged both of them quickly, then lit a cigarette. "I drove from the Alentejo. Five and a half hours." Then she looked to their faces. "So?"

Joaquim shook his head. "Fernando has the azulejo."

She stared at her brother, the cigarette burning down to her fingers. "No."

"It's true."

"Then tell me everything."

"That's going to take some time."

Behind them, the front door of the Factory House creaked open. "We have time," said a deep voice.

They all turned. It was Fernando Souza. He was clutching the sapphire azulejo close to his prodigious belly.

Rita seemed to physically melt. Her brother put his arm around her waist to keep her from collapsing.

"Rita, please," Fernando said.

"Don't fire me," she replied, nearly weeping.

"I won't. Probably." Then he noticed Ainsley and fixed her with a curious stare. "Who is this woman?"

"This is Ainsley Walker," said Joaquim.

"She's been working for me?"

"Yes."

Fernando extended his hand. "Amy Lee Walker, it's a pleasure."

Ainsley didn't bother to correct him. "Likewise."

"Now," said the elderly Souza, "I suggest we go to my suite at the pousada. There, I want to hear everything. From the beginning."

CHAPTER FIFTY-SEVEN

The Pousada do Freixo was a former flour factory west of downtown Oporto that had been converted to a luxury hotel. Downstairs were floor-to-ceiling murals, formal gardens, an infinity pool, French décor, and a classic restaurant that was open late for dinner.

Ainsley saw none of that.

She was inside a third-floor suite, sitting on the couch between Rita and Joaquim, replaying every moment of the last week for Fernando Souza. It was almost midnight. She'd been talking for the last four hours.

Fernando had been impressed. "So you found a way to the Douro Valley from the dead man's cell phone?"

"Yes," replied Ainsley, "to the Quinta do Navalho."

"Where this man João acted oddly."

"Yes."

Fernando had placed his beefy hands on his thighs and was leaning towards them. He seemed like the type of man whose attention was hard to gain—but equally hard to lose.

Ainsley emptied the last of a water bottle into her glass.

Two other empty bottles sat nearby. Her mouth had been dry from the talking.

"I think he was told to slow me down. He knew my name."

"So what happened to the girl who helped you?"

Ainsley shrugged. "I don't know."

"Is she alive?"

"I truly don't know. I thought she'd stolen the azulejo. Should I call her again?"

Ainsley pulled out her phone. She'd put it on silent before entering the Factory House. There were two voicemails, three missed calls, and sixteen text messages.

All from Bia.

"Oh my God," she said, "she's been trying to call me."

Ainsley leapt off the couch and walked outside to the balcony and slid the door shut behind her. The temperature had dropped to nearly freezing. Below, from the formal gardens, came the sound of a trickling fountain, and spread out, far to the left and right, was the Douro itself, dark and forbidding and sensual at this hour.

She sped through the messages, listened to the voicemail. Bia was very much alive, though she sounded groggy. She said that she'd started the port wine tasting at Framington's, then felt woozy, then passed out. She'd woken up twelve hours later in a guest room in the onsite hotel, remembering nothing else.

She was still in the Douro Valley.

Listening to the messages, Ainsley chewed on her lip, thinking. It was impossible that Bia had passed out for twelve hours from a simple port wine tasting. After all, she was no stranger to grapes. She'd lived with wine her whole life.

No, it sounded more like someone at the winery had slipped something into her drink.

Maybe Bia'd been too blunt in her asking for the azulejo.

A better explanation, however, was that since João had known that Ainsley was coming—which was a mystery in and of itself—João's brother at Framington's had been waiting for Bia.

The difference was that Ainsley had managed to slip away. She remembered that João had poured that twenty-year port wine out of sight, into a new glass. She'd refused to drink it.

Ainsley dialed Bia. It went to voicemail. She was probably passed out again. Ainsley had heard that a roofie could affect a person for days. Still, she left a message warmly acknowledging Bia, apologizing for leaving the Douro Valley without her, and asking her to meet at the pousada.

Then she ended the call and stared across the Douro, its black sheen pricked by reflections of white streetlights on the opposite bank.

More questions arose in her mind. How could they have known that Ainsley and Bia were coming to the Douro Valley? And who was *they*? The British Association in the Factory House? Those men were stiff but they didn't seem like killers. Simon himself had said that he was merely the last step in a long chain of causation.

Then she remembered something else.

A piece of a conversation.

Ainsley rushed back into the suite. Fernando gestured to the couch, but Ainsley went over to the swivel desk chair instead and leaned on the edge of it, her forearms on her knees.

"Fernando," she said, "I don't think that the British Association stole your sapphire azulejo."

He twisted his bulk to face her. "But the pricks just blackmailed me and my family."

Joaquim and Rita were perched on the edge of the bed. They suddenly were all ears.

"Simon told me in the kitchen," she explained, "that he was merely the last in a chain of events."

"So?" said Joaquim.

"So maybe he's just the messenger. Maybe something else is forcing him to use the British Association to force you to blackmail your nephew."

Fernando was extremely still, his head cocked slightly to the left. "I'm listening."

"If the British Association had been behind the theft, they would've brought the azulejo to one of their wineries. Maybe Taylor Fladgate, maybe Croft, maybe Warre, whatever."

"Framington's isn't British?" said Rita. "It's an English name."

Fernando shook his head. "No, not anymore."

"Who owns it?" said Joaquim.

Ainsley lifted an index finger. "ConBev. According to João."

Fernando pounded his fist into his palm. "That's right. It was a recent acquisition."

Joaquim was listening closely. "I know ConBev. That's one of the biggest beverage distributors in the world. It's worth billions of dollars."

"It's private or public?"

"Public," said Fernando. "And they would benefit the most from preserving the exclusivity of port wine. This old government regulation keeps out the trash producers. It preserves the high profit margins."

"And the high profit margins are all the bean counters care about," said Joaquim.

"Period."

"So how could ConBev have physically stolen this?" said Ainsley.

Fernando looked towards Rita. "You change the security code after every guest, yes?"

"Absolutely."

"Who was the last guest?"

"You won't like the answer," said Rita.

"Tell me."

"Lionel and Catherine Hampstead."

Fernando dug the heel of his palm into an eye socket. Then he shook his head. "They're not even my friends. Mafalda knew them from her last marriage."

Joaquim had pulled out his smartphone and was typing. "Ainsley, you said that you met Catherine Hampstead?"

"Yes."

"Her husband Lionel—have you met him?

"No."

"I've met him a few times," said Rita. "He's tall, quiet, intelligent, always working in the background. Catherine does the entertaining."

That made sense. Ainsley knew that, for many couples, the person who did the talking rarely held the power.

"And he works in finance?" said Joaquim.

"He works at an investment bank in London," said Rita.

"Which one?"

The property manager thought hard. "I think it's called Wolfenham."

Joaquim paused. "Wait, hang on." His fingers flew madly on his phone. "I am searching for Wolfenham Bank and ConBev together. Are you ready for this?"

Ainsley was on the edge of her seat. "What is it?"

"It looks like Wolfenham bought a forty percent stake in ConBev last year."

CHAPTER FIFTY-EIGHT

Nobody spoke for a moment.

Then Ainsley said, "No way."

"Look for yourself," said Joaquim, gesturing to her.

She ran and sat beside him on the bed and peered over his arm to his phone. She felt his tricep against her chest.

On the small screen was a headline in the *Financial Times* from four months earlier:

Wolfenham increases exposure to beverage sector.

He clicked to the next page. Another headline, the same week, from the *Wall Street Journal*:

Wolfenham CEO defends ConBev investment at annual share-holders' meeting.

"Wow," said Ainsley. "There's the reason."

"It's money," added Joaquim. "Lots of it."

The sapphire azulejo lay on the coffee table in the middle of the room. Ainsley looked at it with new respect. She thought of the billions of dollars of international investment money that were depending upon its delivery to the hands of a single obscure Portuguese politician.

Meanwhile, Fernando had turned a bright purple. His

jowls were quivering. It looked like a mixture of fear and rage. "The English banks have been interfering in our politics for centuries. What made me think that things had changed?"

Nobody answered.

"So I guess it was Catherine Hampstead," said Rita.

"Not necessarily," replied Ainsley. "Her husband may not have told her about his plans. She compared herself to a prisoner when I met her."

"And the guard never tells the prisoner the truth," said Joaquim.

"So will we ever know?" Rita said. "I mean, we can't just ask them."

Fernando stood up. "No, we can't ask them. And we will never know definitively. They're too smart, too powerful. But I do know that the Hampsteads will not be welcome on my property again."

"But your wife—" Rita said.

"I don't care what Mafalda says. They are off the list." He wagged a stern finger in the air. "No more."

Ainsley cautiously cleared her throat. "Fernando, what are you going to do about your nephew?"

The purple drained from Fernando's fleshy face, and he seemed suddenly darker. He dropped his chin into his chest and sat down.

"I don't know," he said. "I need to go home and think about this."

Gripping the arm of the sofa, Fernando pulled himself to his feet with great effort. He crossed the room heavily, side to side, like a steamship groaning through a tempestuous sea.

"Miss Walker," he said, "you may use the suite tonight."

"Thank you," she said.

Ainsley felt her throat constrict. There was a much bigger question she wanted to ask, but she couldn't be the one to broach it.

Then she didn't have to.

Fernando had stopped at the door, his hand resting on the knob. "Also, Miss Walker—have you been paid for your work?"

Ainsley felt her heart hammering in her chest. She didn't want to overstep her bounds and embarrass anybody. "No, not yet."

Rita cast her eyes down.

"It's quite late, *senhor*," said Joaquim nervously, "so maybe we should speak about this another time."

Fernando bristled at the suggestion. "No, at this moment, I prefer to be direct." He nodded towards Ainsley. "Senhora Walker has protected my family. She must be rewarded."

Half embarrassed, half proud, Ainsley felt a tiny shoot of hope begin to sprout in her chest.

"We don't have any money, senhor," said Joaquim. "My business is barely hanging on. Ainsley agreed to take this job on contingency."

Fernando tilted his head. "*Em contingência?*"

Joaquim nodded.

A cunning look drew across the old man's face. "So you expected me to pay if the azulejo was discovered? But you couldn't tell me that. Why?"

"We were afraid, senhor," said Joaquim, "that Rita would lose her job."

"And if not, you just weren't going to pay her anything?"

"No," replied Joaquim firmly, "we were going to pay her, somehow." He looked at Ainsley with the saddest pair of eyes she'd ever seen. They made him seem vulnerable, a new expression for him.

Rita immediately ran to the old man's side. "*Perdoe-me, senhor*," she said. "*Eu lhe implore.*"

The quinta owner looked down at his employee. Then he

patted her arm. "This isn't your fault. They would have found a way to steal the azulejo."

Rita seemed to dissolve. A trickle of three tears worked their silent way down her cheek. Ainsley understood just how valuable a job was in Portugal.

"Oh, thank you, senhor—" she said, kissing his hand.

"But you should've told me."

"Oh yes, senhor—"

"How much did you agree to?"

"Three thousand euros," said Ainsley, interrupting. She'd recovered her confidence now that Fernando appeared to be favoring a quick payment.

"That's not cheap," he said.

Ainsley frowned. For an international investigator, that was very cheap.

Joaquim stepped in. "She also paid for her own plane ticket."

Fernando weighed the options. Ainsley didn't have the heart to tell him that the contract was already signed. If he didn't agree, Joaquim would be on the hook for it. There could be no mercy, either. The hounds were at her door.

"I will pay," he said.

Ainsley felt the breath whoosh out of her body. She hadn't realized that she'd been holding it. "Thank you, Fernando."

"It will be delivered to this room tomorrow morning."

She nodded. "Then I will definitely stay here tonight."

He looked to the others. "We will speak later."

Fernando left the room. The moment that the door silently closed behind him, Rita collapsed onto the floor. "I saw my life passing before me," she said.

"You're very dramatic," said Joaquim coolly.

"You weren't going to lose your job!" said Rita.

"There are other jobs."

"Not anymore." Rita suddenly leapt to her feet and

launched herself onto Ainsley. "You are an angel sent from heaven."

"No," said Ainsley, "that is most definitely not true."

"You are to me. Thank you." The woman pulled back, more tears streaking down her face. "Can you believe that I have to drive back to the Alentejo tonight?"

"Stay," said Joaquim.

"No," said Rita, "I have a meeting with the water company in Sintra in the morning. They are like God. I can't stand them up or our guests don't shower."

Joaquim shrugged. "Take some money for petrol."

He handed her forty euros. She kissed him on the cheek. "*Obrigada, irmão.*"

The door closed silently behind her. Now there was just the two of them, Ainsley and Joaquim. The air between them felt supercharged.

"If Fernando hadn't agreed to pay, I would've sued the pants off you," she said.

"But my pants are still on," he said.

They stood looking at one another. Ainsley placed one foot girlishly behind the other. "So did you inquire with the front desk about getting your own room tonight?"

"Not yet," he said, casually pouring himself a small whiskey from the wet bar.

"Maybe you should."

"Yeah, maybe."

"You can't stay here. This is my suite."

He grinned. "I know. Besides, sleeping with your boss would be unseemly. Grounds for a lawsuit."

She paused. "You know, I'm technically unemployed now."

"That's true," he said.

"Even though I still haven't received my last paycheck."

Joaquim rushed to encourage her. "Oh, he's good for it. Fernando is utterly reliable."

"He'd better be."

"He is. Trust me."

"Why should I?"

Their eyes locked. Ainsley felt like she was on a moving sidewalk that emptied out straight into his arms. A moment later, she was looking up into Joaquim's eyes. She felt one hand encircle her waist, and another on the back of her head.

As their lips met, she closed her eyes.

CHAPTER FIFTY-NINE

The muffled sound of water hitting tile gently brought Ainsley back to consciousness. She blinked, yawned, looked around.

The bed was a modern one, with thin gold coverlet and luxurious white sheets. She was still in the suite at the Pousada do Freixo. The orange rays of dawn were shining through the gauzy curtain, underneath which were the glimmering waters of the Douro.

She'd slept with him. There was no alcohol, no poor judgment. It'd been an easy decision: Joaquim was simply the most interesting, attractive man she'd met in a long time. In Pinhão, he'd even come to her rescue, which couldn't be said for anybody else. And since he was no longer paying her, the nasty taint of money-for-favors had been removed.

As she wound her hair around her fingers and thought about last night, a little smile appeared at the corner of her lips. Then her mind wandered, away from the man showering in the bathroom, towards something else.

Three thousand euros.

She did the math in her mind. Depending on the

exchange rate, that translated to about four thousand dollars. She would pay David his two thousand dollars, pay for the airplane ticket, pay for all the expenses she'd incurred here—and still have a few hundred left over.

She'd come out ahead, by a little. Enough to keep her head above water, for at least another month.

There was a sharp knock at the door. Ainsley leapt up, remembered that she was naked, then slipped back into her clothes from last night. Tossing her hair around her neck, Ainsley stumbled over and looked through the peephole.

It was Bia.

She flung the door open and embraced her friend. "I thought you had screwed me."

Bia pulled back, looking at Ainsley's messy hair and backwards shirt. "No, I think someone else did a good job of that."

"Get in here," said Ainsley, smiling.

Bia sat down on the sofa. Ainsley filled the coffeemaker and joined her. "Now, start from the moment we separated," she said.

The story took ten minutes. Bia didn't really have many extra details to add, since she'd been unconscious, except to note that the employees who drugged her had been the same ones who'd faked the robbery scene in the backroom.

"Martim and Goncalo," said Ainsley.

"Yes."

"It did seem odd," said Ainsley, "to think that you'd use ether to knock out a man twice your size."

Bia held her palms up. "I'm not a crime boss. I don't know anything about that stuff. All I do is give protection to azulejo thieves."

"And João at Quinta do Navalho—"

"—was probably under orders to delay you. Just like me.

They probably shared the same package of roofies. But you were smart enough to avoid it."

"It's not your fault," said Ainsley. "But my other question hasn't been answered yet."

"Who killed Vasco the Italiano?"

Ainsley nodded. "My only guess is that someone was following us. How else could they have known we were coming to the Douro Valley? Or who we even were?"

"That makes sense to me."

"Remember how I said that I felt something following us in Évora?"

"Yes."

"I thought it was the spirits of the town. But maybe it was an investigator contracted by ConBev."

Bia laughed. "An investigator following an investigator."

"Who then committed murder."

A sadness filled the space between them. Then the shower turned off. Bia looked towards the door. "So who's in the bathroom?"

"A friend."

"I see. What's your friend's name?"

The bathroom door opened. Joaquim stepped out with a bath towel wrapped around his waist.

"Who's this?" he said.

"My friend Bia."

"Your friend, the azulejo gangster?" he said. "Back from the dead?"

Ainsley did a quick introduction. Bia regarded him warily. She was the type of girl who didn't trust good-looking men. "I feel like we've met before," she said.

"Me too," said Joaquim.

"Have you been to—" said Bia.

"—that restaurant in Cascais?" he finished.

"Com Licenca?"

"Yes!" Bia shot to her feet. "I knew I recognized you. Do you remember? I was the girl—"

"—under the table—"

"That one time—"

"—you and that other girl—"

"—and you and that other guy—"

"—of course they all know you, you're the one from America—"

Totally confused, Ainsley sat back. They'd clearly met before. Soon, they'd switched to rapid Portuguese. Ainsley could tell from their body language alone that it had been a friendly connection, not romantic.

Finally Bia turned to Ainsley. "This is your boss?"

"Not anymore. You two know each other?"

"Kind of," answered Joaquim.

Rita answered more strongly. "Yes. We've met twice. Last year."

There was a sharp rap at the door. Joaquim and Bia resumed their fast conversation, while Ainsley went to answer it.

A small man in a polo shirt and blue jeans was standing with a package.

"Ainsley Walker?"

"Yes."

"From Fernando Souza." He handed over an envelope. "And this too." He handed her a small box. Her name had been written on a notecard taped to the outside.

"Thank you," said Ainsley.

"Have a nice day," he said.

She closed the door and ripped open the envelope. Inside was a stack of one-hundred-euro notes. She thumbed through them. It was three thousand exactly. Ainsley heaved a sigh of relief.

Then she opened the box. It was a bottle of Souza port

wine. A handwritten note said, *Sincerest regards, Fernando*.

"A Souza port wine?" said Joaquim. "What year?"

Ainsley read the label. "Nineteen eighty-seven."

"That was a vintage year," said Joaquim.

"I remember," said Ainsley. "Your sister told me about it."

That was a generous gift. Rita had said that it retailed for over a thousand dollars. She put the envelope and the bottle in her white bag and zipped it shut.

Then Ainsley sank back into the couch, arms and legs flung out. She faced the glass doorwall that showed the Douro River. Then she exhaled mightily. It felt like a huge weight had been lifted from her shoulders.

The case was over.

———

Bia came over and sat down next to her. "Now what?" said Ainsley.

"We go to the U.S.," said Bia.

"We?" said Ainsley. "You were really serious about that?"

The Portuguese girl's face grew dark. "Of course. There is no future for me in this country."

"You'll need a job."

Ainsley glanced at Joaquim. "Didn't Fatima tell me that she was leaving?"

In the bathroom, Joaquim was shaving. "She's going to Brazil to travel. It's hard to find a native Portuguese speaker."

"I could work for you," said Bia.

"You would be perfect," he replied.

"Of course I'm perfect," said Bia.

Ainsley shook her head in disbelief. This was working out too neatly. The family had recovered the sapphire azulejo, she herself had been paid the agreed-upon amount, and Bia had found work in the U.S.

Something had to go wrong.

Joaquim washed the lather off his face, toweled it dry, and applied aftershave. "Ladies," he said, "I would love to make more plans about the future, but unfortunately I need to get on a train to Lisbon. My flight leaves at six pm tonight."

"If you wait, I can join you," said Ainsley.

"No," he replied, "you are going to rest today, Ainsley. You've worked hard enough."

"Are you sure?"

"I've already paid for another night. It includes a complimentary session at the spa on the second floor."

Ainsley felt her heart quaver. "You are a sweetheart."

"Only," he said, "to those who deserve it."

She turned back to Bia. "So when will you be ready to leave Portugal?"

The girl thought for a moment. "Three days."

"That's all?"

"I don't need to do much," said Bia. She ticked off the tasks on her fingers. "Inform my grandmother. Tell my network to find new protection. Figure out what clothing to bring. Cancel mobile phone plan. That's all."

It made sense. She had no car, no property, no husband. She lived lightly.

"What about a work visa?" said Ainsley.

Joaquim interrupted. "No, no, trying to go through American immigration is like swimming in sludge. She'll be waiting forever. She should come on a tourist visa, then apply for the work visa when she's already in the U.S." He paused. "Working for me, of course."

"I can wait for you," said Ainsley.

"Would you?"

"Sure. I'm unemployed. I can even help you pack."

"Let's book a flight tonight."

The two women embraced. After Joaquim left for the train station, they ordered a breakfast from room service.

Ainsley pushed away the empty plate when she was finished. She was starting to get the sleepy feeling that follows a big meal. "I should really take a shower," said Ainsley.

"Why?" said Bia.

"So we can go out and see Oporto."

Bia was trying to stifle laughter.

"What's so funny?" said Ainsley.

"You never stop, do you?"

"Not really." Then Ainsley felt an enormous yawn seize her face. When it had passed, she said, "Just give me a couple of minutes to digest."

"Okay," said Bia.

The girl watched Ainsley crawl over to the bed and collapse upon the duvet.

"Just give me a couple minutes to rest," murmured Ainsley, "and I'll be ... up and ... ready to ... go..."

Bia smiled. "I'll be here."

A minute later, Ainsley's eyes had closed, and a small snoring sound was issuing gently from her mouth.

It'd been a long journey.

LISBON

EPILOGUE

Three days later, Ainsley stepped out of the taxicab at the Lisbon International Airport. She was ready to head back to the States, back to home, back to her regular life. It didn't suit her, exactly, but she had little other choice.

Out of the other side of the taxi stepped Bia, dressed in a white top and a white pants.

"It's impossible to keep white clothing clean while travelling," said Ainsley.

"I don't care," said Bia. "This is a rebirth. A new beginning."

"Did you decide to tell your parents?"

"No, but my father will hear about it later. I'll fight that battle later."

She and her grandmother didn't like each other much either. Inside their apartment, Ainsley had endured a front-row seat to the familial strife, as Bia had packed her bags while arguing with the elderly woman. There had been tears, anguish, signs of the cross, rending of garments.

It hadn't been Ainsley's business, and when the fighting became too vicious, she'd stepped outside the apartment, onto the landing where she'd first met Bia, and dialed some very expensive long-distance phone calls to her insurance company. She'd learned that the wrecked rental car had been pulled out of the vineyard—she couldn't imagine the logistics needed to do that—and she'd given all the information about the accident. While the inspectors were evaluating the incident, there was nothing to do but wait.

Now, at the airport, the taxi driver pulled their bags from the trunk. Ainsley tipped him generously. They pulled their bags through the automatic doors and entered the terminal.

At the ticket desk, Ainsley forked over her confirmation code and passport to the desk agent. The computer beeped; a roll of paper spooled out of the printer. The desk agent affixed it to the suitcase, checked the weight, and then tossed it onto the conveyor belt.

As Ainsley and Bia waited in the security line, the Portuguese girl began shifting her weight from foot to foot. Her fingers clenched and unclenched.

"I've been dreaming of this for so long," she finally said. "Leaving it all behind. Going to a better place, more opportunities. It's difficult to believe that now it's happening. So quick. No trouble."

"I actually think it's harder to go home."

"Maybe." Bia's eyes were glistening now. "Thank you for everything you've done."

"I'm happy to help," replied Ainsley.

"It feels like this is our destiny."

Bia flung herself upon Ainsley, who squeezed her in return. It was necessary to avoid a meltdown, which was a looming possibility. That would be understandable, of course —the prospect of leaving your homeland with nothing but a couple of bags and a smile would be frightening to even the bravest among us.

Furthermore, Ainsley and Bia were actually confronting

the same problems—no jobs, going to a land that felt alien. The only difference was that for Bia, the United States held that magic, that ineffable spirit, that makes travelling and adventure so alluring.

For Ainsley, though, it was just home. This journey had been a mere delay, a few extra days of bought time.

A travelling addiction was stronger than any other addiction, for one reason—nobody ever told you to stop doing it.

At the front of the security line, Ainsley untied her shoes, dropped her bag on the belt, then stepped into the scanner and held her arms above her head. She was passed through, briefly wanded, then allowed to recover her shoes and bag. When Bia had passed through, they moved towards their gate.

Moving down the concourse, the two women paddled through the great swarms of humanity. Ainsley felt perspiration dampening her armpits. She was oddly excited. Some people brought home pictures, food, or art from foreign journeys.

At the gate, they chose a pair of seats next to one another.

"We have thirty minutes until boarding," said Ainsley. "I'm going to buy a book for the plane."

"Okay," said Bia.

"Can you watch my bag?"

"Of course."

Ainsley headed to a nearby bookshop. She found the English language section and browsed the mystery section. It was limited to stories about murder. She usually tried to avoid those, but there wasn't much choice.

She chose a detective mystery with a one-word title. It would be the type of book that you forgot about the moment you finished it. Ainsley preferred stories that stuck with you for days, weeks, even months after you finished them—stories with details, with strong voices, with a sense of spirit behind the words.

She paid for her purchase and began walking back down the concourse. She looked at the book in her hands. It most likely ended with the main character getting everything she wanted. Fantasy fulfillment. That wasn't how real life worked, of course.

At the gate, she found her bag sitting on a seat, right where she'd left it—but Bia was gone.

Ainsley spun around, cursing. Had Bia deserted her again? She thought she could trust the girl. It felt a little late in the relationship to be playing these trust games.

Then she spotted her. Bia was about forty meters down the concourse, the opposite direction from the bookshop, escorted by a heavy, waddling man. And she was walking away. On either side of them strode a pair of serious-looking military types.

A million possibilities zoomed through Ainsley's mind. Bia was being kidnapped. Bia was double-crossing her. Bia was going for a walk with some new military friends. None of it made any sense.

She grabbed her bag, ran out to the concourse—and began to run.

Breathing heavily, her cheeks puffing, she flew past one surprised face after another, her arms pumping, her legs stretching. The airport melted away, and she was back on the oval cinder track of her long-ago athletic days.

As she drew closer, she could see that the escorting man was wearing the official outfit of a Lisbon police official. His body shape looked oddly familiar.

"Bia!" she shouted. "Where are you going?"

The girl stopped and turned. She had tears in her eyes, and her nostrils were red.

"I don't have a choice, Ainsley," she said.

The chubby escort turned around. Ainsley felt her heart drop into her shoes. She came to a stop.

It was Augusto.

The head of the azulejo task force.

"You?" said Ainsley. "What are you doing here? With this girl?"

"This woman is being detained for questioning," he said.

"Questioning about what?" barked Ainsley.

"About her involvement in the theft of valuable azulejos from the public streets of Lisbon."

Ainsley rolled her eyes. "Yes, Augusto, this is O Paizão. You were right. She has been associated with azulejo thieves. But please don't detain her. She's leaving the country. She won't ever touch another azulejo again."

A wry smile decorated Augusto's face, but he said nothing.

Meanwhile, Bia was looking at Ainsley as though from a great, inseparable distance, a sad expression on her face.

"Ainsley," she said, "you don't understand. Augusto is my father."

Silence.

Ainsley was rendered speechless.

In the blink of an eye, the remaining pieces of Bia's story fell into place. The reason for her access to the police department. The reason nothing was ever done about Lisbon's azulejo thievery. The reason she felt such need to leave her life behind.

Ainsley let her imagination run wild. Bia had probably been forced into the business by her father, so that they could keep all the kickback money in the family. And that was, most likely, the reason he'd stopped her at the airport. Bia couldn't be allowed to leave. She was threatening to destroy the family business.

"It's legal," said Bia. "I can't stop him."

"But—"

"Just go without me," she said. "It was too good to be true. I'll never get out of here."

"I won't leave," said Ainsley.

Augusto cut in. "You have had success here," he said, "but this is not your country. We are not your people. You should leave now."

"What he's really saying," said Bia, "is that if you don't leave, he will prosecute you."

"For what?"

"Murder."

Ainsley's eyes nearly popped out of her skull. "He knows—"

"—about Vasco. Police talk."

Ainsley stammered dumbly. The military guards had faced Ainsley full on now, their large hands planted on their hips. The intimation was clear.

There was nothing to say or do. "We have no choice?"

Bia looked utterly despondent. "Don't forget me."

"I won't," said Ainsley.

"Goodbye," said Bia.

Ainsley tried to form another response, but nothing came out. She watched Augusto turn Bia around. Then she watched the four people march away, down the concourse, until they were gone.

Her arms hanging dumbly at her sides, Ainsley felt as utterly alone as any human can possibly be.

The female gate agent came on the intercom: "Now boarding passengers for United flight one-seven-thirty..."

That was her flight. Ainsley needed to board the plane, but she couldn't make her legs move. Home had just lost its last remaining bit of attractiveness, but she couldn't stay in Portugal either.

She would go somewhere else.

Dejected, Ainsley returned to her gate and approached

the desk agent, who was taking people's tickets and passing the bar codes underneath a red electronic scanner.

"Excuse me," Ainsley said, "but I need to change my ticket."

"For this flight?"

"Yes."

"Where do you want to go?"

"I don't know."

The desk agent paused. "You don't know where you want to go?"

Ainsley shook her head.

The desk agent grew casual. "Why don't you go to Spain? The tickets are very cheap. The flights to Madrid leave every hour and they're never full."

"I will do that," said Ainsley.

The desk agent was still swiping boarding passes under the scanner. "Just wait until I'm finished here, please."

Ainsley unslung the bag from her shoulder and dropped it onto the counter. "Take as long as you need. I'll be right here."

PLOTWORKS PUBLISHING

If you enjoyed this story, please leave a review at the place where you purchased it.

Then visit Plotworks Publishing to follow Ainsley Walker on her next exciting gemstone travel mystery!

Turn the page for a sneak peek—

THE SPAIN TOURMALINE

AN GEMSTONE TRAVEL MYSTERY

J. A. JERNAY

THE SPAIN TOURMALINE

As she trailed Zamorano through the darkened streets, Ainsley discovered the sensual side of Seville.

The brisk night breeze tickling her cheeks. The scent of orange blossom. The food carts on the streetcorners, offering *churros con chocolate*. The drunken revelers spilling out of crowded tapas bars onto the cobblestones.

Semana Santa. Holy Week.

She followed him through the Plaza Espana, a huge semicircular public space filled with glazed tiles, fountains, bridges, and art deco design. Then she followed him out of the historic center, across the gorgeously illuminated Triana Bridge, to the neighborhood of the same name on the other side.

Ainsley regretted the fact that she had nearly written off this city. In her mind, she compared Seville with her own hometown, a grim, humorless place where dutiful obedience was demanded, where bedroom lights were turned off by nine o'clock every night. It was like comparing a pair of sexy heels with a pair of sturdy black nurse's shoes.

Ahead of her, Zamorano was scampering along a row of

residential buildings, *foot foot cane*. Then she he disappeared down an outdoor staircase. This was the place. She looked up at the structure. It was a centuries-old building, walls painted the color of old blood, scabbed with wrought-iron.

Without pausing, Ainsley ran down the outdoor staircase and pushed through a heavy coffered door. She plunged into a dark passageway. At the far end was a single overhead light illuminating a residential door.

Behind her, the heavy coffered door clicked shut.

As she plunged further into the darkness, hearing her own shoes clacking on the floor, Ainsley felt her heart hammering against her sternum. Ahead, Zamorano was a mere shadow scampering in the darkness, *foot foot cane*.

As she drew closer to the spiral staircase, she saw a splash of red and black paint on the residential door. She squinted and peered.

It was a silhouette of a bull being murdered.

She could see the white *picas* sticking out of its hump, the fur drenched in blood, the lifeless stare as the eyes rolled backwards in its skull.

Ainsley felt a sudden wave of revulsion. This place was overwhelming, suffocating, claustrophobic. Coming here had been a mistake.

She stopped. "I can't go any further," she said.

"Why?"

"I don't know you, I don't know this city, and I hate the bullfights. I'm going back to my boyfriend—"

Before Ainsley could turn back, she heard the *thock* of Zamorano's cane grow louder on the floor as he drew closer. Then she felt his fingers catch her by the arm.

"I want to show you something," he said.

She heard him unrolling a paper. Then she heard the sound of a match striking. An orange flame illuminated half of Zamorano's face, the buck teeth, the pink eyes. It was a good face, ugly but kind.

He slowly lifted something up to the light. She recognized it.

It was the flyer. The one that read *La vuelta de la espada de Pepe*. The matador with the ferocious facial expression, the blood-red gemstone decorated the hilt of the sword.

"You have seen this?" he said.

"Of course."

The man fell silent. His eyes intensely searched Ainsley's face. Spanish people had stares that seemed to spring from their very souls.

"You must choose," said Zamorano. "It's either yes and you come with me, or no and you leave. But if the answer is yes, you cannot turn back."

Ainsley looked towards the door with the painting of the murdered bull. Then she looked at the bullfighter on the flyer. Zamorano gave her a knowing tilt of his head. He was letting her put two and two together.

"If that's the case," she said, "then I want to leave."

Ainsley backed away from the small man, from the painting —then finally turned and fled down the hallway, back towards the heavy wooden door that had clicked shut behind her. In the darkness, she fluttered her hands across the coffered door, trying to find the way out. When she found the knob, squarely in the middle, she grabbed it with both hands and yanked hard.

It didn't budge.

"You need a key," said Zamorano's voice.

"To get out?"

"Yes."

"Can I have it?"

"I don't have one."

"Why not?"

"I don't live here. But he does."

"Who?"

"Him."

Ainsley slowly turned around. At the far end of the hall-way, the painted door had been opened. In the doorway stood the silhouette of a stocky man, his arms held away from his sides.

"Who are you?" she croaked.

"I am called Pepito," said the man in a booming voice, "and you must be the one who finds gemstones."

PLOTWORKS PUBLISHING

Visit Plotworks Publishing to follow Ainsley Walker on her next exciting gemstone travel mystery!

Then explore a new series by J.A. Jernay—the Cosmo Bennett Mapping Thrillers!

Turn the page for a sneak peek—

J.A. JERNAY

BOUNDARY

A COSMO BENNETT MAPPING THRILLER

FROM THE AUTHOR OF THE AINSLEY WALKER
GEMSTONE TRAVEL MYSTERY SERIES

BOUNDARY

Cosmo and his assistant Noah shuffled down the dirt shoulder of the boulevard in the midday heat, sweating and miserable.

Each was lost in his own thoughts. Cosmo dreamed of hitting a heavy punching bag at his gymnasium. Noah dreamed of passing level nineteen of Operation Earlobe, an obscure RPG he'd abandoned last semester.

The morning's meeting had been a complete bust.

"I don't think we should continue," said Cosmo finally.

Noah didn't respond, but Cosmo took no notice. He continued: "I don't think anybody here takes our task seriously. I don't think this propaganda map was as influential as they say. I don't think this map has driven the civil unrest. I think social media and centuries of tribal warfare are more to blame for the unrest than anything else."

He looked over at Noah, waiting for a response. "What about you?"

The graduate assistant came back from his reverie. "Huh?"

"Did you hear anything I said?"

"No."

"I was just saying this is pointless and we should go home."

"I don't have a problem with that."

They arrived at Vida e Caffé. It was a chain café, with hundreds of similar franchises scattered across the southern part of the African continent. The branding was modern and inviting. A hundred people sat beneath umbrellas at small tables on the large outdoor patio.

An arm was waving at them. It was Christopher, their fixer, a cup of tea on a ceramic saucer in front of him. Two other cups awaited them.

"Hello sirs," he said. "I ordered us all a rooibos. It's a vanilla tea that is extraordinary."

Cosmo and Noah pulled out the chairs and sat down. The driver quickly sussed out that something was wrong.

"It was a bad meeting?" he said quietly.

"Yes," said Cosmo, "there was no progress made."

"I'm very sorry."

Cosmo sighed. "I think we have to leave."

The fixer looked confused. "But you just sat down—"

"The country," he clarified. "We have to leave Fabajouti. We can't seem to do any good here."

Christopher looked crestfallen. "I do understand your frustration."

Noah said, "If it's okay with you, we'd probably like to just get in the car and go back to the hotel."

The fixer rediscovered his manners. "Of course, as you wish—"

"But we'd love to try the tea first—" added Cosmo.

"You two enjoy the rooibos," said Christopher, "while I fetch the car. The parking lot is very jammed and it will take quite a while to remove. I've already paid the bill."

Before they could object, the driver had shot to his feet.

He clapped Cosmo on the shoulder and left the patio. They watched him cross the boulevard to an off-street parking area that was crammed tightly with vehicles. On his approach, the attendant began shifting other vehicles.

Noah sipped the tea. "This does taste really good. I don't drink enough tea."

"I like tea," said Cosmo. He sipped from the cup. "This one is good."

"What's your favorite?" asked Noah.

"Maybe pu'er."

"That one's bitter, right?"

"Yeah. It's fermented."

"What about Earl Grey?"

"A cliché."

"I think I'm more of a fruity tea guy," said Noah.

Cosmo nodded. "Yeah, they have their charms."

"You ever try chamomile?"

"It's good for sleeping," said Cosmo, "but otherwise it's—"

His comment was cut short by a massive fireball that erupted from the parking lot across the street.

————

In a split second, Cosmo and Noah instinctively rolled off their chairs and onto the ground beneath their table. Their eyes met. Each was filled with terror.

Then the shock of the overpressure hit. Cosmo felt the force of the blast wave hit the left side of his body. The highly compressed air rattled the left side of his skull. It even sent his lips and cheeks flapping to the right.

The initial sound of the explosion was deafening, but that was soon replaced by a symphony of falling destruction. A thousand pieces of metal, plastic, glass, and upholstery rained down upon the boulevard, the grass, the other cars.

A shower of tiny shrapnel hit on the patio of the cafe. One hit Noah in the hand and sizzled his flesh. He shook it off.

They waited another few seconds for the shrapnel rain to end. Then Cosmo and Noah lifted their heads.

The patio of the café was transformed into pandemonium. The patrons started to pull themselves up from the ground and flee out to the street and in the opposite direction. The street itself was coming alive with panicked people running in every direction.

"What the actual—" said Noah.

"Christopher!" interrupted Cosmo. "What about Christopher?"

He scrambled up to his feet. Without waiting for Noah, he sprinted out of the café and across the boulevard, weaving through the stopped cars. The air was acrid with chemicals and the heat had somehow intensified even further.

The parking lot was a field of wreckage. The bomb had exploded in the middle of the space, shredding every vehicle and person within twenty meters. Pieces of concrete and metal and glass had been blown across the scene.

"Christopher!" he shouted again. "Christopher! Don't do this!"

He saw a shoe with a foot still in it. He saw a red string of guts entangled in a hubcap. A wave of nausea gripped his stomach. He covered his nose with his t-shirt and backed away.

He tripped backwards over a piece of metal, stumbled, and fell to the ground.

That's when he saw it.

A long strip of shredded fabric. A yellow-and-green printed tropical shirt.

It was bloody and torn.

Cosmo turned his head and retched onto the asphalt. All the tea he'd just drank came out.

He somehow pulled himself to his feet and staggered back to the café. Noah was waiting at the far corner, on the sidewalk, pacing frantically.

"So?"

"I found him," said Cosmo. He forced the next words out. "A little bit."

Noah's face went white. "Oh my God."

Cosmo didn't say anything. He just gripped Noah by the upper arm. "Walk with me. And don't look back."

———

The pair moved briskly down the boulevard, away from the scene. People were running past them, mouths open, eyes full of fear, but Cosmo maintained a steady pace. His face betrayed an intense desire to appear as normal as possible.

"So we're just going to leave the scene?" said Noah.

"Yep."

"Why?"

"Don't make me answer that, Noah."

"I think we should talk to the police, cooperate, tell them everything—"

"In a different country," Cosmo replied, "in a different scenario, you'd be right. But not here, not now."

Noah looked back over his shoulder at the scene.

"Look straight ahead," Cosmo said through his teeth, "and listen to me. Our Mercedes is gone. Christopher is ... gone."

"Shit—"

"And I'm going to suggest something else that could blow your mind."

"What?"

"It's possible that we were the intended target."

"That's insane."

"Is it?"

"How do you know?"

"I don't. But it's a possibility. Here's another one. It's possible that we are going to be used as scapegoats. We were the last people seen eating with Christopher. Do you want to be put in a Fabajouti jail on suspicion of a crime?"

They walked for another half minute in silence. Behind them, the chaos grew distant.

"Where are we going?" Noah said finally.

"Back to the hotel."

"And then?"

"We're leaving, like we planned."

"We're not going home, are we?" said Noah.

Cosmo's mouth grew hard and his jaw jutted out. He stared straight forward at an invisible point on the horizon. "No, we're not."

PLOTWORKS PUBLISHING

Visit Plotworks Publishing today for all these titles—and more!